Other Than That, Mrs. Lincoln

Other Than That, Mrs. Lincoln

By Bill J. Burch

Published in the United States by March Hare, Ltd.

ISBN : 978-1-7378052-0-5 (Paperback)

ISBN : 978-1-7378052-1-2 (ePub)

Interior Design by Booknook.biz.

Cover design by Erika Alyana of erika.alyana@gmail.com

Contents

Chapter I

Elizabeth had lived in, or at least visited, most of the major cities in America, but Washington D.C. was the only one where the smell was improved by the passing of a herd of pigs. This particular herd was some two dozen Berkshire pigs being shepherded down Pennsylvania Avenue by a Negro boy and his assistant – a Louisiana Catahoula Leopard dog. The boy walked behind and the dog trotted to the outside of the herd. Elizabeth assumed neither was being paid for their services, but the dog seemed far more attuned to the task, running back and forth and threatening a nip each time a pig turned wayward.

Elizabeth, walking on the cobblestone sidewalk, stopped and leaned her angular body against the unpainted lap siding of a hardware store. Her sepia toned face blended chameleon-like into the faded poplar boards as she watched the procession. She had always been fond of pigs. Her first two chores as a five year old slave were the caring for the three year old daughter of her owners, and the feeding and watering of a litter of shoats. She was fond of all of her dependencies, but she found the piglets somewhat easier to train.

Even when the streets were tolerably dry, there was a stench from the road apples deposited by the horses, pigs and goats so that Washington bore the perpetual odor of an outhouse. The olfactory assault was intensified by the breezes sweeping across the muddy tidal basin of the Potomac River and over the open canal used as a sewage depository. To the southeast of the White House was the rendering plant where her late friend Henry LaRon had worked. A wind working its way northward was enough to knock an ox to his knees. The Dearborn wagons coming around every morning to handle the night soil were over-matched. "Politicians turn out more manure than any other creature on earth," Elizabeth was fond of saying. It's no small wonder that foreign diplomats considered Washington a hardship post.

She wondered how the Catahoula, without a detectable sign from the drover, knew to divert the herd from Pennsylvania Avenue and onto 7th Street towards Clary's Abattoir. Lacking sufficient time today to pursue the young man and slake her curiosity, Elizabeth indexed his shabby clothes in her mind's closet. After over forty years as a seamstress and dress-maker, she frequently remembered people not so much by their faces, but rather by their choice of apparel and the definition it lent to their bodies. And she doubted if that young man owned more than one change of clothes.

She pivoted and entered the mahogany doors into what served as her sectarian cathedral – the clothier firm of Harper & Mitchell's - wherein Mr. Harper engaged in trade with Mrs. General McClean, with whom Elizabeth was only casually acquainted. Mrs. McClean, with a 'noblesse oblige' smile, nodded a greeting in her direction.

Mr. Harper, whose fondness for Elizabeth was decidedly north of a mere mercantile relationship, greeted her with his usual "All the pleasantries of the day to you, Mrs. Keckley." His phrases always reminded Elizabeth of his mahogany doors: well polished with linseed oil so they glistened and shone, but sufficiently wiped down so as not to be sticky.

Chapter I

Mr. Harper extended a yard or so of cashmere from a bolt while Mrs. McClean fondled the cloth between her thumb and forefinger. "Tell me frankly, Mrs. Keckley, do you think this would make a suitable morning robe?"

Elizabeth hesitated as she eyed the cloth and said, "At the risk of seeming rude, I have a matter of some importance to discuss with Mr. Harper that would take only a minute or two in his office and then I would be free to give you my ideas."

"Of course," Mrs. McClean said.

Mr. Harper gestured Elizabeth toward his office with a sweep of his open hand. He closed the door behind her.

"Mr. Harper, you extended me credit when I first came to town on nothing more than the fact you thought I had an honest face. Some proprietors won't deal with a Negro under any circumstances, and yet you let me walk out with over $200.00 in materials with no security whatsoever, except my pledge to return the next day. You pay me a generous commission on all the cloth I purchase for my clients. In short, you have been a godsend."

"Thank you, Mrs. Keckley," said Mr. Harper, steeling himself for the salvo he feared was yet to come.

"But that new cashmere is not of good quality. Good cashmere is made only with the soft undercoat of the goat, and the longer coarse hairs must be combed out. It's a tedious, time-consuming task. That bolt of cloth, I'll warrant, came from an English mill where they are not as fastidious as the Asians. But I would sooner have my tongue pulled out than say that to Mrs. McClean and cause you to lose a sale."

"Thank you for your concern, Mrs. Keckley, but we are the largest clothier in Washington D.C. precisely because we sell only the finest material at a fair price. Now go tell Mrs. McClean exactly what you told me. We'll return that bolt to the manufacturer, and I wouldn't be surprised if you secured Mrs. McClean as a patron."

When Elizabeth returned, Mrs. McClean had wandered over to the silks. She listened patiently to Elizabeth's lecture on the demerits of English cashmere and immediately said, "I'm invited to a supper at Willard's this Sunday and I don't have a decent dress to wear. I want you to make me a dress out of this material. You choose the laces. You can take my measurements now or you can come by my house this afternoon."

Elizabeth was caught off-guard by the suddenness of the request. "It's quite impossible. I'm over-subscribed and short-handed as it is."

"Pshaw! Nothing is impossible. Besides," Mrs. McClean looked conspiratorial, "I happen to know you are desirous of working for the ladies of the White House. I also happen to be a good friend of Mrs. Lincoln and I have it in my power to procure you her work."

Elizabeth wanted to do cartwheels down the aisles. This indeed was her unfulfilled ambition and the reason she had come to Washington.

"Do you know Portia, the young quadroon owned by Colonel Burkey? She's a veritable witch with needles and thread and the Colonel wishes to rent her out. He'll be at my house at two o'clock."

"But, I'm not certain I'm in a position to take on another employee," Elizabeth mumbled as a sort of half-apology.

"Horse feathers," said Mrs. McClean. "The colonel wants $200.00 a year for Portia. I'll front him the money and deduct it from you as you finish my dresses. Then you'll have Portia for the remainder of the year."

Mrs. McClean augured a look deep within Elizabeth's head. "If you're squeamish about hiring a slave, then pay her a salary or set the money aside to buy her freedom. You'll still make out handsomely. I trust all of our dealings aren't going to be such a wrestling match. Remember, two o'clock."

Chapter I

She talked over her shoulder as she fastened her bonnet and headed for the door. "Come by then and you can make the financial arrangements with Colonel Burkey and take my measurements. And bring the laces you select."

Elizabeth felt the calm that always followed when a whirlwind blew away. Turning towards Mr. Harper, Elizabeth said, "And which one is the general, her or Mr. McClean?"

"That woman could march cats through a fish market without a one breaking ranks. And if she sets her mind on introducing you to Mrs. Lincoln, don't you doubt it for a moment."

———•••———

Elizabeth had five minutes to spare as she approached the Georgian townhouse of General and Mrs. McClean. She grasped the brass knocker in her right hand and slammed the tiny lion's head smartly against the door. Soon, a rather imposing black man in well-tailored livery opened the door. Elizabeth recognized the man as someone involved in a rather nasty altercation at Tall Freddie's just a week ago. Tall Freddie's was a bar and restaurant in the Murder Bay section of town, and when she saw straight razors being drawn, Elizabeth had made a hasty exit. The man before her had obviously come to no harm and if he recognized Elizabeth, he gave no indication. "This way, please." he said, pivoting and heading for a large waiting room on the east side of the house. A mature, but vigorous, white man and a young black woman with an oak-leaf complexion were sitting on a sofa covered in a floral-themed Aubusson needlepoint. Elizabeth hoped the girl had made the dress she was wearing, for it was apparent to her well-trained eye that a seamstress of considerable skill had been involved in its crafting.

The man rose and said, "Allow me to present myself. I'm Colonel Junius Burkey. And this is Portia."

Portia made a perfunctory curtsey and sat back down. With that sixth sense that can only be developed by years of living in bondage where the ability to read the whims and moods of others frequently led to physical safety, Elizabeth intuited that drama was afoot.

"I'm Elizabeth Keckley. It's a pleasure to meet you both."

"Mrs. McClean has taken the liberty of preparing a document outlining our respective obligations. If you wish to consult with counsel before signing, I'll certainly understand."

"I'm certain Mrs. McClean has covered everything adequately. Do you have a pen?"

Colonel Burkey, seizing the chance to display a prized object, produced a gold pen from the inside pocket of his coat. "This was made for me by my friend, the jeweler Richard Cross. Isn't it exquisite? It's the latest; the ink is actually carried inside the pen. Unfortunately, I seem to have damaged the nib when I dropped it the other day. Pray be careful, or your hands could be covered in ink."

Elizabeth took the pen in her magical hands, dutifully admired it, and signed with a flourish. Not a smidgeon of ink ran amok.

"Well, I'll leave you two to get acquainted. If you don't object, I'll drop in next week to ensure the transition has come about smoothly." Colonel Burkey turned and headed towards the front door, seemingly unaware that tears had begun to run down Portia's face.

Elizabeth put her arm around Portia and stood silently. After a short while, the doorman returned and said, "Mrs. McClean will see you upstairs now."

As Elizabeth entered the room Mrs. McClean said, "I prefer my shoulders exposed and my bosom well-covered. And at my age I prefer a comfortable waist – I don't want to be corseted in like a German sausage. Leave that to the younger women."

Elizabeth's fingers nimbly pulled the tape measure over and around her body. "Do you need to write those numbers down?" asked Mrs. McClean.

"I'll remember," Elizabeth said matter-of-factly.

"Elizabeth, I think we shall be friends. I intend to help you in any way I can. Just remember, although it may seem as though I stampeded you into this, I think the outcome will be to the greater good of everyone involved. This will all become clearer as time goes by, but I'll be here to help you in anything you may need on Portia's behalf. The Colonel's wife is a dear friend of mine..." Her voice trailed off softly. Elizabeth was beginning to understand.

"I'll expect you here Sunday at ten o'clock with the dress," said Mrs. McClean as she snapped back into martinet mode. "And I've scheduled you a meeting with Mrs. Lincoln early next week at the White House. She will be interviewing mantua makers at that time. Don't let her know we have already decided on you. Let her think it's her idea." Then, like Eve and the serpent, they both smiled warmly.

Downstairs, Portia had dried her eyes, having summoned some inner reservoir of strength. "Let me carry one of your valises," Elizabeth offered. "It's fifteen blocks to my house."

They were no more than two doors from the McClean mansion when Portia grabbed the wrought iron handrail of a neighbors step and silently deposited her breakfast on the cobblestone sidewalk. Elizabeth extended her a kerchief to wipe her mouth. "How far along are you?"

"Better part of three months. Do you know how to keep it from becoming four?"

"I know how to make cotton root bark tea, if that's what you really want to do?"

"Will it hurt?"

"No more than getting kicked by a mule."

Portia managed a thin smile. "Have you ever taken it?"

"Thought about it once. Thought better about it and didn't. Glad I didn't. My boy George hung the moon."

Elizabeth sat the valise on the sidewalk. "Let's rest a spell." She commandeered the suitcase into a chair of sorts and sat. "Did you steal all of their silverware? This thing must weigh fifty pounds."

"I'm carrying in my belly the only thing I took from that house, and I certainly didn't steal it. But it's lost all of its value to me now. Can we do the cotton root bark tonight?"

"No, tonight we start on Mrs. McClean's dress. We'll have our little tea party Sunday night after the dress is delivered. Here comes the omnibus. It goes within two blocks of my house."

Although it was only early afternoon on a mild winter day, the two horses pulling the omnibus were both foaming generously at the mouth. Elizabeth knew a certain amount of foam was caused by the bit, and was probably salubrious. But this foam was thick and tinted, as though they had been grazing in a pasture of red clover. Elizabeth thought about not boarding, but decided two more riders wouldn't add that much of a burden to the beasts. About thirty of the forty seats were occupied. There were two seats together about five rows behind the driver. Portia slid in first and they balanced their packages on their knees.

The horses started their uphill ascent on 7th street. As they neared the busier mercantile district near Pennsylvania Avenue, the bus exceeded its capacity and two lads in their late teens or early twenties were standing in the aisles. The driver turned and looked at Portia and then at Elizabeth. Elizabeth was in a reverie, mentally making Mrs. McClean's dress.

"Move to the rear, please."

Elizabeth was jerked back into the present. Anger started to build in her as she realized they were being ordered to relinquish their seats to two young men who looked strong enough to pull a plow.

"But she is with child."

"And she will be with the chief-of-police if she doesn't step to the rear."

Anger and rage burned within Elizabeth as they ceded their seats to the young men. She spoke in a Gullah accent so she would not be understood and pasted the driver with an African curse – "May your fingers turn into fish hooks and may your ass itch for five hundred years."

"Hice un chune, sistuh," rejoined Portia.

After several blocks the number of departures exceeded the number of new riders until at last Elizabeth and Portia were the sole riders. The universe had shrunk until there were only three inhabitants. The last three people on earth. There were no laws, no customs, no nothing, save the vast expanse of eternity that awaited them.

At the terminus of his route, the driver asked, "How much further to your house?"

"Two blocks."

"I'm ahead of schedule. I'll take you so you don't have to slog through the mud with your valises."

"Thank you, but only if you'll allow me to pump a bucket of fresh well water for the horses. They seem to be in danger of foundering."

Elizabeth worked the pump handle methodically, until it primed and proceeded to fill the oaken bucket with cool water. Repetition of mechanical actions always freed Elizabeth's mind for unfettered, runaway thoughts, and she veered towards tomorrow's meeting with Mary Todd Lincoln. She knew her destiny was entwined with the White House but as of yet she could not fathom her role. Perhaps tomorrow would provide the first clue.

Chapter II

The note delivered Sunday evening to Elizabeth's home instructed her to meet Mrs. McClean at eight o'clock the next morning at Willard's Hotel. Mrs. McClean was sitting in the lobby of the hotel on a comfortable looking couch, drinking coffee and reading a copy of Harper's Bazaar when Elizabeth arrived. She folded the paper when she saw Elizabeth and sat it beside the silver coffee urn on the side table.

"Good morning, Elizabeth. Sit down."

It sounded more like an order than it did an invitation.

"Your dress was the sensation of the party yesterday. I have the names of five or six of the ladies who wish to be introduced. But first things first; today is Mrs. Lincoln's day."

"Young man," she said as she snared one of the hotel employees walking towards the dining area, "Please bring another service for my guest, Mrs. Keckley."

He looked as though he had been asked to sacrifice his first-born. He scurried away and consulted with a man behind the registry desk. The man walked from around the desk and approached the couch and said "Is there a problem, Mrs. McClean?"

"Why yes, there is. Whoever was in charge of washing these

dishes did not do a thorough job. They're still slippery and wet."
With that she lifted her cup and brought it down forcefully
against the edge of the coffee table. It shattered into pieces.
"See – they keep slipping out of my hand." She then lifted the
saucer and repeated the accident. "Could Mrs. Keckley and I
please have some china that we could hold on to?"

The man was at a loss for words and stood there motionless.
Mrs. McClean made a movement towards the porcelain pitcher
holding the cream and that was signal enough for the man to
pivot and head for the dining area. She had not once raised her
voice nor allowed the pleasant smile to slip from her face.

As he hurried away, Mrs. McClean turned to Elizabeth and
said, "I saw a dress here in Harper's that I want you to adapt
for me. It's on the Empress Eugenie, but I want you to adjust
the bust line with bows or something. I don't know why the
royalty in Europe, with the possible exception of Queen Victoria,
don't have a sense of modesty. They keep the entire dairy on
display."

She rustled through the paper searching for the lithograph,
and Elizabeth wondered to herself if this woman had ever been
denied anything that she truly desired.

When the manager returned with two sets of cups and
saucers, his mollified customer casually said, "Please add the
cost of the breakage to my bill. Some of the fault was possibly
due to my clumsiness."

Mrs. McClean filled both their cups from the silver coffee
urn. "So, how is Portia working out? Didn't I tell you she was
gifted?"

"Yes, the credit for your dress goes directly to her. She's
a quick learner. Thank you for prodding me in that direction."
Elizabeth looked at Mrs. McClean evenly. "She's a little under
the weather this week, but she'll be fine."

Mrs. McClean gave an imperceptible nod.

Chapter II

"Now Lizzie, here's the room number that Mrs. Lincoln is staying in upstairs." She slipped a piece of paper to Elizabeth. "Unfortunately, it's on the fifth floor. The stairs will do your constitution a world of good. The General and I were at the World's Fair in New York City in '53 and saw a demonstration of Elisha Otis's elevator with its safety device. He was hoisted about thirty feet up and ordered the single cable suspending the cage to be cut. A man with an ax chopped through that rope as cleanly as you'd chop a turkey's neck, but the elevator only fell a few inches. They're putting them in all the hotels in the North. I suppose technology will catch up to our little burg sometimes. But until it does, we'll have to fight the stairs."

The women talked fashion and dresses for fifteen or twenty minutes until it was time for the appointment with Mary Todd Lincoln. As Elizabeth stood, Mrs. McClean said, "Mrs. Lincoln is really a lovely person, but she has a hair trigger temper whenever provoked. That shouldn't be a problem for you, but it's best to be forewarned."

Elizabeth trudged to the fifth floor. Despite her excellent physical condition due to the combination of frequent walks and strong genetic architecture, she still had to pause several minutes outside the designated room to allow her breathing to return to normal. Once recomposed, she knocked on the door.

"Entre vous!" said a lilting voice on the other side of the door.

Elizabeth was in a quandary. Not sure if that meant 'come in' or 'wait a moment,' she stood in the hallway suspended. Finally the voice said, "Come in." There were two women seated by the window, one reading a newspaper and one crocheting a collar, and one woman standing confidently in the middle of the room.

Elizabeth's well-honed powers of observation led her to believe the three women were cut from the same bolt of genetic cloth – probably sisters. And her much sharper third eye alerted her there would be no introductions offered to confirm or deny this insight.

"You must be Elizabeth Keckley, the dress maker that Mrs. McClean recommended. I understand that you have worked for some of my lady friends in St. Louis. You gave satisfaction, no doubt. Who have you worked for in the city?"

"Among others, Mrs. Senator Davis has been one of my best patrons," replied Elizabeth.

Mary's eyes lit up at the mention of Varina Davis. "I was hurt in so many ways when I heard that Mr. Davis resigned his Senate seat and returned south. He and Mr. Lincoln were both in the Congress in 1847, and Varina and I dined frequently while our husbands were off politicking. I was so looking forward to renewing our friendship."

Mary turned to include the two seated women in the conversation. "Varina and I first met at a levee to welcome the new Congressmen to Washington. After exchanging pleasantries for about fifteen minutes I asked Varina, 'Why don't we meet for breakfast tomorrow?' Varina smiled and said, 'Would two o'clock at Willard's be convenient?'

The ladies laughed.

"She hasn't changed in that regard," said Elizabeth. "She once said that she liked to see the sun rise, as long as she was in a gown and returning from a ball."

"And how did you find Mr. Davis?" asked Mary. Her voice was warm and cheery but Elizabeth sensed that this was dangerous territory; Mary was probing to see if Elizabeth could be trusted to keep family secrets and not gossip.

"I had limited dealings with Mr. Davis, but he was always cordial and pleasant."

Mary knew this to be a half-truth at best, but it was the very answer that she wanted to hear. "And you worked for Mrs.

Lamaire in St. Louis. Did you know that we grew up together in Lexington? She was the only one with enough sand to go out with me and steal watermelons. These two, looking playfully at her sisters, "were too afraid of getting caught. Why does a stolen watermelon always taste the sweetest?"

"The same with a stolen kiss," said Elizabeth. "It's the danger – the excitement. It's the spice that turns a broth into a soup. As it says in Proverbs, 'Stolen waters are sweet, and bread eaten in secret is pleasant.'"

Elizabeth could tell that this comment pleased Mrs. Lincoln. She also knew somehow that at that moment she had been hired. Mary reminisced further with her sisters about Mrs. Lamaire and finally returned to Elizabeth.

"I tell you frankly from the start, we are from the West and we are poor. I cannot afford to pay high prices, but if your terms are reasonable, I think that we have a bargain."

"I assure you my prices are very reasonable. We won't have a problem with that."

"There is a cotillion next Tuesday. Do you think you could fashion me a gown out of this?" Mary lifted a rose-colored, moiré antique swatch of cloth from the table where her sister was sitting and crocheting. "You can pick up the material from Harper and Mitchell's and post it to my account. I've already spoken to Mr. Harper."

The next half hour passed with Elizabeth measuring and Mary expounding on her likes and dislikes in fashions. Finally Elizabeth was convinced that she understood exactly what was expected, so she made her good-byes and exited.

———•✦•———

Elizabeth entered the White House for the first time the following Tuesday with the finished gown in tow. She was led upstairs to Mrs. Lincoln's room. The same two sisters who were at the hotel were present. As she walked in Mary said, "Why have you come at this late hour, Mrs. Keckley? Why have you deceived me so? I haven't time to dress. I shan't dress. Mr. Lincoln will just have to go to the ball with the other ladies."

What a spoiled, petulant bitch, Elizabeth thought. "But I thought I would be in plenty of time. Let me dress you."

"Yes Mary, let Mrs. Keckley dress you. There's plenty of time," assured her sister.

"Let me do your hair," she cajoled. "I can have you ready in no time."

The sisters, who Elizabeth noted, also had not begun to dress, exited and went to their quarters. As soon as her audience disappeared, Mary turned cheerful, almost ebullient. "Did you know that the French ambassador will be here tonight? I always look forward to an opportunity to converse in French. Do you speak any foreign languages, Lizzie?"

"I grew up speaking Gullah, if that can be considered a foreign language."

"I'm not familiar with that. What is it?"

"It's an African dialect spoken by the Negroes in the low country along the coast of South Carolina and Georgia."

"I have a natural ear for languages. You must promise to teach me at the earliest convenience. We can talk about people when they're present without them being the wisest."

"Fsutt'n," said Elizabeth.

Within fifteen minutes Mary was dressed and coifed.

As Elizabeth was fastening a pearl necklace around Mary's neck, Mr. Lincoln walked into the room reciting poetry.

"You're in a poetical mood tonight, Father."

"Yes Mother, these are poetical times," said Mr. Lincoln. "It appears that Madame Elizabeth has met with great success. Your gown is stunning. However, our cat has quite a long tail," referring to the nearly six foot train. "Perhaps it would be in better style if some of the tail were up nearer the top."

"Isn't that just like a man?" Mary said to Elizabeth. "What he admires on other women, he wants to hide on his wife. This is precisely why I need to learn your 'Gullah.' We could be discussing the foolishness of men at this very moment." With that she extended her arm to Mr. Lincoln and he escorted her down the stairs.

Chapter III

Elizabeth's requirements for lodgings in a new city were straightforward and twofold: she wanted to be uphill from the commercial district and she wanted her bedroom window facing east to let in the morning sun. She had always been an early riser. She was a morning person. Indeed, she was like a morning glory, a true heliotrope. She needed more than just light; she needed to feel the rays of the sun sliding along her skin, entering her pores and feeding her spirits. Her best thoughts were morning thoughts; decisions made after sundown always ended in disaster. She had committed, for instance, to marrying James Keckley under the light of a half-moon. Equally as disastrous was her moonlit decision to move to Baltimore and open a school to teach young colored girls her methods of cutting and sewing dresses. That failure had at least led Elizabeth here, where as soon as she finished her third cup of coffee, she would bound down the stairs and out into the treacherous streets of Washington, D.C.

Her desire to be uphill from the business section was an offshoot of Newton's Laws of motion: *"A body propelled downhill in the morning will continue to exhibit momentum throughout the business day."* Still, it was sometimes difficult to lean into the day in this hellhole of a city. The mud alone was enough to derail all but the most determined of pedestrians. Very few streets were paved, due mainly to the short-sightedness of the city fathers. The general tax did not shoulder the cost of paving; rather the houses and businesses were apportioned on their front footages. But the streets were so wide that the costs were too onerous to bear, even by the store owners who would be the main beneficiaries.

"An ill-conceived city," Elizabeth often observed. Washingtonians fondly pointed out that this was the first "topsy-turvy" city ever built. All other cities were built on trade and commerce, and government followed. This was a city built only to serve as a seat of power, and businesses and merchants moved in later to catch the drippings and droppings from the public trough. Elizabeth knew that this distinction of being the first concept city probably lay with the city of Houston, conceived by those crafty speculators A.C. and J.K. Allen, who convinced the Republic of Texas to locate their fledgling government on the uninhabited banks of Buffalo Bayou. The generous donation of several choice lots to the newly elected President Sam Houston didn't seem to hurt their cause. She didn't often mention this due to her sense of social astronomy and the knowledge of her proper orbit in the American firmament. However, when Elizabeth had worked as seamstress to Varina Davis, her husband and now President of the Confederate States, Jefferson Davis, had opined that St. Petersburg in Russia might hold the honor, but relented when Elizabeth explained there was already a Swedish city there on the Neva River before the Russians began building their Capitol. She further argued that Washington should be excluded on the same grounds. There was already the existing municipality of Georgetown on the Potomac. It was simply melded into the new federal district.

He relented, but he stared at Elizabeth for the longest time.

She couldn't tell if he was stunned that a former slave had an active brain, or if he was upset at being bested by the hired help. He was a cold one; salmon could spawn in his veins. As keen as Elizabeth's antennae were, she still had difficulty reading him.

"Elizabeth," he finally said, "I'm probably violating the laws of my home state of Mississippi by allowing you to educate yourself. I might have to declare my library off-limits to you if you continue to accumulate knowledge and use it to best me in arguments." This little joke was as close to a touch of humanity that she ever perceived in Mr. Davis.

Varina Davis was quite the opposite – she was as warm as a Franklin stove on a February morning. She was the second Mrs. Davis, the first died of malaria within four months of her marriage. Although eighteen years younger than Jefferson, Varina was well schooled and quick, and many felt she was his intellectual equal. Both were avid readers and their Washington library was one of the best stocked in the nation.

When employed by the Davises, Elizabeth would arrive precisely at eight o'clock. Varina, however, was a late sleeper and would not rise until the early afternoon. This allowed Elizabeth the luxury of reading five or six hours a day. The library was weighted toward legal texts, a subject that held scarcely any interest for Elizabeth, but there were collections on philosophy, history, religion, and architecture. Without a conscious effort, she was digesting more intellectual fodder than was being dispensed at the finer universities.

Her favorite read by far was Alexis de Tocqueville's *Democracy in America*. It was the most insightful look at the institution of slavery she had ever encountered. Instead of pontificating and preaching, de Tocqueville did something so revolutionary there should be a field of study devoted to its methodology – he talked to people and recorded their observations. He talked to farmers in the East, merchants in the North, and planters in the South. He even talked to the slaves themselves. He talked to people who had manumitted their slaves and to people who had freed their slaves because slavery was no longer economically feasible. He also spoke to people who had grown so dependent upon their slaves that they had lost the skills to fend for themselves. The only group he seemed to have missed, regrettably, was the large plantation owners of the Deep South, where the most egregious sins were leveled upon the captives.

Varina was the first to predict to Elizabeth that there would be hostilities between the North and the South, "You are so very handy, Lizzie, that I think I shall take you south with me."

"When are you planning on going south?"

"Soon. Very soon."

"But I thought Mr. Davis had another two years to his term?"

Varina turned and looked over her shoulder into the full length mirror to admire the train of her dress. "You do know that there will be war, don't you? Mr. Davis will resign his seat in the Senate and we will go south."

"But who will fight?"

"The North and the South, of course. Once that scare crow in a top hat, that Mr. Lincoln, comes to Washington, the South will rebel. They will never submit to the humiliating demands of the Abolitionists. They will fight."

"And who will whip?"

"The South, of course," said Varina with total conviction in her voice. "Throughout history, the people who have fought for their convictions have always emerged victorious. Once the North realizes this, they will concede rather than engage in a long and bloody war."

Varina continued to eye her new dress from different angles. "You had better come south with me, Lizzie. I fear the Northerners will blame the Negroes for the war and will be inclined to treat them harshly. Besides, you'll be back here shortly. Once the South raises an army, we'll march on Washington and I shall live in the White House."

Elizabeth plowed these memories over in her mind as she plodded downhill against an opinionated wind, clutching her bag tightly in one hand and holding her muffler closed around her neck with the other.

Elizabeth's appointment with the Queen Bee of this throbbing cesspool was not for three hours hence, and she had left early to visit her friend, the widow LaRon. Eunice LaRon lived in the Murder Bay section of Washington, just southeast of the White House. This aptly named area housed the free blacks, some enslaved blacks who were allowed a measure of freedom by their owners provided they returned every Friday night to their masters home to part with their weekly wages, and a large number of slaves who had begun streaming into the Capitol since the election of Lincoln with little more than the clothes on their back and a vague hope in their hearts. In short, it was an inferno; desperate people with no money, no skills to acquire money, and no training to handle money if they happened to chance upon some. It was precisely this type of person that lunged from an alcove on 14th and C streets and grabbed the straps of Elizabeth's bag.

He was a skinny lad, with that ashy skin that looks like a sycamore tree when its bark is peeling, with fear and panic dripping from his eyes. He had clearly underestimated Elizabeth's strength as well as her attachment to the contents of her bag. It was not the forty or so dollars that impelled Elizabeth to struggle so tenaciously; it was the tools of her trade that caused her to fight like a lioness protecting her cubs. The bag contained tapes and thimbles and scissors. It contained exotic tools such as sewing awls, which she only needed to use on rare occasions, and shears and lace bobbins.

They were pulling the bag back and forth much like lumberjacks working a two-man saw, when a voice said, "Leave off, or I'll dispatch your worthless soul to the bowels of Hell!" Elizabeth turned to see a smallish man pointing a derringer directly at the head of the intruder, who relinquished his claim to the bag and beat a hasty retreat down the muddy street.

"Thank you for your bravery," said Elizabeth.

"It was not bravery, Mrs. Keckley. It was pure stupidity. I acted without thinking."

"Thank you anyway. And how do you know my name?"

"I'm J.L. DeBonet. I'm an actor over at Ford's Theater. I've seen you delivering costumes that you've created for the characters in our plays. I'm afraid we've never been formally introduced."

He extended his hand and Elizabeth grasped it enthusiastically. She could feel his hand trembling. "If you release my hand I fear that I might faint from fright. I'm not the sort who engages in altercations. This gun is merely a stage prop. It's not loaded and even if it were, I wouldn't have the faintest notion on how to cock and shoot it. And those words that I said are merely my rehearsed lines in an upcoming play. As I said, I'm not brave at all – merely rash and foolish. I hope I don't faint."

"My friend's house is around the corner. Come and let her make us some tea while you recover," Elizabeth responded. He was becoming more blanched by the minute. She secured his elbow and propelled him towards Mrs. LaRon's.

Once inside, introductions made and tea steeped, J.L. composed himself in a comfortable chair and stared blankly out the window. Elizabeth related the morning's events to Eunice, who shook her head from side to side. "In broad daylight," she lamented. "In front of God and everybody. What's this world coming to?" They shook their heads and J.L. silently drank his tea.

"I've been afraid to live here ever since Henry passed. Don't laugh and don't scoff at me for what I'm going to tell you, Elizabeth, but I'm considering going back into slavery."

Elizabeth sucked tea into her wind-pipe and coughed violently. When she recovered, Eunice continued, "I'll still be free, but I'm going to move back to the plantation on the Wye River. I always loved the Eastern Shore and I have so many friends and relatives there. Mrs. Claggett has manumitted her slaves and they are all paid a wage as farm hands. I'll return as the cook. I've been in written communication with Mrs. Claggett and we've reached an agreement. Do you know what I miss the most about the plantation? It's the chickens. I love the way they look. I love feeding them. I love gathering the eggs. I like to see the roosters strut and I like to wake up in the mornings to their crowing."

Elizabeth returned her cup to its companion - a blue saucer with a chipped edge.

"I miss farm life myself."

Suddenly reconstituted, J.L. ejected from his chair. "I saw the blackheart lurking at the corner of 14th and C, peering around the building. My bones told me that he was up to villainy. As I was undetected by him, I secreted myself into the doorway of Peterson's Lumber. As Mrs. Keckley stepped off the boardwalk and into street, he made his move. He grabbed the valise and yanked, but Mrs. Keckley held firm. When he saw that she didn't intend to yield, he reached into his pocket and pulled out a folding razor. That primal part of the mind that impels a man to act long before his reason is engaged, bade me to reach into my pocket and produce this derringer, which I happily had on my person solely to be used as a stage prop in tonight's production." J.L. was becoming more animated.

"No wait! He had a gun, not a razor. Or perhaps there were two of them, one of which was holding a knife. I cried out 'cease and desist.' The one with the knife made a movement towards me. I calmly leveled the derringer at his head. 'Your next step will be the first step that you take into Eternity.' He halted his advance, but holding the knife by its point, raised it over his head and threw it at me with great force. Fortunately it was the handle end that slammed into my chest. It clanged harmlessly on the cobblestones. That's when I said, 'Leave off, or I'll dispatch your worthless souls to the bowels of Hell.' They broke and ran like frightened rabbits."

Elizabeth and Eunice looked at each other dumb struck.

"Where can I buy a hunting knife?" J.L. asked excitedly. "I'll need one to cement my story."

Elizabeth and Eunice looked at each other blankly, as J.L. made script changes to the adventure. Soon, he noticed the looks of disbelief being exchanged by the two women.

"I don't know what kind of friends you have, but my friends are theater people. They want – no, they demand – to be thoroughly entertained. They would be disappointed if I didn't craft and polish this story for maximum effect. People go into theater because real life is so monumentally boring and mind numbing, and they have a chance to create something every night that is exciting, or poignant, or at the very least, interesting. I'm merely splashing a little color on the drab canvas of life. I would have thought that you two could appreciate that life isn't always a field of clover. It's frequently brutish and nasty and we have to snatch happiness out of the bottom of a pickle barrel whenever we can. Death can come quickly and unannounced; and when people die they tend to stay that way."

Eunice wasn't as fortunate as the fabricated hero in J.L.'s play; that last statement went point-first into her heart.

"Come look at Henry's knives, and pick out one that's suitable. I'm giving them away anyway."

"Only if you allow me to return the kindness. I would like

for you both to be my guests at tonight's play. It's perfectly dreadful. But I have a prominent part. It's called *The Mulatto*. If you've ever thought that your opinion of white people could sink no lower, just wait until you see us dressed in black-face and imitating Negroes."

As Eunice led J.L. into the kitchen, Elizabeth heard him say, "And how did Henry pass, if I may ask?"

"All of Henry died at Clary's Abattoir two years ago, and most of me along with him. But I can tell the story now and only cry dry tears, if you want to hear it."

Chapter IV

A small sign above the door said 'Clary's Abattoir.' The local citizenry referred to it as the 'slaughter house.' The workers, like Henry LaRon, who sweated there fifty-four hours a week called it the 'blood box' or simply 'the box'. The unpainted, rectangular building was built for the sole purpose of efficiently converting animals, mostly beefs, into foodstuffs to grace the tables of homes and restaurants.

Along one outside wall was an earthen incline of some twenty feet leading up to an enclosure on the second floor. After the cows were herded up the dirt ramp and nestled in a restraining pen, the door was opened and the animal forced onto a metal-lined chute that descended to the first floor. The chute was kept well slicked with tallow so the cow would slide to the bottom at an increasingly brisk pace. Henry would stand slightly to the left of the chute holding a twelve-pound maul over his shoulder. His first task was to swing the maul at precisely the right moment, meeting the oncoming cow slightly above the eyes. The impact, if timed correctly, was enough to kill the animal, or at least, to render him unconscious. On those rare occasions when the initial impact failed to do its job, Henry kept another maul, lighter in weight and tapered to a point, which he would quickly grab and swing down on the top part of the skull where the bone was much thinner. Provided the maul found its target, it was always lethal. But as a third wave of defense against a recalcitrant cow, a revolver hung on a nail. Henry had only used the revolver once in a three-year period, which is why all the eighteen other workers liked Henry working as the 'greeter.' The noise of the revolver in the confinement of the building was shattering to the ears of the workers, and the owner didn't like the additional cost of the bullet.

Once he felled the animal, Henry's next task was to take a twelve-inch butcher knife and slit the throat of the animal, severing the carotid artery. He would then slide a rope with a slip knot around one of the rear legs of the carcass. The rope was attached to a pulley powered by a steam engine which took the carcass out of Henry's area and over to the bleed pit. Henry would clean his work area with a hose coming from a cistern on top of the building. He would hone his knife on a leather strop after every cow, and clean his maul to ensure a good grip on the hickory handle. He would then pull a rope to open the spring-loaded door on the second floor and yell, "cow," beginning the process anew.

On a normal day, Henry dispatched forty or fifty beeves. If the slaughter was hogs, the tally was less. Henry was content in his job, allowed to work at his own pace, and paid nearly as much as the white men.

"Well done, Henry. Well done," Mr. Clary said. Henry was wiping bear grease off his hands with a calico rag. He had rebuilt the pump that supplied the water to the boiler in less than four hours. Although he didn't say it aloud, Mr. Clary was doing math in his head; four hours without machines yielded seventeen processed cows, whereas with machines it would have been twenty-five. "Yessir Henry, well done. In fact, I think you've earned a vacation. Your train ticket to New York is already on my desk. We'll leave Friday morning. You still have kinfolk there? In between reminiscing with them and sight-seeing, maybe one day you can meet me at Wilson's Pump and we'll look around and see if they have anything to help us modernize this old plant." Mr. Clary had placed his order this morning via telegraph.

Since Henry was the most mechanically minded of all of Mr. Clary's employees, it was only natural that he accompany Mr. Clary on the trip to be trained in the construction of the new system. Having an uncle in the city where he could be lodged free of charge only added to the conviction that Henry was definitely the man for the task.

"We'll buy a wagon and a team in New York and you can drive 'em home. I know where I can get a bargain on four Morgans." Not only had Clary bought the horses that morning via the wire, he had also pre-sold them locally for a price that more than covered what he would have to pay Henry for the six-day trip.

Henry had never ridden on a train before nor had he spent a solitary night alone since his marriage to Eunice some fifteen years prior. Eunice mollified his anxiety somewhat by persuading Elizabeth to make a modest adjustment to her planned trip to New York in order to be on the same train as Henry. Elizabeth was combining a business trip and a small vacation. She would spend three days in New York dealing with the millinery shops and clothiers, and then accompany her friend Frederick Douglass on a four city speaking tour.

"I'm as nervous as a four-balled house cat in a room full of rocking chairs, Elizabeth. I feel so out of place traveling with all these rich white folks."

"We won't so much be traveling *with them* as *behind them*," Elizabeth said. "We will be confined to the last car. But don't worry – trains are pretty much run by black folks. All of the porters and bag boys will be there with us."

That evening Elizabeth won enough money playing poker with the night shift porters to cover the cost of her trip. She could have won more but she folded a hand with four Jacks so Henry could win a pot.

———•·•———

Henry's uncle was waiting as the train pulled into the station and Henry disembarked from the coach car nearest the caboose. "Hey, hey, hey," called out Uncle Willie. The two men embraced in a bear-hug. "How's Eunice gittin' along?"

"Eunice is fine. She's as fine as elderberry wine. Probably finer now that I'm out from underneath her feet for a few days."

"You remember Elizabeth Keckley?" Henry asked Willie.

The two men laughed and talked and briefed each other on family matters as they walked toward the terminal. As they neared the front of the train, they almost collided with Mr. Clary as he emerged from his first class car. "Mr. Clary, this is my Uncle Willie."

"William Mayes at your service, sir. Let me grab that bag for you. I have a buggy in front. Can we give you a ride to your hotel?"

"I'm staying at the Tremont. Would it be out of your way?"

"Not at all. We're going right by there," Willie responded. "That landau hitched to the bay is ours."

Mr. Clary sat in the back while Elizabeth and Henry and Willie sat side by side in the front and continued their easy conversation about everything and nothing.

"How long are you going to be in town?"

"Over the weekend and into the middle of next week."

"Hallelujah! I've put together a baseball team and tomorrow we're going over to Hoboken to play the Colored Union Club.

You can play for me if you remember anything that I taught you." They both laughed.

Henry turned to include Mr. Clary into the conversation. "Mr. Clary plays on a team in Washington. They have uniforms and everything."

"It's true. Next to making money I love baseball better 'n anything in this world."

"Hoboken is just across the Hudson river from New York. Perhaps you can come over and watch us?"

"I have business on Saturday morning, but I should be free in the afternoon."

As they pulled in front of the Tremont, Willie gave him the pertinent information and off-loaded his bag. "Thanks for the ride and I'll see you Saturday. Henry, I'll see you tomorrow at 8 o'clock at Wilson's Pump and Engine Co. Can you get him there?" he asked Willie.

"It's not six blocks from my house. He'll be there."

It was a beautiful fall day in late September – crisp and clean. Mr. Clary was excited as he approached the sandy lot in Hoboken. He knew that baseball was only a game, but he watched for the past fifteen years as it worked its way into the American psyche much like a tapeworm. Once in a man's system there seemed to be no remedy. It just nestled there, benign parasite that it was, feeding at its leisure. Mr. Clary had been bitten about ten years ago, and it turned into a smoldering love fest. He couldn't wait for the first warm day of spring to gather his friends and teammates and head to the vacant park just west of the White House. Although his expectations were low concerning today's outing, his insides were still atingle. Perhaps Willie would ask him to address one or both teams after the game, and he could give them a pep talk on the finer points of the game. Baseball wasn't as simple as it looked to the casual observer. It had the strategy of a chess match with every pitch and every bat nuanced. Fielders have to be shifted, runners on base have to know how big a lead to take, depending on the score, the strike count and the batter's ability. Managers flash instructions to the players with a series of silent hand gestures. Managers were like Generals; their tactics switching in response to what the other manager was instructing his players to do. It looks so simple and yet it is so layered and subtle. He would have to keep his talk simple – not overwhelm them with too much at once.

Elizabeth had coerced Frederick Douglass into accompanying her to the ballpark. He was dressed as though he were giving a funeral oration. "For God's Sake, Frederick, don't you ever just relax? This is a baseball game. Not a lecture."

"Elizabeth, these are momentous times. We are poised at a crossroad in History. The Negro is on the cusp of Destiny. We must do all in our power to assure that momentum is not lost. We must extend our fullest energies to achieving the black man's proper place in society."

"Frederick, I'm on holiday, for God's sake. Take the starch out of your shirt for two hours and let's enjoy the ball game. I want to learn about the game and I want to watch Henry and I want a beer."

"Elizabeth, baseball is just a silly game played by boys who should be men. Do you honestly think that something as inconsequential as a baseball game can ever have a role in elevating our race to an equal status with whites? The notion is absurd. This is a waste of time."

"Well, at least let me waste it in a pleasant mood and get me a beer. Here comes Henry's team." Elizabeth stood up and whistled between her teeth.

Henry's team batted first. The first batter was just a nubbin of a man, his size better suited to being a jockey than a baseball player. The first two pitches were balls, barely outside the strike zone, and Clary noted the excellent velocity with which the pitcher threw. On the third pitch the batter whirled around and instead of swinging he cushioned the ball softly against the bat and trickled it slowly towards the third baseman. Clary watched the third baseman run in to field the ball, but when he looked back, the runner was already crossing first base. Clary had never seen a man with such speed. He collared a peanut vender and bought a ten cent bag of salt-boiled peanuts.

The next batter slammed a screaming ground ball towards center field when the short-stop emerged out of nowhere and snared the ball in his glove. Without looking he under-handed the ball to the second baseman, who deftly touched the bag and in one motion leapt into the air and threw the ball to first base. Double Play! Clary was stunned.

The next batter was Henry. The first pitch was a strike – a fastball that seemed to violate the laws of motion. It sped towards home plate about four inches higher than Henry's waist, but as it neared home plate, it abruptly dove towards the ground. The next pitch was another fastball and Henry connected with a 'splat' that sounded like a musket fired at close range. The ball flew so far over the fielder's heads that they didn't run in pursuit, but merely turned and watched in reverence. "I'll be damned," Clary muttered beneath his breath. It was as though the swing had caught Clary in his solar plexus. He had to sit down. Acid churned in his stomach. "Must be bad peanuts." Clary suffered through four more innings and two more cannon launchings by Henry before he left the ball park. "What a waste of talent" Clary thought to himself. If only there was some way he could use Henry on his team in Washington. "Wishful thinking" he told himself. "Even if Henry were allowed to play, I suspect he wouldn't do that well against the superior competition. And that must have been the tightest wrapped baseball in America, with a core of at least 4 inches of India rubber. Still..." Clary trudged toward the ferry. "I felt fine this morning, now I feel like throwing up. That'll teach me to buy peanuts from street venders."

———— ·•· ————

Other than watching helplessly as a man slipped off a ferry and drowned in the Susquehanna River, Henry's return trip to Washington was uneventful.

After installing the new equipment, Mr. Clary approached Henry about trying out as the 'greeter.' "Just like hittin' a baseball, and it pays three dollars more a week."

Henry was a natural. His sense of timing was exquisite. That twelve-pound maul became an extension of Henry's very arm. "Cow"... slide...whack! Cow"...slide...whack!

It was a good life. Only once did Henry have any misgivings. A herd of Herefords were being processed; and it was shaping up to be a routine day, until about the fifteenth cow.

When cows were pushed onto the chute, their eyes became fixated on the chute, about three feet in front of their hooves. They never seemed to notice Henry awaiting them at the bottom. But this fifteenth cow was different. About ten feet into her descent, she turned those baleful eyes directly at Henry and lowed in a voice that froze him. He couldn't swing. The cow stumbled a little as she reached the bottom and quickly righted herself. She turned her back on Henry and stood motionless.

"Need help, Henry?" shouted the man in the bleed pit.

"No, I got it."

He removed the revolver from the nail and placed it point blank against the skull. One shot and the heifer fell in place.

For the longest time, Henry would wake up in the middle of the night and hear that plaintive mooing. He would see those large eyes boring into his soul, and he would stay up the rest of the night.

Herefords were introduced into America by Henry Clay, the Great Compromiser. Due to their overall hardiness and their thickly marbled and juicy steaks, they were becoming America's most dominant breed. Henry dispatched plenty of Herefords in the years since his staring contest with the heifer, but never encountered a similar problem.

On a sultry summer day in 1860, Henry met another Hereford that broke the monotony of the day. He noticed the maul was working loose on the hickory shaft. He could feel it shift slightly as he swung. At lunch time he searched for a nail to drive into the tapered end of the handle that ran through the maul. A nail would widen the shaft and tighten the fit. Unable to find a suitable nail in the plant, he made a mental note to bring a fourteen penny nail from home the next day. When the whistle blew at 12:30 signaling the end of lunch, Henry took his position and hefted his sledge. "Cow", he yelled.

Twelve hundred pounds of beef came sliding toward him. As Henry swung, the twelve-pound ball of metal slipped off the end of the shaft and crashed through the window. This sudden shift in balance caused Henry to stumble in front of the approaching cow. Even female Herefords are horned, and the one on the right side of her head caught Henry below his chin and entered his skull. Henry was dead immediately, but the Hereford couldn't dislodge him. She shook her head violently, but Henry swung from side to side like a cornhusk doll. The worker from the bleed pit ran over and took the revolver off the nail, and one shot ended the macabre dance.

Chapter V

Elizabeth treaded up the stairs of the White House and down the west hall to an open door. William, the honey bear of a man who escorted her, motioned with his hand for Elizabeth to enter. Mrs. Lincoln was standing at the window with her back to the door. She stood without a trace of movement. It would have been impossible for Mrs. Lincoln not to have heard her approaching, given the percussions set off every time Elizabeth's heavy shoes struck the bare wooden floors and the swishing of her furbelow as it scraped the floor with each step.

After an interval Elizabeth said, "Should I come back in a while, ma'am? William said you were ready to receive me."

Mary still did not turn to face Elizabeth, but lifted her right hand with the index finger extended indicating, Elizabeth assumed, that Mary needed another moment.

Finally, she turned and Elizabeth could see she had been crying. Not a hard cry like something had just happened, but that deep, soft crying women do occasionally to cleanse the soul. Elizabeth had once tried to explain this phenomenon to her then husband, James Keckley, but gave up in exasperation, exclaiming "It's more like bookkeeping for the heart. It balances everything inside." James looked at her as though she was explaining how to fly by flapping his arms quickly.

"Today is March 10th. It's the birthday of our little son Eddie who died eleven years ago. He was only three years old when the fevers took him. Strange – I didn't even know it was his birthday until I found myself crying. Have you ever lost a child, Mrs. Keckley?"

"Praise God, no. I only have one son George and he's safely studying at Wilberforce College."

"I know Wilberforce. Do you know Mr. Chase in my husband's cabinet? He was a founder and endower of the college. I guess even Lucifer himself does a good deed on occasion. I lobbied against his appointment, but Mr. Lincoln had his mind set. Have you met Mr. Lincoln yet? He's a great lawyer. He can walk around an argument and look at the back side better than any man alive. But he has no judgment of people. Mr. Chase, indeed! The man is only concerned with furthering his own interests. He has no loyalty and no integrity. And that Stanton is as crooked as a Virginia fence."

Mrs. Lincoln spat out the words with real venom. She had changed directions quicker than a quarter horse. Elizabeth's friend Artemas once described a weather occurrence that sailors call an 'ox-eye'. When at sea, sometimes in the distance, one can see a dark cloud no larger than an 'ox-eye'. Experienced sailors run to lower some sail. The 'ox-eye' grows so quickly that within minutes you're in the middle of gale force winds. The 'ox-eye' that had puffed up around Mrs. Lincoln dissipated as quickly as it had arisen. No storm this time, just a stiff breeze. But Elizabeth made a note in the ship's log. She'd heard gossip about Mrs. Lincoln's outbursts, but thankfully was spared seeing one today.

Mary Todd Lincoln seemed to be one of those magnetic people who no matter where they stood in a gathering exerted a gravitational pull on everything in the room until they were the exact epicenter. She was a small woman – maybe five-two. Her eyes reminded Elizabeth of Medusa; dangerous to gaze upon, but impossible to ignore. She looked like a banty rooster. Elizabeth had won a fair amount of money betting on cock-fights back home, and she could pick those with a taste for the kill. *"And this is someone I would never bet against."* Elizabeth pegged her age in the early forties. She was still an attractive woman, due mainly to those magnetic eyes. *"Old age won't be kind to her,"* thought Elizabeth. *"White women don't age gracefully anyway; and this one is already fifteen pounds above her fighting weight. But I still wouldn't bet against her."*

"Now tell me, Lizzie – I'm thinking of painting this room blue. I'm going to renovate this ugly old house. If Mr. Lincoln won't take my advice on something as simple as appointing Judas and Brutus to his cabinet, then I'll busy myself with a project. Do you know anything about paints?"

"My friend Artemas does. He was the painter for the restoration of the Cathedral in Baltimore. I believe the Cathedral and the Capital Building had the same architect, a Mr. Hoban. Artemas will be sailing in tomorrow. I'll present him, if you wish."

"Splendid! Bring him around at 10 o'clock Thursday."

Up until now, the White House had been as silent as a mausoleum. Suddenly, Elizabeth thought the opening volley of the war Varina Davis had predicted had been fired. The yelling and whooping sounded as though a cavalry were riding horses up the stairs. Mary didn't seem concerned. "Come and meet my boys," she beamed.

Two boys, barely out of knee britches, charged up the stairs, each leading a harnessed animal. The older was reined to a pony; the younger had a rope around the neck of a heifer.

"Get those animals out of here right now, or I'll start cutting switches," threatened Mary. Both Elizabeth and the boys knew the threat was hollow.

"We're going to the fort on the roof," rejoined the older boy.

"You're going to your eternal reward if you don't march both of those beasts out of here right now," Mary said, sounding a bit more serious. "But before you go, come and meet Mrs. Keckley."

The boys approached, and she rested her hand lovingly on the shoulder on the older boy. "This is William, known to us affectionately as Willie. Willie will be twelve in February, provided God grants me the will power to restrain myself."

Willie removed his cap and bowed with an exaggerated swoop. "I am deeply honored Mrs. Keckley, if I can be of any service at all, please feel free to call."

Elizabeth suppressed a giggle and answered, "Thank you, William. I am so pleased to make your acquaintance."

"And this is Tad. He's ten."

Tad bore an unnatural resemblance to a Jack-o-lantern, with the possible exception that a Jack-o-lantern had fewer and better teeth. Tad blandly walked over to Elizabeth, pressed her hand to his cheek, and said, "Hello, Miss Jib. Would you like to go outside and see our goat?"

Elizabeth had grown up speaking Gullah and was accustomed to the soft and lazy-lipped way that most slaves spoke English, so she possessed a fairly accomplished ear. But she had some difficulty understanding Tad. He sounded as though he had just returned from an elocution class, but had forgotten to take the marbles out of his mouth.

"Perhaps later, Tad. I have business with your mother at the present."

What a loving child, Elizabeth thought. He continued to hold her hand.

"If you don't take those animals out of here right now, I'm

personally going to lead them over to Clary's," reprimanded Mrs. Lincoln.

"I guess this is the first time that they've had these animals in here," Elizabeth said.

"Yes, how did you know?"

"Because cows can't walk down stairs."

Tad couldn't tell if he was being teased. He looked at his mother to see if he could pluck some clue from her expression. Unfortunately, his mother was as nonplussed as he was.

"I've never heard that, Elizabeth. But again, I've never seen a cow in a house. Are you sure we can't lead her out?"

"She won't go. She'll balk at the top of the stairs, and if you push her, she'll only buckle and fall."

Mary looked at Tad, then the heifer, then back at Tad. "Go get your father, Tad."

Tad bolted from the room. Mary eyed the heifer as though she were considering calling in a butcher. Presently Mr. Lincoln entered the room. He didn't so much walk as he jangled. His movements didn't flow smoothly. Elizabeth thought that he looked like a praying mantis. His extremities were too large for his body. It looked as though he had more than two legs and he was taller than she had remembered. He was also uglier. He looked bemused.

"I grew up on a farm," he said, "But I never heard that." Tad had obviously apprised Mr. Lincoln of the dilemma. "Cows must be like bureaucrats; easy to get 'em in but darn near impossible to get 'em to leave."

He grabbed the harness and led the heifer down the hall and to the top of the stairs. As predicted, she balked at the top of the stairs. Mr. Lincoln walked to the side of the animal and reached under her belly with both arms. He tensed and straightened, lifting the befuddled calf up to his chest. Elizabeth quickly did her farm math – a calf weighs about 80 pounds at birth and about 800 after a year. By her best guess, Mr. Lincoln had just hefted about 400 pounds. She wasn't sure that even Artemas could do that. As he slowly lumbered down the stairs, Mary said, "Mr. Lincoln may not go down as our wisest president, but I'll bet that he'll go down as our strongest."

"Do you realize that you just lifted about four hundred pounds?" Elizabeth asked admiringly.

"I deal with Congress. I have to clear away four hundred pounds of bull every day just to get to my office. At least here I encounter the entire cow. With Congress I'm dealing mostly with rear-ends," he said from the bottom of the stairs.

Small laughter hung in the air when Mrs. Lincoln screamed in a voice shrill enough to kill lice. Mr. Lincoln bounded up the stairs. His secretaries, Nicolay and Hay, rushed down the hall from their shared office. Elizabeth's eyes flew to the boys, to see if their safety was imperiled. They seemed to be in no danger, but were staring at their mother wide-eyed. "What is it?" shouted Mr. Lincoln.

"There!" Mrs. Lincoln said in a broken, pitiable voice, as she extended her finger and pointed at a mouse couched timidly along the wall. It wasn't even a full grown mouse, more like a baby mouse out for his first stroll. Tad walked over and scooped him up in both hands.

"Don't worry, Mother. I'll take him outside." Mary hugged Elizabeth and Elizabeth could feel her shaking. "My boys have a small zoo downstairs and yet we don't even have a house cat. If you don't rid this house of rodents, I'm moving back to Springfield," she said to Mr. Lincoln. She couldn't stop shivering.

"Artemas has a special poison that he uses for rats. We'll talk to him about mixing you some when he comes Thursday. He got it from the South American Indians when he was sailing down there. It's very potent."

"I must lie down. Could you put a cold compress on my head, Elizabeth? I'm afraid I'm coming down with one of my headaches."

"Of course," Elizabeth said as she guided Mary towards the bedroom.

"*I like her*" Elizabeth noted to herself, "*but the woman is as strange as riding boots on a rooster.*"

Chapter VI

Thursday was a typical wintry day in Washington, D.C. It was freezing as the sun climbed out of the Chesapeake Bay, shook itself dry and gave just off enough heat to begin the slow melt of the thin layer of ice covering most of the city. Elizabeth had long maintained that Washington weather was the worst in the world. Cold in the north could be fought and at least neutralized. You could always put on more clothes or get closer to the fire. The cold in Washington didn't affect the body so much as it did the soul. It probed around your body like an oyster knife looking for a near invisible seam, and when found, it opened you up in a way that could not be treated with the traditional weapons of winter warfare. Only politicians, with their eternally lit lamps of smugness and self-righteousness, seemed immune.

As a child Elizabeth had adopted the unshakable idea that the people of a region were responsible for the weather. The south was warm and languid because of the lava-like blood that oozed through the veins of black and white alike. The people of the north were distant and icy, causing those long and solitary winters. Washington was the navel of the country, taking its cue from the politicians who plied their trade there. It was neither fish nor fowl, but insincere, changing on a whim, always keenly attuned to the shifting winds of public opinion. Hence, you could leave the house in the morning wearing two coats, and walk home in the evening carrying both across your arms. It was an unending cycle of freeze and thaw – freeze and thaw. Eunice was fond of saying, "A week of winter in Washington is like a year in Purgatory."

Portia was proving to be heaven-sent. Not only was she as magical with needle and thread as Mrs. McClean had advertised, but she also had managerial skills. Elizabeth could outline the work load for the day and Portia would apportion it out to the other girls. Elizabeth could return in the afternoon and find most every task had been completed. Elizabeth, having apprenticed under overseers, always laid out more work than could be achieved in a normal work day.

Artemas offered a forearm to Elizabeth for support as they began the ascent up the steps to the White House. They were among the first to use the steps today and the hoar frost provided adequate footing. Robert, one of the servants employed in the White House, greeted them inside the massive doors. Elizabeth noted how dowdy and worn his clothes were.

"Mrs. Lincoln is upstairs. Come into the waiting room and I'll announce you."

Elizabeth and Artemas followed Robert into the anteroom. A balding, middle-aged man, nattily attired in a seersucker suit, was the room's solitary occupant. He shot straight out of his chair upon seeing Elizabeth and Artemas. "The tide must be up in the Potomac and every piece of foul jetsam is washing ashore," the man exclaimed.

"It's rather like some strong-armed sea man was emptying the captain's chamber pot and threw its contents all the way into the White House," shot back Artemas.

"I'm barely hired and I'll be dismissed my first hour for precipitating a race riot," Elizabeth said to herself.

Artemas glared and continued, "It's jetsam when it's tossed overboard and called flotsam when it washes ashore, you weak-kneed land lubber. It would be easier to teach a pig how to shave than it would be for me to teach you how to be a proper sailor."

At that, both men broke into wide smiles and embraced in a bear hug.

"Elizabeth, this is Doctor Ephraim George Squier, the most unfit man for sea travel that God ever allowed on the deck of a ship."

"I'm afraid he's limned me fairly. How many of your and Uncle Salty's meals did I merely warm up for the fishes?"

"Most every one, as I recall."

Doctor Squier squinted at Elizabeth. "I trust that you're able to get Artemas to cook for you on occasion. A rare treat, indeed. I've dined at The Eutaw House in Baltimore, Antoine's in New Orleans, and the St. Charles here in Washington, and I swear, Artemas is the finest chef of the lot. I'd give a week's wages for another bowl of your turtle gumbo."

"I often wondered if it tasted as good on the way up as they did on the way down. The credit goes to Uncle Salty. I just helped him in the galley when time permitted. I was really the ship's carpenter; a wood butcher as it were."

Dr. Squier looked at Elizabeth and continued, "When we were anchored off the Galapagos Islands, Artemas and Uncle Salty discovered that the giant tortoises couldn't up-right themselves if you rolled them on their backs. So they loaded up the decks of the ship with foundered turtles, an ingenious way to ensure meat for a sea voyage. Sadly, so many ships started to do it, that I hear that it's caused a scarcity of turtles. What was the name of that ship?"

"The Beagle" Artemas answered.

"How long were you aboard?"

"About two years. Uncle Salty and I signed on at Montevideo and mustered out at Tahiti. Too much time at port to suit Salty. Too many inland excursions looking at rocks and animals and bugs, but mostly he hated hanging around with all those dry-land sailors."

"That Mr. Darwin published his book about all that about two years ago. Caused quite a kick-up with the religious folk back in England. I got an extra copy if you'd care to read it. You're part of history."

"Thank you, no. I've only read one book in my life, thanks to you, and I don't feel the need to read another."

They both laughed and again the doctor looked at Elizabeth. "I taught this pirate how to play chess to relieve the monotony of a sea voyage. Once he became slightly adept, we began to wager upon the outcome of the matches. He not only relieved the monotony of sea voyage, he also relieved me of most of my money. Believing Artemas was benefiting from that run of good fortune often times bestowed on beginners, and lacking any more hard specie, I proffered a vellum bound copy of *The Compleat Angler* 'gainst 4 Half Eagles. It was as though Paul Morphy himself was looking over Artemas's shoulder and guiding his hand. Maybe twelve moves in, and Isaac Walton's classic descends from the hands of a gentleman to the clutches of a wharf rat." They both chortled.

"Whatever happened to the volume? I'd pay handsomely to redeem it."

"That's not possible. But I'll tell you where you may go and read it. Or to be more accurate, where you may go and read half of it," said Artemas.

"Why only half?'

"Well, every evening at grog-time, Uncle Salty, who had no schooling, would ask me to read him a page or two." Artemas leaned into his story with relish. "He loved listening to that book. Over and over. Night after night. I damn near memorized that thing. He had a plan; after we quit the sea, we would go to England and fly fish at each and every stream and pond that old Isaac Walton had fished. In the fall of '54, we laid over on the Dutch Isle of Tortola. Uncle Salty became enamored of a local beauty named Rosita. Rosita wanted her bedroom wall-papered like she had seen in London. Eager, but lacking the proper materials, Uncle Salty suggested the pages of 'The Compleat Angler'. Rosita agreed, but was insistent that only the odd numbered pages be facing out, a request to which Uncle Salty readily conceded. Except for the page that described the making and mixing of paints; he made me promise that even or odd, that page would be facing out."

"So, my beloved tome is now decoration for a brothel?"

"No one mentioned the term 'brothel'," countered Artemas.

"No, but someone mentioned the word 'Salty.' And knowing that scoundrel, 'brothel' is the proper word. So, tell me. Was the paint page even or odd?"

"Happily, it was odd."

"And the beautiful vellum binding?" asked Dr. Squier, resigned that the story couldn't take a turn for the worse.

"We took that back aboard and sewed chain mail on the ends, borrowed a brass hasp off a foot locker for a clasp, and converted rosary beads into a carrying strap. Uncle Salty presented Rosita with a most attractive purse the next day. She must have appreciated it; I didn't see him on board for four nights". Everyone laughed.

Elizabeth fought to not reveal how thoroughly she was enjoying this conversation. God, she envied the freedom of men. And she particularly liked this man, who could so casually talk of brothels in front of a woman with no trace of embarrassment.

"So, how is the defiler of fine arts these days?"

"Uncle Salty is dead." Artemas said solemnly.

"No. How?" The bonhomie was suddenly sucked into the cracks of the plaster walls.

"Ultimately, it was those damn turtles. We had on-loaded about a dozen at the Cayman Islands. Three weeks into the sail across the Atlantic, Uncle Salty and I were top side. It was evening and a gale was quickly approaching. The whitecaps had swelled to about fifteen feet. We'd just butchered two of the turtles and thrown all of the edible parts into copper pots. I began to take the pots down to the galley to transfer them into the steep tubs. Uncle Salty was hauling water out of the ocean using an oaken bucket and pouring it on the deck to clean up all the blood and guts."

Artemas stared vacantly as though he were watching the events unfold.

"Salty had the second dog watch that evening and he was almost late. I guess that because of the lack of time, he wasn't belaying the line as he tossed it over. He was merely wrapping it thrice around his fore-arm and heaving. As I climbed up after my second trip, I saw Salty readying to heave for a final bucket full. It must have been over 6 on the Beaufort, for I saw that the captain had sent sailors hurrying to lower sails. 'Rain's going to do your work for you,' I said. But it was too late. The bucket was in the air. Then all the evil forces in the universe aligned. The ship dipped into the trough, and just as the bucket collided with the passing wave, one of the turtles came sliding down that slippery deck and caught Salty squarely in the haunches and he was yanked cleanly over the bulwark and into the sea. I dropped the pots and ran aft. I could see him bobbing like a cork. As he disappeared into the storm, Uncle Salty smiled, and gave that smart salute that the Limey sailors use to debark a ship."

Artemas wasn't crying, but tears had begun to leak down his face.

"I ran to the bridge and shouted, 'Captain! Man overboard! Permission to launch a jolly boat.'"

"'Permission denied' came back the captain with no hesitation. 'It's too dangerous to turn this ship against the storm. Take command of the bridge, Artemas, whilst I survey the situation.' As he walked away, he turned and said, 'He's already dead, as cold as that water is. I've lost one man and I won't lose six more on a foolish rescue attempt.' Captain knew I was too true a sailor to desert my post, and that left at liberty, I would deploy a jolly boat. So there I stood; steering that ship away from Salty, more water washing down my face from my tears than from the rain."

"I'm so sorry, Artemas. I truly am. I know how much you loved the man. We won't be meeting his equal anytime soon. A true sailor! I liked the cut of his jib."

Artemas smiled. He appreciated Dr. Squier trying to use a sailor's phrase in Salty's honor. Salty would have appreciated it also.

"He would never tell me his real name. What was it? And why wouldn't he tell me."

"My father, Salty's older brother, died in a cholera outbreak in 1813. It also killed the family that owned Salty and most everybody in the little town of Mystic. They had already manumitted my father, but Salty was still a slave. After burying my father, Salty gathered me up and we walked down to the docks and signed on 'The Susan,' a whaler bound northward to hunt minke whales. Salty signed on as the cook and I was a cabin boy, all of ten years old. His real name was 'Saturnas.' I couldn't say it as a child, and it came out as 'Salty.' He liked it much better. He always said the heaviest burden of slavery was carrying around the stupid names that white people gave them." Elizabeth cackled, having known far too many slaves with names like Tiberius or Jovian or Morpheus.

"So, what brings you to the White House, Artemas?"

"Well, like I said, Uncle Salty was so taken with the paint page, that at every port we scoured the town buying walnut tree leaves, or copperas, or verdigris, or anything else that we thought would yield another tint or shade. Then we would experiment when we got back on board; grinding, pounding, boiling, mixing; sometimes all night. When we got back home in Oxford, word of our paint mixing spread, and the waterman started coming to us to paint their boats. One customer from Annapolis had been commissioned to refurbish the Cathedral in Baltimore, and hired us to do the painting. Mrs. Lincoln is considering redoing the White House, and Elizabeth has brought me to consult with her.

The Cathedral and the White House had some overlapping architects; maybe there's thought that the painter should overlap also," Artemas said in jest.

"And what about you, Dr. Squier? Are you here on business, or have you come to rob the local graveyard?" asked Artemas. He shot a smile at Elizabeth and said, "Dr. Squier has the amusing hobby of collecting skulls with holes drilled in them."

"Trepanation, my dear boy – Trepanation! It's been practiced for centuries. I've been appointed Commissioner to Peru by Mr. Lincoln. Remember it was Senora Zentino in Cuczo who gave me my first trepanned skull – the one from the Aztec ruins. By the by, do you perchance still have that apparatus you built for me? I have a patient who suffers from headaches so severe that most days he's unable to lift his head off the pillow. He wants to be trepanned to see if it relieves the pressure."

"*This is a bizarre conversation, even by a white man's standards,*" Elizabeth noted silently to herself. Then aloud: "You know someone who wants you to drill a hole in their head?" Elizabeth asked, not entirely convinced that this conversation was serious.

"I do indeed. Most assuredly!"

"Coincidence that you should mention it," said Artemas. "I used it just last week. I keep a double handful of Dorset sheep on my place in Oxford, mainly because I like the way they look. Well, it's rutting season, and one of the young rams decided to challenge the old buck. The old stud got the better part of it, and the young ram wobbled off, blood dripping from his nose. The next day, there was a knot the size of a musket ball over his right eye. He didn't stand up for three days and the knot got bigger. I figured I was going to lose him anyway, so I sedated him with that Peruvian concoction that you fleeced those natives out of."

Dr. Squier allowed the volley to go unreturned; being totally absorbed in the story and desirous of hearing its conclusion.

"I strapped your contraption on his head and started to drill. The details are too gory to re-tell, but suffice it to say that the pressure was relieved and his head returned to its normal shape. Now, the only problem is keeping the flies and gnats out of the hole."

"Would it be possible to cut a section of bone from a cow or deer skull?" asked a high-pitched voice from behind them.

They turned in unison towards the door to see the angular Mr. Lincoln slouched against the frame. "Why, Mr. Lincoln! I didn't hear you come in," said Dr. Squier. "Have you had the pleasure of meeting Mrs. Keckley and Mr. Artemas Hardesty?"

"Madame Elizabeth and I are acquainted. Mr. Hardesty and I have never met. I fear that if Artemas decides on permanent residence in our city, then I'll no longer be the tallest man in town. Stand back to back with me, and let Dr. Squier chalk us off squarely." The two giants backed into each other.

"I think Artemas has a solid inch on you, Mr. Lincoln," said the doctor.

Mary Lincoln had entered the room. "You're still the biggest thing to come out of Illinois. Or perhaps history hasn't written the final chapter on Senator Douglas yet? Maybe his star will ultimately be set higher in the firmament than yours," she teased. "Did you know that I was squired by both of them, but I chose Mr. Lincoln?"

"In generations to come, I think the highest honor will go not to either one of us, but to Mr. John Deere. Without his invention of the tempered steel plow and moldboard, Illinois would still be Indian Territory. A man couldn't go fifteen feet in that sticky gumbo dirt without having to stop and clean his plow. I think that when the world grows wise, inventors will be held in higher esteem than politicians."

"From your mouth to God's ear," Elizabeth prayed to herself in keeping with her private conviction that politicians were about the lowest form of life, under-ranked only by fugitive slave catchers and wife-beaters.

"Did you know that Mr. Lincoln has an invention of his own and a patent on it?" Mary proudly asked.

"Indeed? What is it?" asked Dr. Squier.

"It's a device to assist a river boat in freeing itself if it gets caught on the shoals," said Mr. Lincoln "As a young man, a friend and I took a flat boat with goods from Indiana down the Ohio and Mississippi Rivers to New Orleans. We spent as much time unloading the craft and freeing it from sand bars as we did navigating the river. So I worked on an idea to solve the problem. Would you care to see a model?"

"Very much!"

Mr. Lincoln walked into the hall and shouted up the stairs, "Nickolay! Hay! Would one of you fetch 6469 and bring it hither, please?"

Presently, one of the young secretaries, carefully bearing the miniature boat, eased into the room.

"Patent #6469, issued in 1849 – Never built –" Artemas eyed it intently for less than a minute.

"May I be so bold as to offer some suggestions?" Artemas started talking about buoys and baffles and pumps and cunt lines; and he and Mr. Lincoln, completely absorbed in boat building, walked up the stairs and into Mr. Lincoln's office. Artemas looked as though he had made that trip a hundred times before.

"Most singular individual I've ever encountered," Dr. Squier said to no one in particular.

Elizabeth watched Mary's spirits sink. She had initially veered the conversation so that it was about her, but had miscalculated how the introduction of the patent would spin out of her control.

"Being a poor student and observer of human nature, I'm curious, if it's not prying, as to what you saw in Mr. Lincoln to lean you in his direction. I recall that at the time, Mr. Douglas was more widely known and his star was ascending more rapidly," Dr. Squier asked hesitantly, well aware that he was walking barefoot in a briar patch.

"Being from Kentucky, I considered myself a good judge of horse flesh. I saw Mr. Douglas as more of a quarter horse, and Mr. Lincoln as more of a thorough-bred. I always intended to become a first lady, and deemed the Derby to the White House to be at least a mile and a half race. A thorough-bred always wins in the long run. Mr. Lincoln was country and unpolished, but after fifteen minutes of conversation, I knew that his constitution was fashioned out of Mr. Deere's stainless steel." Mary was happier now that the conversation was once again centered on her.

Artemas returned to the room. "Mr. Lincoln bids you to come to his office. He said to show yourself in, as you are well familiar with these halls."

"Would you and Mrs. Keckley be my dinner guests this evening? Perhaps we could reprise our chess contests. Do you still wager, Artemas?

"Money, marbles, or chalk! Whatever your pleasure would be. And as a treat, I have brought a sufficiency of turtle gumbo over from the Eastern Shore. Maryland terrapin has a most unique taste. Unless your house sways, it would be an honor to see you eat one of my meals and finally retain it."

"Here's my card. Shall we say eight o'clock?" With that Dr. Squier jauntily bounded up the mahogany stairs.

Mary turned to Artemas and said, "So, let's talk paint."

Chapter VII

"Some of these walls I intend to paint; others will be wallpapered. Do you also have experience with wallpaper?" Mary asked.

Elizabeth hoped that Artemas didn't feel the need to list his exploits with Uncle Salty and Rosita on his resume.

"I have men who are skilled in that, ma'am. I personally don't have the knack."

"But will you personally supervise their work?"

"Not on a daily basis. My other interests on the Eastern Shore preclude me from daily oversight. I do, however, guarantee their work. I'll make periodic visits, if we reach an agreement."

"Will the men have to sail over daily? I'm afraid that won't leave much of a workday."

"No ma'am, I'm buying the house of my friend Eunice LaRon not six blocks from here and I'll quarter the men there. She lives in the Murder Bay section, but she's moving to the Eastern Shore."

Mary could tell that she was dealing with a first rate mind for business. "Will you use slave-labor?"

"If there are any slaves used by me, they will be paid a fair wage."

Artemas knew there was some secret agenda, but as of yet,

he couldn't identify it. He would have to wait until Mrs. Lincoln revealed it. There were plenty of painters in the Washington area, so there had to be a reason why she would prefer someone from out of town.

"So tell me, Artemas, do you propose using milk-based paint or an oil-based paint for these walls?"

"I prefer milk-based paint on plaster walls. Oil paints yield richer colors, but they tend to trap moisture behind the paint, and that leads to bubbling and peeling."

"I trust that you are sufficiently capitalized so that you can purchase paints, rugs, wallpaper and fabrics and invoice me monthly. Congress authorizes a $20,000.00 budget for repairs, but I'm told that there's a small lag time between invoicing and appropriation. Does that present any problems?"

"No ma'am. That's exactly how it worked on the Cathedral in Baltimore." Artemas thought he now understood. Mrs. Lincoln had slipped the word 'fabrics' ever so gently into the conversation. She probably intended on buying materials for her dresses and paying for them out of the renovation funds. He quickly calculated that any risk to him was minimal, so he let it pass.

"Would you make repairs to the horse hair plaster where it's crumbling even if we're going to wallpaper over it?"

"I would, if it were my house."

"Why don't you walk these halls and rooms and give me some rough estimate on how long it might take for repairs and painting."

Artemas strolled down the hall. When alone, Mary looked at Elizabeth and said, "Tell me about yourself. My lady friends in St, Louis told me that you were married. What about Mr. Keckley? Where is he now?"

Elizabeth was certain from the directness of the question that Mary grew up in a slave-owning family. All of the niceties and pretensions of polite society were stripped away in such families and communication was direct and pointed. Owners spoke to their slaves in the same way they spoke to their children. Nothing was sugar-coated or softened. The straighter the question could be asked, the quicker one could get to the answer. It was very efficient - until one tired of being treated like a child.

"On the skinny end of a whiskey bottle would be my guess. The last time I saw that bottle was in Petersburg, Virginia. About eleven years ago. Friends tell me that it hasn't run dry yet, but the drinking was almost a virtue compared to some of his other habits." Elizabeth's voice carried no trace of bitterness, but there was no doubt that to her, that chapter of her life had been written, edited, and filed.

"Was there any issue?"

Elizabeth hesitated. "No, but I have a son."

Mary allowed the cryptic remark to float suspended, and then disappear into the walls. "I find this old house oppressive. It weighs on me in an odd manner. It smells of death and sadness." She sucked in a moderate breath through her nose as if to test her claim. "I just feel it, Elizabeth. I hope Artemas can lock the evil in these walls with a good coat of paint. I know the curse comes with the house and we can't remove it, but I hope we can seal it in until we leave."

Elizabeth also had felt the same sense of dread, but said nothing.

"Since we are to be friends, Lizzy, I fear I must tell you some things about myself. Did I ever tell you how Tad got his name? His Christian name is Thomas, but when he was born, Mr. Lincoln took one look at him and said, 'He's all head. He looks like a tad-pole.' And that was true. After 18 hours in labor, thanks to Dr. Wallace, that big head finally pushed out. But it also pushed out most of my insides and what remained of my sense of modesty. To be honest, I've never fully recovered.

My womanly waters flow to an unnatural extent. And when my monthly times come, I turn into a dragon. Mr. Lincoln calls me 'Death eating an onion.'"

Elizabeth had seen that dragon poke his head out of the cave and breathe fire to scare the villagers into compliance from time to time. But she had only heard reports of the occasions when the dragon was in full fury, burning down the houses and devouring the children.

Elizabeth smiled.

"It's fine to smile now, but if you're ever around when the crimson curtain descends on me, remove yourself with all haste. No matter what vile and ugly things I say, know that I love you, and come back in a week. I'll beg your forgiveness and make amends. Remember Romans 7:20 – 'But if I am doing the very thing I do not want, I am no longer the one doing it, but sin which dwells in me.' I would like to blame these outbursts entirely on my monthly visits, but that's not the whole truth. I sometimes fly into a rage when I'm not so burdened, although I am more susceptible during those times. Maybe when I go through 'the change' I'll no longer play host to the Furies."

Mary's candor was gravitational and it pulled hard on Elizabeth.

"Have you heard of that strange sect that calls themselves 'Mormons'? They started in Missouri and Illinois, but are now chiefly in the Utah Territory. Mr. Lincoln says he is considering joining, since they believe in polygamy, and he already has two wives – the one he married and the siren that occupies my body from time to time. And remember, Lizzie, time is the only exorcist that seems to know the proper rituals to purify me. God knows that Mr. Lincoln has tried with patience and understanding; he has the scar tissue to prove it. Promise me – just run. I give you fair warning, because my time will be coming sometime next week."

Mary looked impish and pulled Elizabeth closer and in a lowered voice said, "Don't ever tell a soul, but one time in Springfield during my monthlies, I broke Mr. Lincoln's nose with a leg of lamb."

Elizabeth tried not to, but she laughed aloud.

"You know, of course, Mrs. Lincoln that your family grows the best medicine in the world for menstrual problems?" said Elizabeth.

"You must have been ill-informed. My family grows tobacco and hemp."

"If your sister Ninian is still coming for a visit next week, wire her and ask her to go to one of the slaves and tell her to gather the makings for some 'Jumpin' Johnny Cakes'. It's a special variation of hemp; the slaves call it ditch weed, and if your slaves don't cultivate it, they're the only ones in the South who don't. I'll go in the woods and hunt for some 'Laughing Jim' – it's a mushroom that makes a soothing tea."

Artemas returned from his search. "What a big house. The only thing I can say for certain is that it'll take eight men over three months to do the minimum that you request. Longer, if you want to rehang doors with bad hinges, or repair stair railings where they're broken, or work on the windows that no longer open, or repair the plaster medallions on the ceilings that have broken off. Do you want to do everything, or are some of the rooms more important than others?"

"We'll start on the rooms downstairs that are used for State functions, and the bedrooms upstairs where we live. Once those are completed, we can take inventory and go from there."

Chapter VIII

"Have you ever smoked, Mrs. Lincoln?"

"My father grew tobacco. One spring Saturday, my three sisters and two of our friends prepared a picnic basket and we drove our hauling cart down to a swimming hole about two miles from our house. It was Eden. Oak trees, poplars and sycamores ran down to the edges of the water, and their limbs formed a leafy canopy about forty feet above. We called it our 'Indian Cathedral.'"

Elizabeth took two corn cob pipes from her purse. "Artemas made these for me," she said vacantly.

"Is that a new carrying bag?" Mary asked.

"Bag's old - cloth's new. I bought six yards at Harper and Mitchell's last week. Mr. Harper said the design is not woven on a loom, but rather printed on - much like printing a book. They make it in Paisley, Scotland."

"We called the pattern 'Persian Pickles'. I've always found it pleasing. Perhaps I should have a shawl in that design, but in cashmere or silk. Could you bring some samples by next week?"

"Yes ma'am."

"Anyway, after the picnic lunch, my oldest sister Ninian dared us all to smoke. Naturally we did. We were all giddy and dizzy. Fannie, my elder by two years and my dearest and closest friend, suggested that we all go skinny dipping. We sisters had often swum naked here, but never with others. However, the Bartlett girls were the first to undress and run into the water."

Elizabeth had filled the pipes with the finely chopped contents of her little draw-string pouch. She mashed it down tightly with her thumb.

"Let me show you how to do this," Elizabeth said.

She pulled a small piece of lighter knot pine, about four inches long and not as thick as her littlest finger, out of her purse and walked over to the gas-lit sconce on the wall. She held the kindling to the flame for about four seconds before it ignited. She held the flame above the bowl of the pipe, and sucked in four or five times. The mixture lit.

"Now watch." Elizabeth sucked hard on the pipe. She inhaled the smoke and waited, suspended, for as long as she could, then she blew the smoke out of her lungs forcefully.

"Hold it in as long as you can," instructed Elizabeth.

She walked over to Mary, handed her the other pipe, and extended the lit kindling. Mary sucked in but was immediately choked. She coughed violently.

"This medicine may be more painful then the cramps," Mary said through watery eyes.

"Try again. It gets easier."

Mary did as instructed, and this time managed to retain the smoke for about a five count before she involuntarily coughed it out.

"This doesn't smell like the burley tobacco we grew in Kentucky. It's a richer aroma."

"So tell me more about the swimming hole," Elizabeth implored.

Mary's eyes shone like a pixie's, indicating to Elizabeth that the story was going to get more interesting.

"We'd been swimming and splashing for about half an hour when one of the Bartlett girls shrieked. We looked at her and followed her eyes to the shore. There sat Thomas Simon, our neighbor, and son of one of the most unsuccessful farmers in the county. Roger Simon wasn't a bad farmer; he was just the unluckiest man who ever drew breath. One time he bought a prize breeding bull killed by lightning three days later. Once we had a prolonged drought and when we finally had a crop-saving, gully-washing rain, it stopped at our fence line. One year Roger has the finest tobacco crop in the county, but on the way to the auction the mule pulling the wagon had a heart attack and died. Naturally the wagon was straddling the train track. Train only came through every third day. Naturally this was the third day. Train wasn't able to fully brake for about a half mile, scattering tobacco into the woods as it skidded."

Elizabeth was laughing so hard she had to hold her sides.

"Naturally, it started to rain."

With this latest revelation Elizabeth fell upon the bed and tears came out of her eyes. When she finally composed herself, Mary continued, "Daddy always said that God was just practicing on Job, saving his best work for Roger Simon. Roger didn't have any better luck when it came to sowing a crop of kids either. There sat the pick of the litter, his mind as dull as a butter knife, perched on our wagon and smiling so wide I thought the top part of his head was in danger of sliding off. The girls discretely retreated into the deep water so that they were only visible from the chin up."

Elizabeth and Mary continued to draw on their pipes.

"He had plopped himself on the back end of our wagon, his feet dangling, and chewing on a straw.

'Get away from our clothes, you dirty little devil,' yelled Ninian.

'You want these clothes, you walk up here and get 'em,'

hollered Thomas back. 'Otherwise, stay in that water until you shrivel up like prunes.'

Fannie started to cry. 'Don't be such a ninny!' I said. 'I'll be peeled and pickled before I stand in this creek all afternoon waiting for the sun to go down, or for that cretin to leave. I'll handle this. And I'll teach him a lesson he'll never forget.' I walked out of that creek and right up to where Thomas Simon was sitting. 'Listen, why don't you take your buggy down the road for five minutes so these girls can get dressed and go home. Then come back here and you and I can swim.'

'I don't think you'll be here when I get back,' he said.

'Honey, unless I grow a pair of angel wings in the next five minutes, you've already seen everything I got. Why wouldn't I be here?'"

Mary paused her story to suck on the pipe.

"Lizzie, my hair could have been on fire and he would not have noticed; his gaze never got above my shoulders."

Elizabeth giggled. She took Mary's pipe and re-filled them both.

"This medicine is giving me the vapors. I feel so light-headed. Anyway, Thomas Simon did as told. We girls got dressed and they climbed on the wagon. 'You can't stay,' commanded Ninian.

'I can and I am. I'm going to show him that the Simon luck hasn't changed,' I said. 'I'll see you at home in less than an hour.'

They passed Thomas about a hundred yards down the road. When he drove up, he looked about as smug as a man could look. I climbed up beside him.

'I've been waiting. Are you ready for a swim?'

Thomas nodded with that imbecilic look that men get when there's not enough blood to service the brain.

'I want you to run down to the creek and swim over to the

deep water pool there,' I said as I pointed. 'I'll run down and jump off that little node and into your arms.'

He shed his clothes so quickly you would have thought they were tainted with small-pox. When he swam to the farthest point, I grabbed those reins and whirled that buggy around and whipped that broken-down, apple-butted, jug head so hard that he took off running like a quarter horse. My plan was to throw one piece of clothing into the road every quarter mile or so, but one of my moods descended on me and I ceded him nothing. I tied that nag and beat-up buggy to a fence post at his farm, and I walked home; his stinky clothes under my arm."

Elizabeth was laughing uncontrollably. "What did you do with his clothes?"

"We put them on a scarecrow at the edge of a pea patch out near the road. Either he, or some needy soul, took them in about two days."

Elizabeth liked to watch the defiance dance in Mary's eyes. She reminded Elizabeth of a little bantam rooster called 'The Turk' that she frequently bet on at the cock fights in Petersburg.

"Can I tell you something that I've never told a living soul?" Mary's inhibitions had been softened by the medicine. "When I walked up to Thomas Simon, I was not in the least embarrassed. I was enthralled. I felt so strong; so powerful. I knew he was powerless to look away. And I enjoyed it even more knowing the girls were also fixated on me. I felt as though I were Ophelia doing the drowning scene from Hamlet at Ford's Theater."

"All women like to be admired," Elizabeth offered weakly.

"True enough, but it's more than that." Mary seemed to lose the thread of her concentration. She sucked on the pipe again. "Did you ever go swimming 'au naturel,' Lizzie?"

"When I was living in Petersburg, I had a gentleman caller who would fetch me most Saturdays in his coach, and we would ride out to a place that was eerily similar to the one you described.

He would bring books and we would lie there in the warm sun, naked as jay birds, improving our minds. Sometimes, we would improve our minds two or three times in an afternoon."

Mary and Elizabeth collapsed in laughter. Mary was holding her stomach. Nothing had ever seemed this funny before. They heard the gangly foot-steps of Mr. Lincoln echoing down the hall. Mr. Lincoln didn't come into the room. Rather, he grabbed the frame of the door with his massive hands, and leaned his head in. "Mother, I don't recall you laughing this hard in years. Pray tell, what are you talking about?"

"Recipes," she answered, and both women dissolved into uncontrollable laughter.

Correctly sensing that this party was for women only, Mr. Lincoln said, "Well, I'm turning in. I'll close the door so you won't wake the boys. What's that smell?"

"Just some medicine that Elizabeth brought me for my female problems. I'll be in soon."

With that, Mr. Lincoln closed the door and galumphed on down to his room.

"I know that look on Mr. Lincoln's face well. After twenty years of marriage, I can read him like a book. Mr. Lincoln would like to take his horizontal refreshments tonight."

"Should I be going home?"

"No, he'll still be up when I get there."

This unintended 'double entendre' struck them both at the same time. They laughed for a full five minutes.

Catching her breath, Mary continued, "Mr. Lincoln may be the Commander-in-Chief of the army, but there's one soldier completely loyal to me. He never fails to stand up and salute whenever I walk into the bedchamber." They tittered like school girls.

"Elizabeth, I'm feeling a bit peckish. Do you have anything to eat?"

"I've got some fudge in my purse. But, I made it with the jumping johnnycakes ingredients. It might prove to be too much medicine for one night."

"Oh, fiddle-faddle, Lizzie. I'm starving and I haven't felt this good in years. Bust it out!"

As they sat on the bed nibbling fudge Mary said pensively, "Black people must be more relaxed than white people. I can't imagine a white man lying around naked in the day-time like your gentleman caller."

"My gentleman caller was a white man, Mary." This abrupt revelation was good for another five minutes of uninterrupted laughter.

"He was the father of my son, George. George is as white as flour. He's so white he was able to enlist in the army in Missouri. He's with the troops under General Lyon."

Elizabeth's face became deadly serious. "Nobody knew who the father was and the delivery was rather difficult. After struggling for eight or nine hours with no progress, the mid-wives brought in the doctor and the forceps. At about eleven o'clock at night, George finally was pulled out. The doctor cut the umbilical cord, picked up George, and started to walk to the head of the bed into the candle light and said, "Elizabeth, you're the proud mother of a bouncing baby..... WHITE!!!"

They were both certain that laughing this hard could only result in death.

"Oh Lizzie, this is a perfectly wonderful medicine. I haven't felt this peaceful since I was a young girl in Lexington." Scenes floated in and out of her mind with no invitation. She was at her first debutant ball; she was lying in a clover patch with her sisters; she was walking into church for Christmas services, holding her mother's warm hand.

"The pain is going away. Do me a kindness and come rub my

stomach. My nanny would do it when I had a stomach ache and it was so soothing."

The rapid fire images began to slow down. A solitary image crystallized in her mind. She was standing on a bluff over-looking a wide river. Behind her were acres and acres of her beloved blue-grass. At the top of a gently rolling hill, a rider sat on a horse.

It was the Appaloosa gelding that her father had given her on her sixteenth birthday. The horse was restive. He snorted; he crow hopped; he bobbed his tail up and down - always a sign that he was angry; he raked the ground with his front feet. And she was wearing the blue, watered-silk riding habit he had bought her at Hermes in France, along with the Hermes saddle. The gelding snorted, his nostrils flared, and he danced from side to side.

Elizabeth continued to massage her stomach.

The rider and horse seemed to be waiting for something. There was some hesitancy; something was pending. Some unspoken bond was being set. Rider and horse began to lope down the hill. They were about nine furlongs from the bluff. The gait was steady and even. The rider was in perfect concert with the horse. She was neither urging him forward nor restraining him. Rhythmically, they raced on. She could hear the even clop, clop, clop of the hooves. When the rider and horse were about four furlongs from the bluff they broke into a gallop. The rider leaned forward and tensed her legs. The horse answered. Now it was all out for the finish line. Mary could see foam escaping from the horse's mouth. Suddenly she realized that they did not intend to stop. Onward they strode. Both of their faces were frozen in grim determination to carry out their pact of death. As they reached the edge of the bluff, it was impossible to tell if the horse leapt, or if the rider soared up, her strong legs taking the horse with her. Mary now knew that she was the rider. To her amazement, the horse didn't plummet; he flew, or glided in the air. The sole sound was the wind. It was being pumped by a bellows. She could make out the different tones as the bellows sucked it in, and gently blew it out.

When Elizabeth could hear nothing but Mary's deep snoring, she returned everything to her carrying bag and started out on her trip home.

Chapter IX

Winter was gathering up its instruments of torture and moving north. Spring was subletting for the season and quietly begun moving a few of its things into Washington. Some of the birds had returned and the rich magenta buds had appeared on the red bud trees.

The departure of the Canadian geese was the only seasonal loss that mattered as far as Elizabeth was concerned. She loved to watch them flying in their V formation, always one or two of the flock too stupid to grasp the concept of perfect symmetry. Their honking was a symphony to her ears. Once on a visit to Artemas's house on the Eastern Shore, she had seen geese in flight so numerous that they had no beginning or end. They covered the sky in both directions until they just vanished from sight.

Elizabeth was giving Portia a lesson on the sewing machine while the other girls were engaged in a more prosaic task of hand stitching some ruffles, when she heard a pounding on the door so forceful she feared for the integrity of the hinges. "Good Lord'" she said as she hurried to the door.

"War! War has broken out. The secessionists have fired on Fort Sumner," shouted Colonel Burkey, waving the morning edition of the *National Intelligencer* above his head like a baton. Elizabeth grabbed the paper and began to read. *What will this do to my business,* Elizabeth thought. She blushed, hoping she had not said it aloud. But it was true; her only concern was the effect that it would have on her and her girls. Two small countries to oppress black people would be no worse than one large country.

"Will the North respond?" she asked.

"Mr. Lincoln has already mustered for volunteers. He's raising thirty thousand men for 90 days enlistment. That should be enough to restore order."

"Will you enlist?" Elizabeth inquired.

"I don't know. It's complicated. Is there a room where we can talk privately?"

"Certainly. Let's go to my office."

Elizabeth noted the strange way Portia and Colonel Burkey nodded acknowledgement to each other. Portia had never offered any clarification and Elizabeth had not pried.

As Elizabeth closed the door behind them, Colonel Burkey said, "I don't know if this war news will change anything, but when I left the house this morning, I was coming to tell you that Mrs. Burkey and I are moving back to Scotland. Her mother lives there and frankly, another country may be what we need."

"To save your marriage," Elizabeth inferred but dared not say aloud.

"And what about Portia?" Elizabeth felt her heart sink. Even in such a short term she had come to rely upon Portia. "Will this affect our arrangement in any way?"

"I was going to Richmond next month to sell her. I have a buyer, but I had an idea last night. Why don't you buy her?"

Elizabeth felt her stomach pitch and roll. Elizabeth had made a comfortable pact with life. She didn't want to change the world. She was content to run her business, feel the seasons come and go, read, eat good food, and make love to Artemas whenever possible. The two things that she did not want to do were to be responsible for the death of another human being or to own one as a slave.

"That look of repulsion that you have on your face is the very reason that I think you should be the one to buy her. I would very much desire to see Portia free, but I'm not at liberty at present to manumit her."

No, I don't expect Mrs. Burkey would be in favor of that, Elizabeth thought.

"I could set aside a portion of her wages each week until she repaid me the full amount, like Artemas does for some of his farm hands on the Eastern Shore. And what if I decide against it? What happens to the money that I've already paid for her year's service?"

"I would refund the balance on a pro rata basis."

"And what is the asking price?"

"$400.00 and that's a bargain price."

Elizabeth felt odd haggling over the price of a human being as matter-of-factly as she might negotiate prices for fabric at Harper and Mitchell's. "Let me talk to Portia and if she's agreeable, you've got yourself a deal."

"We'll have to go to the court house in Richmond to transfer the title."

"I'm familiar with the process. I bought my and my son George's freedom about six years ago."

"We can take the train to Richmond any day that's suitable for you. The morning train leaves at 8:00 am and there's a return train leaving at 2:00 in the afternoon. That should afford us ample time to do our business."

As she closed the door behind the Colonel, she noticed that instead of basking in the warm glow of someone who had done a good deed, Elizabeth felt dirty and ashamed.

As she walked back into the work room she looked at Portia and said, "Well Portia, rumor is that you're going to be a free woman."

Portia turned white and hastily explained, "I was only talking to that abolitionist. I'm not really running away to Canada. Honest, Miss Elizabeth."

Elizabeth had to laugh. "No Portia, you and I are going to buy your freedom. You don't have to run anywhere ever again."

Elizabeth walked into the kitchen and began boiling water for some tea, but she couldn't dispel the lumpy feeling she had in her stomach.

Chapter X

The first few months of the war were kind to Elizabeth. The pulse of Washington, D.C.'s business center was steady and strong. As soldiers moved into the Capital, they had to be housed and shod and fed. Hardware and lumber store owners were wealthy overnight. Saloon owners were prosperous. Belle Boyd was hiring fallen angels as quickly as they debarked the Baltimore & Ohio Railroad, ever ready to serve their country by ministrating to the lonely and adrift soldiers. Belle had agents on commission working at the train depot, identifying the women who fit a certain profile – young, unaccompanied, unmet upon arrival, and with a look of fatalism hammered deeply in their eyes. No expense was spared when it came to outfitting one of Belle Boyd's girls – she paid fairly and she paid upon delivery.

Elizabeth's office was on the first floor of her house facing south. She plopped her burl walnut roll top desk, lovingly crafted by Artemas, squarely in the middle of the room. With this as her wheel-house, each Saturday mid-morn, she would navigate through the normally placid seas of financing and accounting. This was cherished time. The cutting and mending and sewing were the back breaking, callus building work of wardrobe farming. Tallying up the profits was the harvest. And a handsome harvest it was, the fruits being piled higher and higher in Riggs National Bank in Georgetown, prompting the tellers to peer over her growing stacks of deposits and greet her as "Mrs. Keckley."

Elizabeth placed her desk in the middle of the room, as opposed to up against the windows, as it allowed her a greater view of the walls. Artemas had created a rich tincture of pumpkin in a linseed-oil based paint that other painters could not seem to duplicate. Not given to pettiness, Elizabeth nevertheless felt smug as her white patrons ogled the walls in admiration, one offering close to a year's wages if Artemas would paint their dining room in that exact shade. That pigment, Elizabeth lied, could only be procured from a tribe of cannibals, far up the Amazon River, and possibly now extinct.

Elizabeth would sit for hours watching the sun being pulled from left to right across the two massive windows, agitating the hues continuously. Yesterday it took seventeen minutes for the sun to vacate the easternmost window and reappear in its westernmost counterpart. But today something happened in that interval. The sun was extinguished. A breeze arose, gentle at first, dusting up the leaves off the ground and giving them a ride. Then it began to play rougher, tearing the leaves off the branches and stirring them into the mix. The wind, once playful and mischievous, honed a finer edge and became annoyed.

Elizabeth heard a knock on the door. She bundled her papers into an untidy pile and laid them on the couch, securing them with a book for ballast. She stood and walked into the parlor. The wind was mean now, bullying things about, and making sounds much too loud.

She opened the door and saw a soldier standing on her porch and trying resolutely to resist the weather. His left hand was atop his head, restraining his military cap from joining into the fray with the leaves and his right hand cupped around his mouth in an attempt to funnel his words to Elizabeth above the droning of the wind. Elizabeth thought she heard him say something about being Corporal Somebody and maybe from the War Department. She couldn't be sure.

The vacuum caused by the wind sucked Elizabeth's breath out of her lungs. A quick gust of wind knocked her against the door jamb. She caromed off the jamb and was hurled against the coat rack standing in her entry hall. She felt something break. Elizabeth realized this was more than a stiff breeze – she was in the midst of a tornado. She crawled back to the door on all fours but the soldier was gone – blown away or by his own volition Elizabeth couldn't tell.

"What was that he said? Did he mention George?"

The lack of air made Elizabeth nauseous. She knew she was going to be sick. Her stomach knotted and contracted but there was nothing to expel. In between these spasms Elizabeth tried to remember what the soldier had said. She could recall in perfect clarity how his mouth had moved, but she couldn't hear the words. "Was it something about George?"

The last dry-heave contraction lasted a full thirty seconds, after which Elizabeth curled on the floor and held her stomach with both arms.

Portia and the girls had heard the commotion and raced down the stairs. As they helped her to her feet, she looked down the street, the dirt devils kicking up sand and making everything blurry and fuzzy. For a fleeting second the whirlwind ceased and she thought she saw a soldier on horseback. He turned his mount towards Elizabeth and smiled. "God, he looks a lot like George." The wind kicked up again and he was gone.

As Portia and the girls walked Elizabeth to her room, she asked, to no one in particular, "Did he say something about George?"

Chapter XI

"Lizzie, can you assist Tad in dressing?" Mary yelled from her room across the hall. "I've laid out his soldier's uniform on his bed. And make him wear those new black shoes. Don't let him whine you into wearing those beat-up brogans. We've never had a family photograph taken and I want everyone to look their Sunday best."

Elizabeth sat at the ornate sewing machine that was a gift to Mary from one of the thousands of patronage seekers who had curried favor with the Lincolns. She was putting in a seam for Mrs. Lincoln. She stopped pedaling, stood up somewhat annoyed at having been interrupted, and headed for Tad's room. *It's not right that a healthy ten year old boy is unable to dress himself,* Elizabeth thought. She was genuinely fond of Tad, but this chore never failed to get her dander up.

Tad was standing at the window watching his goat, Nanko, on the lawn below. *"I wonder if the soft ground would break his fall if I threw him out the window?"* she continued in her silent monologue. *"I'm pretty sure he'd be all right as long as he landed on his head."*

"Let's put your shirt on, honey." The most annoying thing about dressing Tad was that he didn't know how to assist in the dressing. If resistance was needed, he would go slack. If he needed to relax, he would go tense. Elizabeth knew that he didn't do it to be spiteful; he just lacked normal instincts. "Tad, I swear to God I think it would be easier to dress a corpse."

Tad flashed her one of his abundant toothed grins.

"Soldiers wear brogans with their uniforms," Tad protested when Elizabeth brought out the black shoes. "Besides, those hurt my feet. They're too tight."

"Well, the General ordered all soldiers to wear black shoes to have their picture taken today. A good soldier can never disobey a direct order." This idea seemed to gain some traction as Tad ceased his protest. His foot, however, slipped across the rug as Elizabeth tried to push it into the shoe. "Lock your knee, Tad, so your foot won't slide," Elizabeth pled, as she visualized Tad tumbling out the window.

Elizabeth crossed the hall and entered the sitting room where Mr. Lincoln sat reading the daily edition of the *Herald*.

"Madame Elizabeth, would you be so kind as to trim my whiskers? Mother thinks they're running wild."

"Of course, Mr. Lincoln. Bring your chair over closer to the light." Mr. Lincoln folded the newspaper that he was reading, lifted the chair and sat it nearer the light.

Mary stormed into the room shouting instructions to Willie and Tad. On her high energy days like this, she reminded Elizabeth of a steamboat racing down the Potomac. And Elizabeth had on occasion seen those boilers explode. She wasn't anywhere near the danger zone yet, but pressure built up quickly in Mary and she had a faulty blow-off valve.

"Willie! Tad! Hurry! Don't sit there like a bump on a pickle; Mr. Brady only shoots with the morning light. If we're late, he'll cancel the session."

Willie appeared looking positively dapper. Tad looked presentable.

"Elizabeth, can you do something with Tad's hair? It looks like rats slept in it last night."

"Did you ask William to prepare the carriage?" Mary asked Mr. Lincoln

"I did, but its such a nice day, I thought we might walk."

"And give these hellions a chance to mess up their clothes before we get there? They'd be having a road apple fight, or wrestling in a mud hole. No, we'll take the buggy. If it's still nice after the session, we can walk home. Elizabeth, can you accompany us for any last minute adjustments?"

Elizabeth knew that Mary's requests were really demands. "I'd be delighted. Besides, I've never been in Mr. Brady's studio."

"Let's be off like a jug handle," Mr. Lincoln said as he unfurled his long body and stood.

Mary grabbed her dress and flared it out and shushed her baby chicks down the stairs and into the waiting buggy.

The carriage ride down Pennsylvania Ave. caused the usual gaping and staring of the citizenry. "Are you the first President who had children?" Willie asked.

"Of course not."

"Then why do people always stare at Tad and me like we belonged in Mr. Barnum's circus?"

Mary smiled. She was the only Lincoln who truly basked in the attention. She reached toward Willie. "Are you feeling a bit peaked? Let me feel your forehead."

Willie brushed her hand aside. "I feel fine."

The carriage pulled up to Thompson's Saloon, a five story building with four massive windows on each floor. 'BRADYS GALLERY' was spelled out in large black letters between the second and third floor. The boys, who had accompanied their father here several times, were out of the carriage and on a dead run to the saloon. They burst through the swinging doors and ran to the bar. "I'll stand a whiskey for any man who'll drink to the Massachusetts 54th," Willie cried out.

"And I'll stand outside to fight any man who won't drink to the 54th," chimed in Tad. Willie and Tad had picked this up from their last visit to Thompson's.

Being barely ten o'clock, the bar was empty save the bartender. "Your money's no good in here, lads. These drinks are on the house."

Willie and Tad could barely see over the bar. The bartender grabbed a bottle of sarsaparilla from behind him and poured three shot glasses full, pushing two of them towards the boys. "To the boys in the 54th!" With that the three of them downed their drinks.

"Come on boys," Mr. Lincoln said from the swinging doors. "Mother is waiting. Morning, Mr. Thompson. What's the damage here?"

"I wouldn't think of charging those brave soldiers. They brighten my day every time they come here."

"Still, I don't want them to get into the habit of cadging drinks."

Mr. Thompson was an astute business man. He knew that good stories were as marketable as good whiskey, and this town had an unquenchable thirst for stories concerning the Lincolns.

Willie and Tad began to ascend the stairs: Tad running, but Willie merely walking. Mary regarded Willie with that maternal third-eye that women grow to ensure the safety and well-being of their offspring. She could not put it into words yet, but Mary saw something troubling gathering around Willie, and she was concerned.

Mathew Brady's studio could have doubled as a museum, with its ornate chandeliers and fine mahogany furniture. Photographs of every notable in Washington, D.C. covered the walls. Mr. Brady was seated on a cane-bottomed chair examining some photographs as they entered a large room on the third floor. A man stood beside him wearing a military cap cocked at a rakish angle. Elizabeth could not remember seeing a more handsome man. She had once seen P.T. Beauregard, the Confederate General, in Richmond. He was a man so dashing that women's heads would swivel like a piano stool when he walked down the street. Beauregard had that steamy Creole face; but this man was more appealing. Women, when safely nestled away from the men-folk at a sewing bee, would describe him as having bedroom eyes.

Mr. Brady rose as the entourage entered. "Mr. and Mrs. Lincoln, may I present my assistant, Jack Radcliffe."

"Charmed," said Mary. "This is our dear friend, Elizabeth. And these are our sons – Willie and Tad."

Mr. Radcliffe approached Elizabeth and said, "I passed you in the street yesterday. I would like to photograph you one day. You have a most remarkable profile. Doesn't her face reflect pride and struggle and dignity, Mr. Brady?"

"Yes, excellent clay," Mr. Brady agreed through squinted eyes.

Mary was not at all pleased with the attention being lavished on Elizabeth. "I thought that Mr. Lincoln could be seated at the desk, perhaps reading. I could stand to his right, and the boys to the left, and Robert, assuming he shows, could be behind the desk," Mary said.

"I think it might be better balanced if you were the central figure, Mrs. Lincoln. The viewing eyes are going to be drawn to you anyway," countered Mr. Radcliffe. Mary suddenly liked him much better. "However, since we shall be a moment waiting for Robert, I beg to go downstairs and capture a beautiful rose that I passed this morning. All of Washington knows that a flower adorning your hair is your trade mark. May I?'

"Well, thank you. Aren't you the perfect gentleman?"

As he left, Mr. Lincoln asked "Is he a new assistant?"

"No, Mr. Gardner's indisposed today. Mr. Radcliffe is one of my field photographers." By way of clarification, he looked at Mrs. Lincoln and explained, "I have eighteen portable studios. Each is equipped with a dark room and cameras and film. I'm trying to capture this war through photography."

Robert walked into the room. "I trust that I'm not too late."

"You're as timely as a pardon," said Mr. Lincoln. "We're just getting into position."

Robert walked by Elizabeth and nodded a perfunctory "Good morning."

When Elizabeth looked at Robert, she always thought of a pickle. She liked pickles, but mostly as an afterthought. And she suspected most people felt the same way. If you asked a thousand people to name their favorite food, none would say "the pickle." Similarly, if you quizzed a thousand people on their most despised food, again "pickle' would not be mentioned. Robert was much the same; he offended no one, but few were drawn to him. 'Bloodless' would be the closest that Elizabeth could come to describing him. Politics would be an ideal career for him.

Elizabeth had once caught Mary studying Robert as he was engaged in an idle conversation with Mr. Hay. Elizabeth imagined that Mary was trying to peer under that placid exterior and plumb it for any signs of genuine affection. Mothers keep a vigil on the hearts of their children, weighing which ones they can most likely rely on to provide care and comfort in their dotage. *"Who can you depend on to hold the lifeline?"* as Artemas was fond of asking. Something in Mary's eyes led Elizabeth to believe that Mary entertained doubts as to Robert's worth as a stanchion. No, Mary would have to pin her hopes on Willie. Tad was very loving and caring, but he was not capable of becoming what Mary needed. As Artemas says, "A cat can have kittens in an oven, but that don't make 'em biscuits."

No, Willie would have to be her old age hope chest.

"I pray that Willie's there if the storms of life ever wash her overboard. Tad wouldn't be strong enough to man the lifeline, and Robert wouldn't be interested enough," Elizabeth pondered to herself.

"Clouds coming from Alexandria," said Robert.

Jack Radcliffe charmed his way back into the studio, clutching a near perfect red rose in his hand.

"Can you position this?" he asked Elizabeth. "We need to make haste; clouds are moving over the Potomac. Besides, this rose will wilt quickly with envy when it's placed in competition with Mrs. Lincoln," he flattered.

"Damn, look at the white boy plow!" Elizabeth said to herself. *"He must sleep in an oil can. I don't know what he sleeps in, but I doubt if he often sleeps alone."*

As Elizabeth was preening Mary, Willie walked over to the camera and asked, "How does this work?"

Outwardly the camera was merely a mahogany box, not much larger than a picnic basket, with a short brass nozzle for a nose, perched atop a tripod.

Jack Radcliffe removed the lens cap and said, "The image that you see will be etched on these glass plates."

Willie lifted the dark velvet curtain on the rear of the box and thrust his head in. "You've got the box upside down," he protested. "Everybody's standing on their heads."

Mr. Radcliffe smiled and said, "That's the way the image is reflected. After we take the picture, I'll take you downstairs and show you why on a torn-apart camera. These glass plates are coated with chemicals that react with the light. These partitions on both sides of the plate will be removed for a few seconds when everyone is in position to capture the light. Then I'll slide them back down to keep the glass in total darkness. The protected plates are only removed in a dark room, where they will be washed and treated with other chemicals to set the picture."

"I wanna look too," Tad whined.

"After the picture. We're racing the clouds. Everyone in place, please."

"At last! A photograph of the entire family" said Mary, still glowing in Mr. Radcliffe's puffery.

"When I count to three, nobody move a muscle for five seconds. At three, he removed the lens cap and counted aloud to five.

"Perfect!" he said as he re-seated the partitions on either side of the plate. He removed the snugly covered plate and set it in a wooden carrying case. "We should take another, but I fear the clouds have carried the day."

"Now I want to look," shouted Tad as he made a dash from behind the table. In his haste he caught Willie squarely in the ankle with the toe of his new shoes. Willie grabbed his ankle and hopped. "Tad, you're as clumsy as an ox, and you smell worse."

Willie didn't often hurl insults at his younger brother, but the intense pain overrode his judgment. Tad was stunned and hurt.

"Well, your feet stink and you don't love Jesus," Tad volleyed back.

"You're a skillet-headed moron," Willie retaliated.

This betrayal cut Tad deeply. Willie had always been Tad's staunchest defender, protecting Tad from the taunts of bullies about his marble-mouth speech problems and his slowness. He lunged at Willie wildly, but Willie was bigger and quicker. He got Tad in a head lock, and they staggered around the room.

"If they're going to fight, at least let Willie knock a dozen or so of those extra teeth out of Tad's mouth," Elizabeth optimistically said to herself.

Mr. Lincoln jumped up to separate the boys, but he was too late. They fell into the tripod and only a miraculous catch of the flying camera by Mr. Radcliffe prevented it from being dashed to the floor. However, the carrying case holding the glass plate caromed off the wall with a thud, and the glass plate shattered into several pieces. Mr. Radcliffe didn't fare much better. As he bent over to set the camera on the floor, the entwined boys careened into his back-side, smashing his head against the hard plaster wall. Blood trickled down his forehead. Mr. Lincoln separated the boys.

Mary sat there as though she was watching a play with a challenging plot line. "Elizabeth, Robert will ride home in the carriage with us since its raining. Please wait here until the carriage returns and then go to the army hospital and fetch Dr. Stone. Tell him I need him to come look at Willie immediately."

"But I'm not sick," Willie protested, and then he proceeded to vomit a thick, green bile on Jack Radcliffe and the camera.

"I'm so sorry," offered Mr. Lincoln as he pulled a handkerchief from his pocket and extended it to Mr. Radcliff. He cleaned himself and the camera as best he could, biting his lip to suppress his growing anger.

As the entourage wended its way down the three flights of stairs, Mathew Brady slumped into the chair. He slid his hand into his inside coat pocket and pulled out a thin whiskey bottle with the label of 'Hopkins Finest.' He took a two swallow pull on the bottle and cocked it to one side, revealing a final drink. "Want to knock the corner out of this, Mr. Radcliffe?"

"Thanks, but no. It's still morning."

"I didn't know Hell had mornings." He stared vacantly at the wall. "Little bastards," he finally mumbled. "Are you going to come in tomorrow, Mr. Radcliffe?"

"No, I'm going back to the front tonight. I think I'll be safer there."

Chapter XII

"Hello, Willie. Still plowing a straight furrow?" asked Elizabeth.

Willie managed a feeble smile, but Elizabeth could tell he was no better than yesterday. In fact he had been in a steady decline since the debacle five days earlier at Brady's Studio. The vomiting had ceased after three days, probably due to the fact that he had eaten next to nothing. His forehead was clammy to the touch and feverish. A thick gummy paste pooled in the outside corners of his eyes. His breathing was slow and labored, and each inhale sounded like a soup spoon being dragged over a pewter plate. Elizabeth submerged a washcloth in the porcelain water bowl next to the bed. She twisted the excess water out of the cloth and placed it lightly on his brow. This seemed to neither please nor displease him; he merely closed his eyes and slipped into a sleep.

Elizabeth moved her chair closer to the lamp and took a book out of her purse. As usual the setting sun had leeched out Elizabeth's energy, but she had promised Mary that she would sit with Willie until the night nurse came on at ten. Thomas Hobbes was heavy slogging for a tired mind, but reading was better than staring at the walls, although Mary and Artemas had chosen a stunning tincture of myrtle green with hints of darker colors that were teased out by the candle light. She had scarcely opened the book when Mr. Lincoln walked in, gangly arms and legs looking as though an inexperienced carpenter had hastily nailed them onto his body.

"How're the codgers?"

"Tad is as right as rain. He's been asleep in his room the better part of an hour. Willie seems a little improved," Elizabeth lied.

Lincoln collapsed into a Queen Anne wingback chair as though the shoddy construction supporting his legs had given way. He stared at Willie gravely.

"Any news on the war, Mr. Lincoln?"

"Plenty of news, but it's all bad."

The war had been prosecuted for less than a year, but Lincoln had aged at least five. Candlelight reflects more of the soul than ordinary daylight, and Elizabeth liked the way he looked in the flickering flame. He didn't look homely and haggard like he did in the day, but rather solemn and dignified. He looked like a mature chestnut tree with its thick and deeply rutted bark. "What's the read?" he asked Elizabeth.

"The English Philosopher Thomas Hobbes. I'm afraid it's too much of a tax on my unschooled brain."

"How do the winds blow in England? I've never read philosophers."

"It's an ill wind as best as I can tell. Or at least a harsh one. Life is short, solitary, brutish and nasty, unless we enter into a social contract with our neighbors on how we wish to be governed. Hobbes preferred a monarchy to a democracy. Have you ever considered declaring yourself 'King Abraham'?"

"It would certainly be easier to be a king and rule by fiat, rather than constantly arm-wrestling with Congress. What about you, Madame Elizabeth? Which would you find preferable?"

Elizabeth had grown some hard bark on her emotions

over the years, being treated like furniture or some other inanimate household appointment, but tonight that particular question cut her sharply. "I'm black, Mr. Lincoln. No one in this country has ever asked a black to enter into any kind of a social contract. We've been contracted for; bought and sold like a keg of nails, but to my knowledge no one has ever asked us how we would prefer to be governed." She suddenly felt ashamed. Mr. Lincoln had come to minister to his gravely ill son, not to be confronted about the ills of society. "I apologize, Mr. Lincoln. Perhaps my outburst can be attributed to the lateness of the hour."

"Late or not," Mr. Lincoln answered, "You're quite right. I'm the one who should be asking for forgiveness. I spoke without thinking. Perhaps I could borrow Mr. Hobbes when you've finished."

Elizabeth saw no need to announce that it was out of the Jefferson Davis library. Lincoln could see the Davis imprimatur on the inside leaf whenever he opened it. And she certainly didn't want to repeat Varina's casual boast that she would retrieve it when the Confederate army overtook Washington. That boast seemed more and more likely as the war wore on.

"Did you have a formal education, Madame Elizabeth?"

"Not a day in my life. I learned to read with some of the girls that I tended as a slave. I was scarcely two years older than they were and they encouraged me to sit in on their tutoring. I became an avid reader but I can scarcely write anything other than my name."

"I only had one year of formal school myself. My mother, really my step-mother, encouraged me towards learning."

Again Elizabeth was stunned by the contrast between Mr. Lincoln's visage in candlelight as opposed to daylight.

"You should have Mr. Brady do your picture at night by candle light. It's your best look."

"I don't think the cameras work at night. They need plenty of light."

After a comfortable silence of several minutes, Lincoln asked, "How, if I may ask, did you get out of slavery?"

"I was owned by a family named Burwell. The elder Mr. Burwell was a planter. He was a good man, but prosperity avoided him like a preacher avoids a saloon. He started out in Georgia, but he owned too many slaves and not enough land. He had about 50 slaves and not quite 100 acres of land. He grew hemp, which is a pretty easy crop."

"Yes, I've heard hemp will grow anywhere where there's a little dirt and enough room to spit," said Mr. Lincoln.

"Quite true. And it doesn't require the labor that cotton or sugar cane demand. So every year, Mr. Burwell would sell off five or six slaves and that would be his profit for the year. About the time he got the slave to acreage ratio in balance, he decided to go into the cordage business and built a ropewalk building. I don't know if you've ever seen one of those, but they're narrow buildings about a quarter of a mile long."

"I worked in one briefly as a youngster in Kentucky," said Mr. Lincoln. "Tough way to pass the time while waiting for the sun to go down."

Elizabeth smiled. "Mr. Burwell figured he could buy the hemp of other planters and turn it into a finished product. Trouble was, as you just pointed out, not everybody can work a ropewalk. You have to be extremely strong. Mr. Burwell had been selling off his best men because they brought the highest price. The men that were left had to work twice as long as the men at the other cordages to turn out half the product. To cover the shortages, he had to sell off more slaves. After two seasons, Mr. Burwell realized his folly and sold his land and business and eighteen of us moved to St. Louis. He was in such dire financial straights when we arrived that he couldn't even retrieve a letter from the post office because of the postage due."

Mr. Lincoln nodded.

"He mentioned hiring out my mother, old and grey haired by this time, and I went into apoplexy. I couldn't bear the thought. So I began to solicit the women of St. Louis to do their sewing. Soon I had procured more patrons than I could service. For two years I supported eighteen of us with my needle. Once the magnitude of what I was doing set in, the desire for freedom, for myself and my son George, became an obsession. Eventually Mr. Burwell died and I was passed to his daughter Ann, who had married a man named Garland. Soon Mr. Garland died and a planter from Mississippi, another Mr. Burwell, came to settle the estate. I told him of my desire for freedom and he was very supportive."

Lincoln slouched in his chair. He had developed the habit of attentive listening during his years as a trial attorney in Illinois. He would take his eyes off Elizabeth only when Willie would groan or rattle.

"I proposed going to New York to have Frederick Douglass and the Abolitionists lend me the money to buy the freedom of myself and George. We arrived at the price of $1,200.00 for the two of us. But he was also a business man, so he proposed that I solicit six people from St. Louis to guarantee my return, each bound for two hundred dollars. The first five were secured before noon the next day; due I trust to the reputation that I had been able to forge with my clients. When I approached the sixth guarantor, he said, 'Of course I will sign, Elizabeth, and I bid you a good-by.'

'You mean a good-by for a short term.'

'No, I mean a good-by for all time.'

'Whatever do you mean?'

'You'll never come back, Elizabeth. I know that you mean

to. But when you cross that river, the abolitionists will convince you of how evil we are and you'll never come back.'"

Lincoln was perhaps the greatest collector of moral fables in America. His success as a politician was linked to his ability to remember a story and retell it at the proper moment to drive home a salient point. He narrowed his focus to capture this one complete.

"I was devastated to think that someone who knew me would doubt my word. I went home and collapsed on my bed in tears. I was considering abandoning the entire scheme when I heard a knock at my door. It was Mrs. LaMaire, one of my patrons.

'I heard of your plan, Lizzie, and I feel awful. To think that we are sending you to New York to beg for money when you have so many friends here. I will raise the $1,200.00 for you. I have $200.00 put away for a present and mother owes you $50.00 and will add another $50.00. I'll solicit my friends tomorrow and I'm confident that by the afternoon, we'll have the entire amount.'"

Lincoln smiled, confident that he had gleaned a nugget that he could convert into political capital.

Elizabeth continued, "And so she did. So on July 27th, 1855 George and I became free people. It took me a year to repay my dear friends in St. Louis and then I moved to Baltimore."

"And where is George now?"

Elizabeth hesitated. This was a conversation that she really didn't wish to have tonight but there was no way to avoid it. "George is dead. He enlisted with General Lyon in Illinois and he was killed at the battle of Wilson's Creek."

Elizabeth could see the look of incomprehension spreading across Mr. Lincoln's face. Clearly Mary had not told him about George's parentage.

"George had a white father. He was able to enlist as a white man with no questions asked."

"I'm truly sorry. Have you told Mary?"

"I haven't found an appropriate time. But I'll do it soon. I'd rather that she heard it from me if you don't mind."

They sat in silence.

Finally, Elizabeth asked, "May I ask you about a legal matter?" Elizabeth related the story about buying the deed to Portia. "I know that I can't go back to Richmond now that the war's on, but can we do the paper work here in D.C.?"

"My best advice would be, 'Do nothing.' There is a bill in committee now that will emancipate all the slaves in Washington. Portia is a resident of D.C. so she will fall under the new statute. Owners are being reimbursed $600.00 per slave. All you have to do is go to the court house and file."

A metallic taste coated Elizabeth's mouth. She knew that her motives had all been pure, but somehow, here she was, about to make a profit of $200 on the buying and selling of human flesh. She hastily decided to give all of the profit to her charity, but that didn't remove the taste of silver and iron from her mouth.

The candlelight licked those deep furrows that had come to dominate Mr. Lincoln's face in the last eighteen months. "I'm given to understand that you're a friend of Frederick Douglass?" he asked.

"Yes, Frederick and I go back many years. I've even accompanied him on some of his speaking tours."

"I take it that you're an Abolitionist."

"Not in the sense of Frederick or William Lloyd Garrison, the newspaper man. There is a fine distinction, as our friend Hobbes would say. I certainly want to see slavery abolished, but I don't fully agree with their approach. I suspect sometimes that they're doing more harm than good by concentrating on the atrocities of slavery, rather than on the institution itself. I most assuredly know that horrors occur, but the majority of slave owners treat their slaves tolerably well. These owners will never let the scales fall off their eyes if they think that slavery is evil only if accompanied by physical abuse. The evil of slavery is in the institution itself, not in the excesses that an inhumane owner inflicts on his hapless slaves. I can't imagine Varina and Jefferson Davis inflicting harm on a slave, but they are willing to wage war to preserve their way of life." Elizabeth graciously omitted Mary and her family from the example.

Lincoln sat impassively with both his hands wrapped around his left knee.

"The real tragedy of slavery is the thousand indignities that one is forced to endure on a daily basis," she continued. "If you can bear to hear one more of my long-winded stories, I'll tell you about Cletus Gorrod. Cletus lived in my hometown of Petersburg. Kind owner, as they say in the South. Fed and clothed Cletus well. Allowed both Saturday and Sunday off. One Saturday morning Cletus was riding a mule about five miles outside of Petersburg on the road to Richmond. There were two saddle bags across the rear haunches of the mule containing carpentry tools. He was going to his mother's house to make some repairs. His mother had been 'given her time' on her seventy-fifth birthday with a gift of a two room shack on three acres of land. In reality, she was too feeble to be of any further use to her owner and was dumped in the middle of nowhere to fend for herself. This act of Christian kindness had been accomplished with the lumber salvaged from an old barn that had been blown down by the dying winds of a hurricane that came ashore squarely in the mouth of the James River. Cletus would go most weekends in an attempt to restore the place to its former stature, when it had lodged some of the finest livestock in the county. Cletus was slowly plodding along astride his mule when he rounded a crook in the road and encountered three young men sitting astride their horses.

'Morning,' they shouted.

'Morning,' he returned.

'That's a fine looking mule. He belong to you or to your master?'

'Bought him myself. Mr. Henson done allow me to share crop on twenty acres of his land.'

'I'm partial to that animal. What'll you take for him?'

'Can't sell. Need him too bad.'

'Mules cost about ten dollars. I'll give you forty for that one.'

"One of the men had eased a revolver out of a belt holster and let it rest across his leg. Cletus was scared, to say the least. 'Alright, can I drop him off Monday? I need him this weekend.'

'No, I need him now.'

"Cletus heard the unmistakable tumble of the cylinders of a gun cocking. He didn't want to walk, but he wanted even less to die. 'Alright,' he said as he skinnied down from the mule. The man with the gun dismounted and walked over to him. To Cletus's total amazement the man handed him forty dollars in gold coins. He grabbed the hackamores and led the mule to the edge of the road. He seemed to line him up in accordance with some plan that he carried in his mind and lifted the revolver and shot the mule squarely between the eyes.

'Damn it, Charles. We need him facing the other way.'

'There ain't no rules about which way a mule's gonna fall when you shoot him. Just come rope his feet and let the horse pull him over.'

Needless to say, Cletus assumed that he was next.

"After they had pulled the mule into their desired direction, one of the young men got off his horse and with a six inch butcher's knife, opened the mule up from his neck to his scrotum. The man then field dressed the mule removing all of his insides, no easy feat without hanging an animal that size from a tree or a gantry of some sort.

"The man with the gun looked at Cletus and said, 'How much

do you think those old clothes you're wearing are worth?' Cletus didn't answer. 'I'd say five dollars would be generous. Here's another ten dollars in gold. Take 'em off and put 'em in the grass yonder.' Cletus did as threatened. 'Now come climb inside this mule. Just leave your head sticking out.' Once positioned the third man produced a tanning awl and some rawhide strips and began sewing Cletus into the mule. When he was finished only Cletus's head was protruding from the carcass.

'Stage coach comes along here every day about nine o'clock going to Richmond. That's less than an hour. We'll be hiding in the trees. We want to see the look on their faces when they see you. No need to worry, if they don't cut you out, we will.' With that they rode down the dusty road. Out about a hundred yards, one of the riders wheeled around and trotted back to Cletus. 'There's a creek around that bend in the road. You can go wash yourself off there when you're out.' He slued his horse around and trotted back to his companions."

Elizabeth could read in Lincoln's eyes that he had been moved. "What happened to them?"

"The boys went on back to college with an amusing story to tell. Cletus went into a deeper and deeper swoon. Last I heard he was heavy into the bottle and beatin' up on his wife and kids."

They sat in silence for several minutes.

"And just because you're free it doesn't mean the indignities stop. I carry a quart size mason jar in that bag there," pointing with her finger. "Even coming over here tonight, I suddenly had to pee. Do you know there's not a store or hotel that will allow a black woman to use the privy? I had to turn down an alley street and pee into my Mason jar and just stand there and pray to God that no one should happen to turn that corner."

Elizabeth thought she had exceeded boundaries, but once again the nighttime had clouded her judgment. She was too tired to care and Mr. Lincoln didn't seem to take offense.

"I ran on a platform of not allowing slavery to expand into the Territories, but if I ever get the chance. I think I will go for its total annihilation."

Mrs. Barton, the night nurse, entered the room. Willie's breathing was even raspier than before. "Say goodnight to Willie for me when he wakes. And tell Mrs. Lincoln I'll see her tomorrow at ten."

She picked up her bag, Mason jar and all, and headed home.

Chapter XIII

Willie's condition was worse by the following evening. His breathing now sounded like marbles being shaken in a jar. His sweat had a fetid smell, like a cabbage soup that had been left out too long on a stove without reheating. All white people have a strange smell, but this was different, more intense. Elizabeth's Cherokee friend back in Virginia used a word to describe the white man's aroma. She translated it to mean 'wet-dog-in-house.' Eunice LaRon believed that the smell was connected to slavery. Whenever all vestiges of slavery were erased from the hearts of whites, the odor would go away.

Elizabeth noticed the dark patches that yesterday had been only at his toes had now climbed up to his knees as she changed the sheets and wiped down his pistol hot body.. She knew the doctors were scared because they kept coming up with more and better words to describe the condition, but not a single new medicine or treatment. In truth, their nostrums and potions had long been exhausted. They had tried teas of black haw root and ground hickory leaves and Virginia snake root. Now they hovered like witch doctors, hoping that some correct phrase could appease a disinterested god and return Willie to health. Both parents were huddled near the bed tightly holding hands, Mary's mouth barely moving, offering silent prayers of desperation.

She was trading like a Potlatch Indian. "I'll give you Mr. Lincoln if you'll let Willie live."

"I'll get Mr. Lincoln soon enough."

"Then take me, but spare my little Willie."

The disinterested god just stared into the abyss.

"Take the White house, take all the trappings of power and prestige, take all of our money, take the clothes, but please let little Willie live."

She could tell that he was considering it.

And then it all stopped.

Dr. Stone stood up and softly said, "Well, you won't be needing my services anymore this evening." He picked up his ditty bag and left the room.

Mr. Lincoln rose from his chair and stumbled down the hall. Mrs. Lincoln shook like an aspen tree in a faint breeze. Her grief was so profound she couldn't contain it. She cried out loudly and her body convulsed. Elizabeth clutched her tightly and escorted her down the hall and into her room.

All at once, the ice pick of a fever that had been stabbing Willie in the brain subsided. His eyes, which only moments prior had been thickly encrusted were now clear and translucent. His breathing was no longer labored; the fifty pound sack of potatoes that had been sitting on his chest had been removed. *"This must be how my pony feels when I uncinch his saddle,"* he thought to himself. He felt better than he had felt in weeks. He looked around the room and wondered where everyone had gone.

"I've recovered. It's like one moment I was in the deepest pain, but now I'm fully recovered."

"I feel so good now that I would like to get dressed and ride my pony for a while."

Instantly he was standing in front of the mahogany armoire. *"I think I'll wear my soldier's uniform."* Willie thought that perhaps he was still feverish – there seemed to be no lag between his thoughts and his actions. He didn't remember actually putting his feet into his trousers or putting on his coat, but here he was fully dressed.

"I wish I could have William saddle my pony for me and meet me at the South Entrance."

Willie finished dressing himself and took a slow, deliberate look around the room, etching into his mind the exact placement of the furniture, the pictures on the wall, the dark green wallpaper beneath the chair railing that his mother had chosen. He stared as though the image would have to last him an eternity.

Once he had captured an image as faithful as Mr. Brady's camera, he walked out. He felt refreshed, almost weightless. He practically glided down the stairs. William was standing at the south entrance, pony saddled and waiting. William gave Willie a leg up and asked, "Where're you going to ride to, Master Willie?"

"I think I'll go to the war office first to see if there's any news I can pick up for father. Then I'm going to see if they've made any progress on the dome at the Capitol Building. Since I'll be on the east side of town, I'll swing by the Baltimore & Ohio terminal, and I might just follow that line all the way to Chicago and then on to Springfield."

"That's a long ride, Master Willie. Are you sure you're up to it?"

"I guess nobody is ever truly ready for a long ride, but I think I have no choice. I'm as ready as I'll ever be. Take care of Tad while I'm away" He nudged his pony in his ribs with the heel of his boot and trotted away. He looked up at the second story and saw Tad standing in his bedroom window. Both boys smiled and waved good-by and the pony broke into a trot.

Mr. Lincoln blindly felt his way down the hall until he reached the shared office of Nickolay and Hay. "Well, my boy is gone. He's really gone."

Mary was not to be consoled. "Oh Lizzie, I just want to die and be shed of this wretched world. When little Eddie died, I hurt down to my heart and bones. But this hurt can gain no purchase. It goes entirely through my body and consumes me. Oh Lizzie, help me die. I don't wish to live another day." With this, her body contracted and twitched as though she were having a seizure.

'Now Mary, you must think of Tad. You know how Willie adored him. He would want you to care for him."

"Tad!" she bolted upright. "Has anyone told him? I can't do it, Lizzie. Please go to him. I don't want him to hear from anyone but you. Please do it, Lizzie. Please!"

Elizabeth stood and nodded ever so slowly. She turned and walked to the door, turning left in the hallway and entered Tad's room. Tad was standing at the window, looking into the stables where the animals were quartered at night. As usual he greeted Elizabeth with that vacuous Jack-O-Lantern smile.

"Tad, you should be in bed. You're still not well enough to be up and about." She placed her palm on his forehead as she guided him back to bed.

"Tad, I have some bad news and I don't know of any gentle way of saying it; Willie has left us."

"I know. I saw him ride away and he waved good-by. Will he be gone long?"

Elizabeth was puzzled but said, "I'm afraid he won't be coming back, honey. I'm so sorry."

Tad looked at her with a look of incomprehension and pulled the quilt up around his neck and closed his eyes.

Chapter XIV

The nine months following the death of Willie were sad ones in the White House. The War was looking like a bad decision rolling downhill. Confederate victory followed confederate victory. Lincoln was changing generals as frequently as he changed socks, but Robert E. Lee was pushing the Union Army around at will. It seemed to Elizabeth that Varina Davis had been absolutely correct in her assessment of the South's ability to wage war. She fully expected to see grey uniforms marching on Washington streets any day. Mrs. Lincoln had made some temporary repairs to her heart; caulking a break here with tin and mortar, nailing a board there, staunching the flow of blood by applying a styptic to the small leaks. But Elizabeth knew that the workmanship was shoddy and the repairs temporary at best. Mary continued to refurbish the white House and she continued to order new clothes, but Elizabeth knew that these activities were futile attempts to fill the void caused by the loss of Willie. The only positive to this drear backdrop was the fact that Elizabeth's business was booming. Mrs. Lincoln increased her wardrobe weekly but seldom wore anything except the dark crepe of mourning. Most of her other patrons followed the lead of Mrs. Lincoln; using the purchase of a new wardrobe to deflect attention from the daily newspapers that only told of death and dying and a war that grew more untenable day by day.

"Lizzie, I'm going north to New York and Saratoga for a few weeks. I had arranged for Tad to stay with Mrs. Baker, but he pitched a conniption fit when I told him. He only wants to stay with you. Will you consent for him to be in your charge?"

"Of course. But I have business in Oxford and Easton. Would it be acceptable if Tad escorted me? We would be staying at Artemas's home outside of Oxford. It's large and there's plenty of room. I think Tad would be in hog heaven."

"Let me ask Mr. Lincoln. There's much Confederate sympathy on the Eastern Shore." Elizabeth could tell that she had already approved the plan and that her asking Mr. Lincoln was only a courtesy.

"We'll probably go to the Quaker Meeting on Sunday, if you don't object. I promise to return him still a good Presbyterian."

"That would be quite something, since he won't be leaving as one," said Mrs. Lincoln. "I'm afraid he's inherited his church habits from his father. And what would the travel arrangements be? Just how is my most precious child going to disappear from known civilization?"

"We'll take the train to Annapolis and Artemas is sailing one of his boats over for us."

"One of his boats?" Suddenly Mary was piqued. "How many does he have?"

"I'm not sure. I know he employs seven men during the crabbing and oystering season. I've never really asked him."

"Is there anything that our Artemas can't do? Sounds like he would be a fine catch for some lucky lady. Should I be preparing a trousseau?"

Lizzie laughed. "Probably not. Remember! I was born a slave and I don't intend to go back. But if I were ever tempted, it would probably be with Artemas."

"Are you comparing marriage to slavery?"

"Not really. I've been both and I would take slavery every time."

They could hear Mr. Lincoln walking down the hall. He entered the room wearing that somber look that he wore when he returned from the war room after receiving bad news from the war front.

"Lizzie and Tad are going to the Eastern Shore next week. Doesn't that sound like a caution?"

"I'm reminded of the story of the old man who took the stand in a certain judge's court. The judge asked him to state his age. He said sixty. As he was on the face of it much older, but persisted, the court admonished him, saying, 'The court knows you to be older than sixty.'

'Oh, I understand now,' owned up the old fellow. 'You are thinking of the ten years I spent on the Eastern Shore of Maryland; that was so much time lost and did not count.'

As usual, Lincoln laughed the hardest.

"She's going to turn Tad into a Quaker."

"If she can get Tad to sit still for an hour or so, then I'm all for it." Lincoln turned thoughtful. "The Friends are mostly refusing to pay the special assessment of $300.00 to support the war effort. Do you think you could do us a service and collect the taxes while you're there? How can they be both against slavery and against the war that will end it?" Mr. Lincoln seemed to drift off in thought. "If the opportunity arises, could you bring back some of those Maryland beaten biscuits? I had some when we had that meeting at Johns Hopkins' house in Baltimore early in '61, and I'm quite partial to them."

I was in Baltimore at that time, Elizabeth thought, *and I remember the only thing beaten harder than the biscuits was the Constitution. The mayor of Baltimore, who was so helpful to me when I moved there to open my sewing school, along with the chief-of-police, were determined to be hostile to Mr. Lincoln and as a result were arrested without cause or charges, and are still enslaved in prison at Fort McHenry. God, I wish this was one of our sick vigils. It would be fun to get out the Webster word book and have Mr. Lincoln read the definition of 'slavery.'* But Elizabeth knew that the sick vigil rules didn't apply to daytime. She would have to sheath this sword for another fight. But she would not forget.

"They don't travel well, Mr. President. They are really best fresh off the stove. Artemas calls them 'sinkers' when they have to be re-heated. He says they're so hard that they're only good enough to throw at the geese. If you hit one, they're sure to sink. But I'd be pleased to make you some fresh one morning."

"I'd be most appreciative, Madame Elizabeth. Do you also know how to make red-eye gravy?"

"I'm from Virginia; of course I know how to make red-eye gravy."

"Do our friends on the Eastern Shore have such modern conveniences as the telegraph? Could you keep us apprised of Tad's well-being?"

"Easton does. It's about ten miles from Oxford. I'll wire you every day or so."

Mr. Lincoln left the room for a short time and returned holding an envelope. "Madame Elizabeth, I wonder if you would do me the honor of delivering a letter. I would send it regular post, but I read just this morning in the Herald how badly this government is being run, so I would feel much more secure relying upon you."

They both smiled at his little joke. "It would be my pleasure. The letter is not addressed. To whom shall I tender it?"

"Just keep it upon your person and remit it to anyone who asks for it." With that, Mr. Lincoln bowed and said, "Stanton and Chase await me at the war office. I am confident that your journey will hold more good fortune than mine, but I must be off."

———— •✦• ————

They left at dawn. The train ride to Annapolis was both swift and uneventful. As they descended South Street in Annapolis, she saw Artemas standing against the corner of the Pussars Landing building. God only knows what time he must have left Oxford. Ever faithful, ever dependable Artemas. "Hello, Tad. Ready for a sail?"

"Good morning, Mr. Artemas. Can I ride in the front?" Tad took off in a run without waiting for an answer.

Artemas walked over to the carriage and hoisted both trunks over his back as easily as most people would lift a satchel. "We call it the 'bow', Tad. The wind is with us, Elizabeth, let's not tarry!"

Artemas shoved off and as the boat drifted, he raised a sail. The wind sidled in the sail like a cat snuggling up to a warm stove. Artemis held the tiller lovingly in one hand, his eyes leveled on the horizon. "If this wind holds, we should be docking in Oxford in five hours." Once they cleared the Severn River and entered the Chesapeake Bay, Artemas called to Tad, "Come take the helm, while I hoist another sail." Tad was beside himself. Elizabeth could not dispel the notion that she was being ferried to her death by a delirious Jack-o-lantern. "Small movements, Tad! Keep the sail as fat as you can." Deftly, Artemas pulled another sail into place. Artemas walked back to the tiller. "Put your hand on top of mine and feel my movements."

I hope when people see me sewing that I look as much a part of my craft as Artemas does of his, she thought. As she watched him standing like a bronze god, she remembered the lines that Mr. Lincoln had quoted not a week before; *"What piece of work is a man! How noble in reason, how infinite in faculty! In form and moving how express and admirable! In action how like an angel, in apprehension how like a god! The beauty of the world! The paragon of animals."*

"*Why would anyone want to enslave such a creature?*" The question was rhetorical. She knew the answer well.

"*There is nothing purer in life than sailing,*" thought Elizabeth. "*It's only man and nature. Birth station doesn't matter. Money doesn't matter. Social standing counts for naught. Either you can do it or you can't. You can't lie about it; you can't argue about it; you can't pass laws to make it so. Either you can reap the wind or you can't.*" Elizabeth had seen a statue in one of Jefferson Davis's books of a solitary man standing in a small boat, carved from marble in a single piece. "*When I get wealthy, I'll travel to Italy and look at that statue directly. Or maybe I'll pay someone to carve Artemas as he stands now.*" Elizabeth was feeling generous as she eyed Tad standing beside Artemas, maniacal smile on his face and the sun reflecting off his multitudinous teeth, "*Hell, I'll even throw in the Jack-o-lantern.*"

The trees and bushes were pulling them closer. Elizabeth knew that it would be over soon. "That's my place dead ahead. The one with the boat house," said Artemas. Elizabeth had already inferred as much, seeing as how Eunice LaRon was patiently standing on the pier, her broad smile serving as a beacon in a lighthouse guiding them safely to shore.

The boat house was larger than any of the houses Elizabeth had ever lived in. It had two sections under roof large enough to dock the work boats that presently lay tied to pilings. Artemas dropped the sails and grabbed the pier with the gaff pole. He maneuvered the boat around the pier and into the boat house. Tad shot out of the boat and began running down the pier at full speed as though he had some idea where he was going. "The boy needs some ballast. I'm afraid there's too much cargo space inside," Artemas said.

"He'll be fine. He's just a little slower than most. And all those jumbled teeth make it difficult to understand him sometimes, but he'll be fine," Elizabeth said.

Elizabeth and Eunice locked arms and walked toward the house.

"So how's life on the Eastern Shore? Is farm life as rewarding as you had remembered, or are you ready to return to Murder Bay?"

"It's better than I remember, Lizzy. My only regret is that Henry can't be here to enjoy it with me," said Eunice. "It's odd, but I dream about him more and more frequently. And the dreams get more and more real."

"You sound like Mrs. Lincoln. She no longer talks about dreaming of Willie, but rather about his nighttime visits. Are you going to become like her? Am I going to have to walk on eggshells around you too? Two temperamental women may be more than I can bear."

Eunice smiled. "Not likely. But I did have a dream last night that was as real as standing here. Henry was inside Clary's. He was wearing that leather apron that he wore at work. It was covered with blood. But the cows were revolting. They were all outside and they had the building surrounded. They would charge the doors and the walls. Every time they collided with the building, it would shake as though it were going to fall down. Henry looked at me and said, 'This is more than I bargained for. I'm only trying to make a living.'" Eunice looked puzzled. "What do you think that means?"

"I have no earthly idea," Elizabeth said.

Artemas's house was much larger than the boat house. It was a spyglass house. The larger section was a 2½ story New Englander with two dormers towards the southeast. The next section with the main entrance was a very tall one story, some three feet narrower than the first. And the last section, narrower still, was a one story with an end door that led out to the barn and the kitchen. The water was visible in three directions. The trees were mostly pine and there was a large magnolia. There was a cedar lined lane that she assumed led to a main road, but it curved and she could not see its terminus. There was a stable, a barn, and numerous other small buildings scattered over a roughly six acre clearing.

"How much land do you have here, Artemas?"

"A little over 800 acres. There are six families that live here. They work for me mostly as watermen or farmers, depending on the season. Four families have bought their freedom and two families are still enslaved and rented by me from their owners. Everybody has part of their wages set aside each month and put into what we call 'the dime box.' When it builds up enough, we buy another's freedom. The dime box is kept on the mantle of the fire place. Anybody can use the money, as long as they tell Aunt Amelia first and she writes down their name and the amount."

Tad had found his way to the stables and was sitting on an unsaddled horse, contently staring into space. "The boy needs ballast," Artemas said again. "Let's go see if Aunt Amelia needs help with the cooking."

Eunice snorted. "She might need some, but she sure don't want none."

The kitchen was set aside from the main house and connected by a dog trot of some twenty feet. The dog trot was roofed and was covered with wisteria and trumpet vine and some other kind of vine that Elizabeth could not identify.

"I'm not familiar with that vine. What is it?"

"It's hops. It's used to make beer. I brought some back on my last voyage at sea. It grows about a foot a day in the spring time. Aunt Amelia and I have a bet. She has the trumpet vine and I have the hops. Whichever grows the most by the end of summer wins."

The kitchen was one of the largest that Elizabeth had ever seen. It was built like a tobacco barn with its exterior planks running vertical and hinged to allow for quick ventilation. At the far end of the kitchen stood a massive fireplace with a hearth that extended a full six feet into the room. She supposed that was to prevent popping embers from starting a fire. Resting on the hearth was a davit for swinging heavy pots over the fire in the fireplace. Suspended from the ceiling were skillets and copper pots and cleavers and mallets and all manner of kitchen utensils. There were two stoves sitting side by side. On the opposite wall was a sink with copper pipe draining from a cistern built on the roof of the building. Next to the sink was a massive chopping block fashioned from maple. Close to the entrance was a china cabinet that only a craftsman such as Artemas could have built. It held enough settings to rival what Mrs. Lincoln had purchased for the White House. Opposite that was one of the ice boxes that were becoming so fashionable.

"Aunt Amelia, this is Elizabeth."

"Is there anything I can do to help?" asked Elizabeth.

"Not enough room for two, right now, but I'll call you in a spell." said Amelia, as she covered the entire area of the kitchen, lifting a pot, turning on the tap in the sink, opening the ice box door.

Elizabeth understood immediately. Amelia could not have marked her territory any clearer unless she hiked a leg in each corner and peed.

"Let me know if there's anything I can do," Elizabeth said.

Chapter XV

"Can I go crabbing, Jib?" Tad begged.

"Best crabbing is on a rising tide, Tad," Artemas offered. "'Fraid you wouldn't have much luck right now. But if you walk up that shell road and take the second road to the right and go to the big red house and ask for 'Atwell,' you might get him to take you out on the boat and teach you how to oyster."

Tad looked frantically at Elizabeth. "Come here, Tad." She reached into her pocket and withdrew a skein of red string. She deftly tied it around his right wrist. "That's your right side, Tad. Just follow the string."

Tad scampered up the road. When he was out of ear-shot, Artemas said, "That boy couldn't pour piss out of a boot with the directions on the heel."

Elizabeth smiled and said, "He'll do fine. He's just a late bloomer."

"More like a blooming idiot," Artemas said, but not meanly.

Artemas went back to carving on a deer head. "I think Mr. Lincoln just might have had a good idea about making a bung out of a skull. I'm going to try and thread it, so I can screw it in." A Dorset ram was tied to a leg of the work table, and was lazily reclining in the shade provided by the table. Artemas held a set of calipers and measured the hole in the ram's head, and then measured the stopper. He sanded on the stopper for awhile and then re-measured.

"Funny thing, I've accidentally dropped several things on that ram's brain and he didn't react at all. It's like he couldn't even feel it."

"I wonder if humans are the same way?" asked Elizabeth.

"Let's trepan Tad when he gets back and see. But that might not answer the question about 'humans.'"

"You ride that boy like a rented mule," Elizabeth chided.

"Tad must have solved the mystery of the red string. Here they come now."

Peering into the sun, Elizabeth saw salt and pepper coming towards her. Both boys were roughly the same height, but Tad carried a little more girth. Atwell was shoeless, but he didn't seem to notice that he was walking on crushed oyster shells.

"Won't that cut his feet?"

"Didn't seem to the last hundred times he did it. But if it does, I'm sure he'll move over on the grass."

Atwell held something in his right hand that he repetitively threw down toward his feet, but it would hesitate about six inches from the ground and return to his hand.

"What in God's name is that?"

"That's a toy that children play with on the Philippine Islands. I brought it back from my last voyage. They call it a yo-yo."

As they walked up, Elizabeth noticed that Atwell bore a keen resemblance to her dead son George, only much darker. The dagger still went into her heart when she thought of George, but not as deep and it didn't stay in for nearly as long.

"Atwell, this here's Miss Elizabeth. Show her some of the tricks you can do with your yo-yo."

Atwell threw it down, and at the bottom of its descent, it

floated, going neither up nor down, but merely spinning on its looped string. Next, he paused it at the bottom of its arc and made it walk along the ground. Then he caused it to do two complete 360 revolutions. Tad swooned in admiration.

"Atwell, you and Tad take one of the boats down to Claddy's Cove and scare up a bushel of oysters for tonight."

"Can we take the bug-eye?" asked Atwell.

"You don't need that much boat for a bushel, but I don't care."

As the boys headed to the boat house, Elizabeth asked, "What's a bug-eye?"

"It's a boat I designed for oystering. It's wide and flat and doesn't draw much, so I can get in close on the shallows. I built large, prominent hawse holes up near the bow and the kids said it looks like a bug with big eyes."

Elizabeth saw a very large boat emerge from behind the magnolia tree and her heart stopped. "Is anybody on there with them? Can he handle that? Should you go with them?"

Artemas laughed, "As you said earlier; he'll be just fine."

"Need I remind you that his father is the commander-in-chief of a million well-armed men who carry out firing squads with some regularity? Mr. Lincoln has already signed the death warrant on over 200 soldiers, and for far less serious violations than killing his son. And I won't face it alone either. I'll rat you out, Artemas!"

Artemas laughed. "I'm setting this Mason jar of rat poison on the table here. Tell Mrs. Lincoln to be sure that there are no cats or dogs around where she puts it out. It's lethal." Artemas turned very serious.

"Elizabeth, have you ever thought of coming down here and us jumping the broom. I think you would be happy here. I'm richer than most white men. The farming and the fishing practically run themselves now. We could travel. We could go to

Europe and see all of those sights and museums that you always talk about."

"That's certainly tempting, Artemas. The only two things that I have detested about this war is the death of George, and the City of Philadelphia deciding to delay the opening of the first zoo in this country. I've always wanted to go to a zoo. If we could go see the Vienna Zoo, I might consider it. I want to see a crocodile. What was it that Uncle Salty used to say about crocodiles and white people?"

Artemas noted to himself that Elizabeth had not said 'no' to his proposal, she had merely deflected the conversation in another direction. He took that as a victory.

"Uncle Salty said white people had two sets of eye-lids, like a crocodile, when they looked at slavery. That second set of eyelids kept them from seeing clearly. But a predator with armored skin doesn't necessarily need good eye sight."

"And a bull fight. I've always wanted to see a bull fight."

"You are a puzzle, Elizabeth. You wouldn't slap a gnat, and yet you have this blood lust. I've never known anyone so keen on cock fighting and now you want to travel half way 'round the world to see a bull fight."

"How long did it take you to teach that boy to sail?"

"I didn't teach him."

"Then how did he learn?"

"I had business in St. Michaels one day, and I thought Atwell might enjoy the sail over. He was maybe five years old. He sat there and never said a word. When we got back, he jumped out of the boat and ran home at top speed. The next morning I got up at the usual waterman's hour, four o'clock. I walked down to the pier and there sat Atwell, apparently waiting for me. I loaded some crab traps and bait and gear. He climbed aboard and once again sat silently. The next morning when I got to the boat, it was loaded and ready to go. Atwell had mustered himself on as first mate. When he was eight or nine, we sailed up the mouth of the Choptank River over to a sand bar that I thought might be promising as an oyster bed. I lowered the sails and began probing the river floor to see if I was correct. It was dead calm, but then a furious gust of wind, what Uncle Salty called one of Neptune's farts, caught that sail and spun that boom around in a blink and caught me up around the shoulder blades and knocked me clean out of the boat. Like most watermen, I can't swim, but I was marooned on that little sand spit, water barely above my knees. I stood up and watched that boat head out of the Choptank and into the Chesapeake. Then I saw the sails get adjusted, and the boat turned and headed back in my direction. He drew alongside and dropped the sail and I rolled over the bulwark. Atwell sailed us on home. We never said a word, but we both knew that he would do the sailing from then on."

Elizabeth carried a weight in her stomach for the better part of two hours until the bug-eye sailed back into view. Atwell deftly stood with his hand on the tiller, while Tad stood near the bow throwing the yo-yo up and down. Atwell sailed the boat behind the magnolia tree and Elizabeth felt the tension ooze from her body. Soon the boys were walking towards the house carrying a bushel basket between them.

"Can you and Tad shuck about half of those for Aunt Amelia?" Artemas asked. "And put the rest in the ice house." They sat the bushel basket on one of the tables and Atwell took two flat knives off a peg that was driven into a maple tree. He handed one of the knives to Tad and used the other to begin opening the oysters. Tad watched for a moment and then tried on his own. He couldn't locate the seams of the oyster and soon abandoned the task and went back to playing with the yo-yo.

Artemas was still carving on the deer head. Slowly he was fashioning a bung. He walked over to where the ram was standing alongside the table. He sat the bung into the trepanned hole and tried to screw it in. "Almost," he said as he filed the edges.

"Watch, Artemas!" said Tad as he propelled the yo-yo forward - parallel to the ground. The yo-yo returned to his hand. Tad beamed. He repeated the trick, but instead of returning to his hand, the yo-yo string snapped at its maximum extension and became a missile. It didn't travel far; its journey ended at the side of the Mason jar. The jar shattered and the rat poison ran between the planks of the table and directly into the trepanned hole of the ram. The ram didn't stagger or stumble. He dropped like a sack of potatoes. Tad began to scream hysterically and ran to Elizabeth.

"It's all right Tad" said Artemas. "We were going to butcher him in the fall anyway. This is just a couple of months early. Atwell, go fetch Uncle Caleb and tell him we need him to do a little butchering."

"Will that meat be fit to eat?" Elizabeth asked in a doubtful voice.

"The natives in South America used that potion to hunt monkeys. If it was lethal to eat the meat of anything killed with it, I wouldn't be standing here now."

Elizabeth stroked Tad's head, not doubting Artemas in the least, but glad that tonight's meal was seafood. She slipped the carved bung into her dress pocket. "I don't guess you'll be needing this," she said to Artemas. "I'd like it as a keepsake. Maybe use it as a paper weight."

Chapter XVI

The sun doused itself by falling into the Choptank River. The tree frogs began their throaty symphony and the moon was one quarter full – Elizabeth's favorite.

"Atwell, you and Tad go fetch a couple of mules and meet me at the boat house," said Artemas. "We've got company."

Elizabeth could faintly hear oars rhythmically breaking water. Artemas straightened himself and began walking toward the pier.

A small woman rowed the boat into one of the covered slips of the boat house. Once it was securely moored, she reached down and pulled back a brown tarp revealing two young men lying prone in the hull of the boat. "Artemas, this is Melvin and Elvin, out for a little adventure tonight. They were wondering if they could put up at your hotel for a week or so."

"It would be my pleasure, Aunt Harriet."

The boys were so identical they probably couldn't tell each other apart. They stood about six feet tall and had the chiseled bodies of well-worked field hands.

"This is your party, boys, so, strip down to your birthday suits and let's get started."

The boys hastily shed their clothes. Artemas tossed a bar of soap to the boys and hauled a bucket of water out of the river.

"Rub real hard, boys. You're probably safe, but everything we do is prevention in case someone comes snooping around with the blood hounds."

Artemas poured several buckets of water over the boys. He handed them towels and they dried themselves.

"Leave the towels in the boat."

Artemas drug a square box about two feet wide and four inches high from the corner of the boat house over to the edge of the dock.

"This is coffee and peppers and some other herbs. Now Elvin, I want you to pick up only your shoes and step into the box and then climb on my back and I'll carry you down to the mules. You boys are going to live like martins for the next week – never touching the ground. There are fresh clothes for you in the barn."

Elvin did as instructed and Artemas ferried him down the walkway and over to Atwell and the mules. He returned and repeated the ritual with Melvin.

"Show them where everything is," Artemas instructed Atwell.

"Now let's go see if Aunt Amelia is ready for us."

The first thing that Elizabeth noticed about Harriet Tubman was that she tended not to smile. She didn't look angry or unhappy, but something akin to observant. Her large eyes reminded Elizabeth of the great horned owl, so plentiful on the Eastern Shore. Her steely glare missed nothing; aware that every living thing is either prey or predator, usually both at the same time. True, there are some herbivores prowling the jungle, but they are not very interesting. They are better suited for zoos. Elizabeth still planned on going to one of the fine European zoos after the war. But it's the carnivores that make us feel alive in the jungle. Life is most exhilarating when we are engaged in a life or death struggle. Our heart races when we hear the throaty roar of the lion, asking if we would like to engage in combat to the death; not when we watch the peaceful giraffe nibble on leaves thirty feet in the air. Maybe black people are the herbivores of the human race, content to co-exist with everyone, asking only to be left in peace. White people are definitely the carnivores, able to exist only by feeding on the weak and feeble.

Harriet Tubman was even smaller than Mary Todd Lincoln. Her clothing was mannish and her shoes were the brogans favored by farmers. The laces were tied not in a bow, or slip knot, but in a reef knot. Elizabeth wondered if Artemas had taught her how to tie it, since she had occasionally seen him use that very knot on his shoes.

Harriet Tubman leaned in toward Elizabeth, those unblinking owl eyes seared on Elizabeth as though she was a field mouse or a vole.

"You have something for me?"

Elizabeth was puzzled. Was she expected to produce a gift of some sort? "I'm not certain – what do you mean?"

Harriet waited. Elizabeth felt that if she made an improper move, Harriet would seize her in her deadly talons and fly away to God knows where.

"I was told that you would have a letter for me."

"Oh, the letter! Mr. Lincoln didn't tell me who it was for. Of course!" She reached into her purse and retrieved the letter and extended it to Harriet, who made no movement to take the letter from Elizabeth's hand, but gently said, "Feel these hands and tell me what you think, Keckley."

Elizabeth ran her thumbs over Harriet's palms and fingers. "They are strong hands, leathery and well-callused," Elizabeth said.

"And do you know how they got that way?" Elizabeth shook her head from side to side.

127

"They got that way by starting to hoe in a vegetable patch at five years of age from can to can't. They got that way by being dragged over forty acres by a team of oxen, holding onto the leathery reins that cut into my hands until they bled. They got that way by chopping, sawing, rowing. Hands don't get that way by holding a goddam book – Whatever made you think I ever had time to learn how to read? For God's sake, Keck, read it to me!"

Elizabeth swallowed a laugh. She opened the letter and read; "Pursuant to our conversation, please find enclosed a draft from the war department for $400.00 for initial expenses. Best of wishes for success. A. Lincoln."

"A draft? What's a draft?" asked Harriet.

"Take it to the bank and sign it and they will give you $400.00," explained Elizabeth.

"Do you know what business I'm in? I run a freedom train. I suspect that a good bunch of the people that I've helped ride that train to freedom belonged to those very bankers, or at least to some of their biggest customers. If I was to go into any bank in Easton or Cambridge and say, 'I've got a $400.00 draft from A. Lincoln,' I doubt if I would make it half way home. I'd have a draft alright; it would be a draft blowing up the crack of my black ass as I swung from a poplar tree."

"Atwell!" Artemas yelled, "Take this paper from Aunt Harriet and put it in the dime box. Bring her $400.00 in gold coins. Mix up the half eagles, eagles, and double eagles."

As befitting someone who faced life or death situations on a daily basis, once the solution to the problem was offered, Harriet displayed no interest in the post mortem. She shifted her attention to Elizabeth.

"You're hands are soft, but your fore-arms are muscular and your shoulders are wide. You must have thirty pounds and seven inches on me, but I'll wrestle you for the $400.00 right now.

Winner take all! If you don't have it on you, your words good enough."

A bolt of excitement shot through Elizabeth's body. Of all the things that provided the salt to make the monotony of life palatable, gambling and physical activity were two of Elizabeth's favorites. But then reason and judgment, those twin chaperones that turn most adventures into dreary events, gained control. *"How would I tell Mr. Lincoln that his enterprise would have to be postponed because I had out-wrestled Mrs. Tubman for the seed money?"* she asked herself.

"Maybe another time," Elizabeth said glumly.

"I saw your eyes light up. I know that you wanted to," said the wise old owl.

"Do you know what this is all about?" Harriet asked, waiving the letter towards Elizabeth.

Elizabeth shook her head "No".

"Mr. Lincoln wants me to go down South behind the lines and lead the slaves to Washington."

"Yes, I heard Mr. Lincoln talking to Frederick Douglass about it. Are you taking him with you?"

"Would you take a capon to a cock fight? Frederick will make speeches and raise money from his abolitionist friends, but he would no longer be willing to sleep in swamps and fight mosquitoes and eat pilot bread. No, Frederick's a general in this war now, not a foot soldier. I doubt if he has the onions for what I'm doing. I'm afraid that when he scaled that wall to freedom, he snagged his pouch on the barbed wire and left his jewels to be pecked over by the crows. And make no mistake about it; Frederick Douglass is a good friend of mine. More than a friend, isn't he Artemas? I once gave him a hay ride in that very barn over there. I put something on that man that pond water and lye soap wouldn't take off. We had to put extra starch in his pants to keep his knees from buckling when he walked, didn't we Artemas?"

"That's a natural fact, Aunt Harriet. The man had the weak knee for three days."

"Someone read me his book. What a cart of horse shit. He said he was hired out to Edward Covey because Covey was a slave breaker. I know Covey and he can barely break wind, much less break a slave. But in the Lord's plan, everybody has a part, and Frederick's part is to raise money and give speeches to soften the Pharaoh-hearts of the white man; and truth be told, his little talks have probably led to the freedom of many more blacks than my train rides. Yes, everybody has a part. Even you, Keck- I know about your charity work and I praise God for it."

Aunt Amelia came out of the kitchen, covered in sweat. "This food ain't gonna taste no better if we wait a week. Let's eat! Now you can help me, Mrs. Keckley. Ladle out this she-crab soup to everybody."

There must have been six or seven families sitting around the two long tables and benches that Artemas had fashioned out of cedar. The meal was more sumptuous than anything Elizabeth had seen served at the White House. There were oysters, both raw and fried, soft shell crabs, rock fish, she-crab soup, goose livers, corn bread, collard greens, tomatoes, and black- eyed peas, and three types of fowl.

"I couldn't eat another bite even if meant the emancipation of every slave in Maryland," Elizabeth said.

She breathed deeply and leaned back complacently. Suddenly she realized she was in the death stare of the Great Horned Owl.

"Here comes another thing about Frederick Douglass....." Harriet's voice disappeared into the night and her eyes closed and her head bobbed down on her chest. Elizabeth thought this was a dramatic pause, strictly for effect.

"She's out!" shouted Artemas. "Hurry!"

Atwell and the other children set upon her like a pack of coyotes attacking a wounded rabbit. Atwell grabbed her purse, opened it and removed a revolver. Then he took all the gold coins that he had given her and put them in his pocket. A girl several years younger than Atwell was working the pockets of Harriet's dress; transferring hard candy into her own frock. Another child had dived under the table and busied himself untying the laces on her shoes, and re-tying them to each other. Then, like well-sated hyenas, they went back to their chairs, acting nonchalant and licking their jowls.

Harriet jerked erect. "Was I out again? Did I have another spell?"

"Not that I noticed," Artemas lied.

"I have these spells sometimes where I just nod off," she explained to Elizabeth. "Been having 'em since I was thirteen. I was in Burlington's Hardware and Notions Store in Cambridge, and Jack Baker, one of the vilest overseers on God's green earth, was trying to flog a young slave that kept running away. The boy broke free and ran behind me. 'Help me catch that nigger,' he yelled at me. 'I'd gladly help you catch the clap, but I ain't helping you catch that boy.'"

"This got him so mad that he picked up a flat iron sitting on the store counter and flung it at me. It whomped me upside my head and I was out for three days. Ever since then, I been prone to spells."

Harriet crunched the legs off a fried soft shell crab.

"For about a year I hated that man so much I wanted to see him in hell with a head-ache and an anvil shoved up his ass; then I realized that these spells also brought visions, and these visions were the best gift that anyone had ever given me. From that moment till now, I've never been able to hate any man. I hate what people do, but I can't hate the person."

Harriet finished off the rest of the crab. "I know a slaver over in Cambridge who's sailing down to New Orleans next week to sell some blacks to a sugar cane plantation, and if I don't get all of my stuff back in two minutes, I know a bunch of children who's gonna get a boat ride. And Atwell, if you don't come untie my shoe laces, I'm gonna take that pistol out of your pocket and put it where the sun don't shine."

The hyenas moved even faster than before, giggling as they went.

"Now, line up and get a piece of hard candy, and give poor ole Aunt Harriet a hug."

When the last child had received their treat and hug, Harriet said to Elizabeth, "Come walk with me – I need to take a pee."

"There's an outhouse right there," Elizabeth offered.

"I never could stand to pee in a house. Besides, I want to tell you about a vision I just had and ask you what it means."

The two women faded into the shadows toward the boat house. "What do you think of Mr. Lincoln?"

"The more you know Mr. Lincoln, the better you like him. He's a man without pettiness."

"And you would never do anything to harm him?"

"Good heavens, no!"

Harriet looked puzzled. "I didn't think so. That's what's so puzzling about my vision. I saw the White House draped in crepe and I saw Mr. Lincoln lying in a coffin. And I saw your hand over the White house, as though he had died at your hand. I guess I'll have to keep praying for an interpretation." Harriet handed her purse to Elizabeth and squatted. "God, I love the outdoors."

———•••———

As Harriet began rowing away from the boat house she grabbed Elizabeth with her eyes and said, "Good thing you didn't try me, Keck. I'd of tossed your black ass quicker 'n a gnat can swim a dipper."

"I don't think so, Mrs. Tubman."

"Maybe you go south with me and we have plenty of time to find out who's the strongest."

"I don't think so, Mrs. Tubman." Elizabeth smiled and blew a kiss. "You stay safe. Besides, the war 'll be over before you can row down South."

"Hell, the world will be over," chimed in Artemas.

"I got that figured out. I'm gonna take me a sided wagon and I'll have somebody paint 'Small-Pox' on both sides. Them nigger-lynchin' Rebels won't come within five miles of me."

Everybody sat along the pier to watch Harriet row away towards the open waters of the Choptank.

"Look, she's out again," shouted one of the children. "She's out! She's out!" squealed the children in absolute glee. "Wake up, Aunt Harriet. The boats on fire!" The children had never seen such fine entertainment.

The oars hung limply in the water and the boat drifted with the tide down the Tred Avon and away from Cambridge.

"Shouldn't we do something?" Elizabeth asked anxiously. "What if she wakes up and she's lost her bearings?"

"Harriet was born with a binnacle up her butt. She never loses her sense of direction. She'll take one look at the stars and chart a true course in about two seconds." The words had barely escaped Artemas's mouth when Harriet rocked forward, shot a glance skyward and turned 180 degrees toward Cambridge. The children seemed disappointed that the show was over.

"It's time we got these chillins to bed. We have to get up early if you're still intent on driving into Easton tomorrow for the Quaker meeting."

Chapter XVII

"Good morrow. How art thee? Thank thee for sharing the First Sunday Meeting with us. My name is Emma Ward." Emma Ward could best be described as a spit of a woman, two or three inches shorter than Mary Lincoln. She didn't have Mary's fire in her eyes, but she had a presence, a calmness.

"And I am Elizabeth, and this is Artemas, and this is Tad."

"I was told thee would be here today. Welcome!" With that, the small woman turned and walked up the four brick steps and into the wooden frame building. Elizabeth followed her in, Artemas and Tad in her wake. "Where shall we sit?" Elizabeth asked, uncertain as to the color code.

"If it please thee, sit by me."

Churches in Baltimore and Washington had special sections where the black congregants sat. Elizabeth didn't want to break any conventions, particularly since she had come hoping to ask for money.

Slowly the Friends filed in, dressed in their 'plain' clothing. If the rest of the world paid no more heed to fashion than the Friends, Elizabeth would be forced to seek another occupation. The women wore mostly long black skirts, shawls, and bonnets. The men wore broad brimmed beaver hats and collarless coats.

The congregation fell into a complete silence for about fifteen minutes. Elizabeth undressed and re-dressed every member within her field of vision.

Artemas rebuilt the building. He re-sawed the rough hewn timbers, planed the boards for the hardwood floor, and carefully re-crafted the wooden sliding partitions that could be used to separate the building into two parts. He correctly surmised that was a hold-over from the days when the men's and women's worship were separated.

Tad relived every moment of his adventure on the water with his new 'best-friend' Atwell. Atwell had taught Tad how to use the oyster tongs, although Tad wasn't strong enough to lift the loaded tongs back into the boat. Tad was relegated to the job of separating the clusters of oysters using the culling hammer, measuring to be sure that they exceeded three inches in width, and throwing the smaller ones back into the water. And sometimes Tad just idly sat there, allowing a lazy breeze that came in from the open window to the east to use his ear canals as safe passage to its twinned companion on the other side of his head.

From somewhere behind her, Elizabeth heard a garment rustle as a woman stood up and said, "I would like to read from George Fox: *'We...utterly...deny all outward wars and strife and fightings with outward weapons, for any end or under any pretense whatsoever. And this is our testimony to the whole world. ... The spirit of Christ, by which we are guided, is not changeable, so as to once command us from a thing as evil and again to move unto it; and we do certainly know, and so testify to the world, that the spirit of Christ which leads us into all Truth will never move us to fight and war against any man with outward weapons, neither for the kingdom of Christ, nor for any kingdoms of this world.'* For those of you so inclined like me, who believe that this special assessment of $300.00 dollars is a payment in support of war, I would ask you to look into your heart in deepest silence to see if the Spirit of God moves you in another direction. I myself have decided just this moment, to give my assessment to our guest, Elizabeth Keckley, who, I understand, is starting a charity for unfortunate Negroes who have fled their plantations in the South and are now residing in our Capitol in little more than open-air camps."

Elizabeth noted that this woman didn't subscribe to the antiquated Old English, like Mrs. Ward, but spoke like everyday folks. Elizabeth smiled, remembering Mr. Lincoln's facetious request that Elizabeth help collect the special tax from the Quakers. *I'll collect it alright, but I'll also keep it. If he had trouble prying the money loose from a bunch of pacifists, he won't have a chance in hell of getting it from me*, Elizabeth thought. *I don't think I'll tell him, but I might have to drown Tad on the trip back to Annapolis to ensure his silence.*

Another eternity, masquerading as fifteen minutes, crept past. Then a man to Elizabeth's left stood up and said, "There was a man named John Newton, he was my great grandfather on my mother's side. He was a sea captain, and yesterday, I was examining the contents of an old trunk that contained books and papers of his. I began to read his log of the ship 'Greyhound.' Captain Newton was a slaver. He described in full detail the barbaric practice of buying and selling humans. With the detachment of an accountant, he noted the number of slaves bought and at what price, the number expected to die on the voyage, and the anticipated profit. He described the practice of throwing the most defiant slave overboard early in the voyage, to ensure the docility and compliance of the other slaves for the balance of the trip. As I sat there reading, horror piled on top of horror, I began to think that perhaps we Friends are wrong; perhaps there is not a spark of Divinity in all souls. Then I chanced upon an obituary from the London Times, noting his passing in 1807. Mr. Newton had not only converted; he had become a minister, and, based on his epiphany, had composed the hymn 'Amazing Grace.' With that, he sat down.

"I know that song. I learned it at Fifth Ave. Presbyterian Church where I go with my friends Bud and Holly Taft," Tad blurted out as he rose to his feet. "Mother and Father go to New York Ave. Presbyterian, but I like going with my friends better."

Elizabeth was slack jawed. She had never known Tad to be so effusive. What happened next could only have surprised Elizabeth more if Jesus had walked in the door and started distributing free chocolate. "I would like to sing that song for my brother Willie, who died last year, and for Jib's son, George, who died in the war."

Elizabeth was sure that these people were too kind to laugh at Tad and embarrass him, but she wasn't sure if Friends had a prohibition against singing in a meeting. They certainly had no organ or piano or hymn books. Elizabeth prayed for the first time that day, *"Please God, don't let this be too dreadful."*

Then a miracle occurred, surpassing Jesus and the chocolate: Tad began to sing in a voice as pure as the morning air.

"Amazing grace, how sweet the sound
That saved a wretch like me"

Elizabeth had to physically look at Tad to believe that those sweet, dulcimer tones were actually coming from him. *"He's not big enough to sing that deeply, that richly,"* she thought. Never mind the disappearance of the lisp, the stuttering, and the mouth full of marbles.

"I once was lost but now am found
Was blind, but now I see"

Elizabeth had received the news of George's death with something akin to stoicism. It was painful then, and it remained ever so to this day, like a brick tied around her heart. She mourned constantly, but had never cried. Now the tears slid down her almond cheeks. It wasn't sadness; it was the recognition of something real and concrete that was as pure and as untarnished as her love for George – a mother's love for her son.

When Tad finished his pitch perfect singing, he sat done and whispered to Elizabeth, "I'm sorry I made you cry, Jib."

"I'm not crying, Tad, I'm just overflowing a little. Thank you."

The remainder of the hour was spent in silence. Suddenly, everyone stood up and either shook hands or hugged their neighbor. The clerk, seated at the front, facing the members, stood up and said, "There is coffee and sweets in the kitchen of the brick building. After that we'll have the monthly business meeting."

It was at the business meeting that Elizabeth planned on making her plea for her charity, feeling that the field had already been plowed and seeded; she only needed to spread around a little fertilizer.

As they walked out, Elizabeth said to Mrs. Ward, "We aren't familiar with your customs; I hope we didn't do anything to offend."

"We come here in stillness and quietude to try and hear God's voice, and we certainly did today. No, thee did not offend"

After the business meeting Elizabeth, Artemas, and Tad piled into the buggy to begin the ten mile trek back to the farm. It was a spring day with an easy breeze.

"Pretty enough today to make Lucifer consider reconverting," Elizabeth said.

The sun and wind were both at their backs. "Well, what did you think?" she asked Artemas.

"How much money did you collect?"

"Haven't counted it yet, but something over five thousand dollars, counting the pledges."

"I'll match it if you promise I never have to sit through one of those again."

"Now Artemas, I thought if I became Mrs. Hardesty and moved to the shore, we could go to Meeting every week," she teased.

"It wouldn't be so bad if they would let you carve, or whittle, or just do something with your hands."

Thought of in that light, Elizabeth realized that Artemas was already a perfect Quaker. She had seen him stand or sit for endless hours making a tool, or building a piece of furniture, or holding a tiller on a boat. If Artemas went to weekly Meeting, that would be only one more hour added to the hundreds he already spent attuned with the Almighty.

"What about you, Tad? How did you like the Meeting?" she asked as she twisted to face Tad in the seat behind them.

"I liked the eating in the brick house, but I would have rather been outside playing with my yo-yo."

"Well Tad, you're in for a treat. We're coming up to Peach Blossom Creek and maybe I can talk Artemas into taking me to look for a paw-paw patch. You can stay to tend to the buggy and practice your yo-yo."

Artemas's eyes lit up. He steered the buggy into a landing about fifty feet in front of the wooden bridge that spanned the creek. He tied the buggy to a young, but sturdy, gingko tree. "You're in charge, Tad. Don't let that buggy out of sight."

"Alright. But why does Jib need to take a quilt to hunt for paw-paws?"

"That's in case we need to shoo away any bears."

They followed a path along the edge of the creek for about 200 feet until they found a small clearing of matted down grasses, probably contoured by deer as a sleeping ground. Elizabeth spread the quilt and said, "Let's absorb some sunshine."

Afterwards they lazed in the sun and allowed the breeze to lap at their bodies like a mama cat giving a tongue bath to a kitten. Artemas looked at Elizabeth and saw tears pooling in her eyes.

Like any man would, Artemas asked, "What did I do?"

"Nothing, you goose. I still have George heavy on my mind. He was only twenty when he died. Do you think that he was ever lucky enough to venture off in a paw-paw patch with some sweet young thing? God, I hope so. Twenty years is such a short time to explore life's banquet. I hope he got to sit at the table at least once."

Elizabeth stood up and began preparations to go back to the buggy. "You know, Tad is getting to the age where he might have some interest in such matters."

"God help the livestock," Artemas said. "I can't imagine him charming a girl."

"Actually, he's becoming a rather attractive young man. His speech is better, and if he did seduce some girl, at least now he would be able to dress himself afterwards."

Artemas' laughter was short lived as they heard muffled sobs coming from the buggy. Tad was face down and crying into the crook of his arm. Elizabeth hastened her pace.

"What's the matter, honey? Are you hurt?"

"No, I broke the yo-yo." Tad raised both hands, one holding the yo-yo and the other clutching the severed string. Tad was definitely like his mother; crying was all-consuming. It sprang from a reservoir of despair so deep that an observer was convinced that whatever the cause for such anguish it could never be appeased or fixed.

"It's not broken, Tad" said Artemas. "The string breaks all the time. I'll show you how to put a new one on as soon as we get home. We've got about a mile of it in the tool shed."

And like his mother, when the valve turned off, it was immediate and leak-proof. Tad beamed.

Artemas looked at Elizabeth and said, "You might want to shelve that 'paw-paw patch' notion 'til next planting season."

Chapter XVIII

Supper that Sunday night was mostly the leftovers from the night before. The fish and sea foods had been combined into a gumbo. Since the next morning was a work day, they had eaten earlier in the evening. Elizabeth leaned back in her chair and watched two ospreys chase an eagle away. Ospreys didn't like other birds in their area although they hunted different prey. Ospreys were fish eaters and eagles hunted small animals like mice and voles and rabbits. Elizabeth knew there was some analogy to whites and blacks but she was too full and contented to think about it. Besides, the sun was starting to set and Elizabeth had taken off her thinking cap for the day. Maybe she would pick up the threads in the morning.

Atwell and Tad were carrying second helpings to the barn for Elvin and Melvin.

"Looks like we got company again tonight." said Artemas.

A white man on a chestnut Tennessee walking horse was nonchalantly making his way down the cedar lined road toward the house.

"Evening, Artemas."

"Evening Sheriff. Got another bowl if you got a hankerin' for some of Aunt Amelia's gumbo."

"Wish I would have known earlier, but I just now finished eating with the sheriff in Oxford. We got a telegraph from Cambridge about two run-away slaves and I rode down to alert him. We might need to rent your hounds again if we get a fix on which way they went."

"You know the dogs like a good hunt. Just say when."

The sheriff turned directly to Elizabeth and said, "Don't recall seeing you around before. Are you visiting or are you movin' in?"

"Elizabeth, this is Sheriff Birckhead from Easton."

Elizabeth tried to look casual, but her slave antennae were signaling danger. "Glad to meet you. I'm just in for a few days. I had some business with the Quakers in Easton today. But that's over and now it's just holiday." She regretted saying it as soon as the words left her mouth. 'Quakers' and 'run-away slaves' should not be uttered in the same conversation, especially in a conversation with the sheriff.

Atwell and Tad were walking back from the barn.

"Some of the watermen saw two boys, one black and the other white, oystering over at Claddy's Cove yesterday in one of your boats. Would this be them a comin'?"

"*Oh God, please strike Tad mute*," Elizabeth silently prayed.

Tad and Atwell walked past the mounted visitor – Atwell veering off to the left and climbing atop one of the cedar tables, while Tad drifted right and stood beside Elizabeth, resting his hand in the pocket of her dress as was his unconscious habit.

"What's your name, boy?"

"Tad."

"Where you from?"

"Springfield, Illinois."

"Don't know it. Your folks know you're here?"

"Yes sir."

"How'd you git here?"

"Sailed in on Artemas's boat with Jib."

Sheriff Birckhead leaned forward in the saddle; having some difficulty understanding what Tad was saying through his lisp. "Hope you don't mind me askin' you these questions, but it's my job. I'm the Sheriff of Easton and the Postmaster General for all of Talbot County and Provost Marshall of the Volunteer Militia of all the Eastern Shore. It's my sworn duty. I was appointed by Abraham Lincoln himself. Do you know what that means?"

Tad shook his head from side to side.

"It means that I report directly to Mr. Lincoln. I enforce his laws. Like these fugitive slaves- personally, I don't have anything against them, but the law says they have to be returned to their owners. Do you see what a responsibility I have?"

Tad thought he saw and nodded his head in agreement.

"What would you do if Mr. Lincoln asked you to do something and you didn't exactly agree with it?"

"I guess I'd go ask Ma if I should do it."

Mr. Birckhead smiled indulgently. "Well, the grown-up world don't exactly work like that. There ain't no Ma to ask. You got to make these decisions immediately and on your own."

Sheriff Birckhead kicked one leg up over the saddle and rested it around the horn.

"Don't git me wrong, Tad; with all this responsibility comes a lot of power and prestige. Fer instance, what if I told you that I was takin' you to the White House tomorrow?"

Tad panicked. "But Jib said we could stay 'til Wednesday and Atwell and I could go back out on the boat."

"No, you nit-wit. I didn't mean we're really goin' to the White House. I just meant we could."

Tad felt relieved. He was busting to get back on the water.

"Tomorrow I got to get me a posse and start looking for them fugitives. Tell me Tab, if you was a fugitive and wanted to hide from the law, where do you think you might hide?"

"I'd hide in Artemas's barn. It's big and warm and I could make another bed out of straw like..."

"Boy, you don't have the sense God gave a billy goat," interrupted Sheriff Birckhead. "You wouldn't hide close to where you just ran away. You'd head north to Wilmington or Philadelphia." The sheriff thought he might have a decent conversation if he addressed a fellow white man, but he had clearly underestimated the intellectual depth of Tad. "And if I'm going to head out tomorrow, I better mosey on home and git me a good night's sleep."

"I'm gonna be sailing up the Delaware Bay next week," Artemas said. "It's time for the mackerel to be runnin'. Why don't you wait a week and go with me? I'll wager them boys'll be back in Talbot County by the time you leave."

"No doubt! They don't know who's on their trail."

He reined his horse and started back to Easton. As that Tennessee Walking Horse ambled in that smooth way that no other horse in the world could walk, Elizabeth thought, *There go two things I could watch forever; A Tennessee Walker walking away and an arrogant white man disappearing down the road.*

When he was long out of sight, Artemas and Elizabeth laughed so hard that Tad thought they were going to cry.

Chapter XIX

"Miss Elizabeth, there's a young man in the parlor to see you."

"Who is it, Portia?"

"Never laid eyes on him before, Miss Elizabeth. Just some scruffy white boy."

Elizabeth folded the pattern she was sewing into a neat pile. Interruptions still bothered her, but as her business prospered, managerial duties had laid claim to larger portions of her time. In truth there was a growing part of her that welcomed the interruptions as a chance to stand and stretch. In her twenties and thirties, Elizabeth could sit at a table and sew for hours on end, sometimes even pulling an all-nighter. Now she admitted to herself that she was aging.

Portia's description of the boy as 'scruffy' certainly seemed accurate to Elizabeth as she walked into the parlor, although 'one-armed' would have provided a more tell-tale clue. The right arm of his well tailored suit was flattened across his chest and the cuff was tucked into the left pocket. Elizabeth winced to see well-tailored clothes that had not been properly cared for. She could also see that the coat concealed a hog leg that he had stuck into the waistband of his pants. The boy looked too young and innocent to be armed, but this war had caused a lot of boys to grow up quickly. His face was oily and his hair sprouted little random hay bales.

"Hello ma'am. My name is Robert Cole, but everybody calls me Bobby. I'm looking for Mrs. Keckley."

"I'm Mrs. Keckley. How may I help you?"

Bobby stared at Elizabeth blankly. He was too slow witted to work out the mysteries, and he was too awed to ask questions. Finally he stammered, "George never told me he was adopted. When we sat around the campfire at night and talked of home, George always called you 'mama.'"

Elizabeth felt no need to offer a clarification.

"We were together in General Lyon's army in Missouri. We signed up on the same day. Strange that we ended up such fast friends, George with his college learning, and me a farm boy that barely made it through *Ned and the Primer*. George would try to explain to me about the war, but I never really understood. He would talk about the Missouri Compromise and secession, and Kansas-Nebraska, but all that talk just set my temples a-throbbin'. All I knew was one day my pa said, 'boy, you ain't no more help on this dirt farm than teats on a bull. Go on into Springfield and sign up for the army. And don't forget to send that $12.00 a month directly to your mama and me.'"

Elizabeth felt a maternal twinge. Whenever Bobby would gesture with his left arm the empty sleeve of his right arm would ride out of his pocket. He would quickly stuff it back.

"Do you know the game of baseball, Mrs. Keckley? Some people call it town ball."

"I've seen men playing in that empty lot as I walk to the White House. I've never stopped to watch and I don't know the rules, but I did see a game in New Jersey once. But oddly enough, my girls earn pin money by making baseballs when there are not enough sewing contracts."

Elizabeth didn't go into details. She didn't know if Bobby would like to see the girls take the 2½" ball of India rubber and tightly wrap it with yarn, and then hand stitch the 4 pieces of dark leather with exactly 108 stitches. The finished ball had to weigh 5.75 to 6 ounces and have a circumference of 10 inches. These specifications came from *Beadles Dime Base-Ball Player,* a copy of which had been furnished to Elizabeth when she signed the contract. Elizabeth allowed the girls to keep any monies received for the baseballs, minus expenses.

"George was kilt because of baseball – and me," Bobby dead-panned. His face betrayed no emotion and Elizabeth sensed that some better part of this man-boy had died along with her George.

"General Lyon loved baseball. He ordered two corporals to choose nine soldiers each and prepare for a ball game. The winning team would serve as his honor guard in the upcoming battle, riding behind the lines to deliver messages to the field generals."

Elizabeth had never seen anyone so devoid of human characteristics. Nothing on his face moved when he spoke except his lips. His eyes did not narrow nor expand. His eyebrows did not ride up or down to emphasize a point. Even his voice had no modulation. Elizabeth had once been on Lake Anna in Virginia at dawn. The fog had not yet burned off and you could scarcely see ten feet in front of the boat. Lake Anna felt lifeless. No birds making noise, no duck sounds, not even the croaking of the tree frogs. That lifeless miasma was what Elizabeth saw when she looked into the misty bank of Bobby's eyes. All was still and shrouded. Elizabeth was certain that no sun light would ever burn off that fog.

"George and I were picked on different teams. In the last inning, we were all tied up, 4 to 4. George came to bat and hit the ball over everybody's head. By the time they ran it down and threw it back, George had taken three bases. One more base and they would win. The next batter hit the ball on the ground and George started running towards home base. Our fielder by third base picked up the ball and threw it to me. George dove towards home base and I spun around to tag him. 'Yer out,' sez I. The word of the tagger is final in baseball."

If this retelling carried any emotion with it, it was beyond Elizabeth's abilities of discernment.

"We played on 'til my team won. Thing is, Mrs. Keckley, I never tagged George – and he knew it. Two days later when the fighting started, George marched out on foot through a corn field toward the Rebs, while I rode a fine bay, safely tucked behind the lines, totin' messages from General Lyon. 'General sez to move your six pounder over yonder to that hill' or 'General sez to take your cavalry and attack their right flank.'

"General Lyon caught a mini-ball in his eye socket about mid-morning and fell off his horse dead. General Sturgis stepped into his command and fighting kept on until about three o'clock and then it just stopped. Nobody said 'Stop' or 'We quit' or "We surrender', but somehow everybody knew that it was over. Our boys started coming back out of the cornfields and the infirmary units started taking wagons onto the battle field to pick up the wounded. George hadn't come back so I hitched a ride on one of them wagons. I found George in a holler about 200 feet from the road. He was sorta propped up on a split rail fence, and he didn't look none the worse until you got up close. That's when you could see that the whole front of his shirt was dark stained. He opened his eyes and gave me a weak-tea smile. I smiled back and run over to the doctor with the injury caisson and sez, 'Come over here and I'll help git my friend on the wagon.'

"He looked over at George and then turned his back so as George couldn't hear him and he sez, 'I'm only carrying back the boys that can be operated on. Your friend's done been gut-shot and I can't do nothing for him.'

"I walked over to George and sez, 'They're gonna get you on the next trip. They're only taking the boys that are real bad off.' George knew I was lying cause he had that same smile on his face as when I said 'yer out.'

'Will you sit and wait with me 'til they come back?'

'You bet!'

"That's when I told George about missing the tag and how bad I felt about him having to march out through the corn fields and not me."

'It's just a game,' George said. 'In the end it doesn't really matter. It's just a matter of fate that I was picked on one team and not the other.' That's when he made me promise that I would come and tell you about the game. He said to tell you that he was one of the few people in life who really had a choice on which team he wanted to play. He said to thank you for that and that he would love you forever. Them's the last words he ever said."

Elizabeth felt comforted. "Let me pin that sleeve up for you and you can quit worrying about it." As she folded and pleated the sleeve, she asked Bobby, "Where did you buy this coat? It's very well made."

"Tailor in Chicago makes one for anybody who's been shot in the war."

"And when did you get wounded?" she asked.

"That very night. I was sittin' there rockin' back and forth not knowing what to do when I sees this wagon coming down the road. I'm lookin' real hard cause I ain't never seen such a git-up. It looked like an outhouse on wheels, only longer. The sides were clapboarded and it was tall enough for a man to stand up in it. Every time the wheels would fall off into a rut, that little house would lean out 'til I thought the whole contraption would tump over. Finally it stops and this man hops down and says, 'I'm Jack Radcliffe and I'm here to take pictures. I'll give you two bits if you'll help me drag some of these bodies over near this fence'.

'Do you have a shovel?' I asked him.

'Yes, I do.'

'Well, I'll help you if you'll borrow me your shovel so I can bury my friend.'

'It's a deal, but we need to move the bodies first. I got to get set up before the sun goes down. Grave digging's a night time chore anyway.'

"We started totin' those bodies over to the fence line and I asked him why he was doing that. 'The man I work for is doing a history of the war through pictures. And he likes at least three dead soldiers in every picture. People usually don't die where they need to. That's why I have to move 'em.'

'Sounds like a horrible way to make a dollar,' I allow.

'Ain't it though?'

"Well, by the time I'm done burying George, it's about nine o'clock. I start walking back to our line and the sentry thinks I'm a Reb and he fires a shot that catches me dead square on the big muscle of my right arm. Next thing I know the Doc's carving on me like a Christmas turkey. I go under the ether right handed and wake up left handed."

"What do you do now that your soldiering days are over?"

"Nothin' to do. Daddy thought I was pretty shiftless with two hands; you can imagine what he thinks about me with one, and that being my off hand at that. I guess bringing you this message from George was about as far down the road as I been lookin'. Well, I better be off."

"Since you're at liberty, can you run a little errand for me? I've just finished a dress for one of Belle Boyd's girls and I don't have anyone free to deliver it. I'll pay."

Belle Boyd's boarding house was such a restorative to the weary traveler that most of them only needed to rest for an hour or so before they continued on their way.

"I would be pleased to deliver it if'n you give me directions, but I can't accept no money, on account of George and all."

"Just a moment while I write a little note to Belle."

Elizabeth went to her desk and wrote:

Trust that this will fit Jane perfectly. If alterations are needed, I'll stop by this weekend. Bobby, the bearer of this note, tended my son George as he died. If your Jane could return the kindness, I would consider that apt payment for the gown. Thank you. E.

She sealed the note in an envelope. "Don't give this to anyone except Miss Boyd." She shoved the envelope into his coat pocket. "Can you come for lunch tomorrow?"

He looked at her for a long time. "I've made plans to move on tonight and I don't think I can change 'em."

Sadly, Elizabeth didn't think she could change them either.

Chapter XX

"Why would anyone choose to get married in February?" Elizabeth asked herself as she hurried to make last minute adjustments to the gown Mrs. Lincoln would be wearing that evening. She was thinking of Charles Sherwood Stratton, perhaps better known to the world as "General Tom Thumb", and Miss Lavina Warren, who were blissfully joined three days prior on Feb. 10, 1863 at the Grace Episcopal Church in New York City. The Stratton's were traveling to Washington to visit his brother, a soldier in the Union Army, as part of their honeymoon tour. When informed of their expected visit, Mr. Lincoln extended a Presidential invitation to a reception at the White House. The reception served a dual purpose; it would also mark the cessation of formal grieving for the death of Willie, which occurred exactly one year ago this month.

Mrs. Lincoln had professed an eagerness to doff her mourning clothes and get on with the task of living, but Elizabeth knew that Mary's heart would always be shrouded in crepe. If Mary was rebuilding her shattered life, the repairs were barely underway and, Elizabeth knew, nowhere near complete.

Mr. Stratton was almost as well known as Mr. Lincoln, and given the way the war was progressing, probably better liked.

Through the shrewd handling of Mr. Phineas T. Barnum, the circus promoter, Mr. Stratton had performed around the world, delighting and enthralling the royalty of Europe. Queen Victoria was particularly entranced, having been entertained by the Lilliputian General on several occasions.

More than 2,000 people attended the wedding and over 5,000 people paid to attend the reception at the Metropolitan Hotel. To ensure there would be no shortage of pretzels and snacks, Mr. Barnum had the foresight to sell tickets to the gala affair at $75.00 per person.

Mary seemed to actually be looking forward to the reception tonight. When Mary was in high spirits her walk was almost a trot; when her demons were upon her she walked as though she were slogging through mud. Not only was the pace more deliberate, but her gait was altered as well. Her arms were held away from her body and her fists were clinched, as though she were wading into a barroom brawl. But tonight she was under full sail - the first time in many months that Elizabeth had seen her so animated.

Mary spotted her son Robert leaving the office of Nickolay and Hay. Robert was home from Harvard for a short break. "Are you engaged this evening, Robert?"

"Not at all, Mother."

"Then you must come to the reception for Mr. and Mrs. Stratton. It's at eight o'clock."

"Our notions of duty are entirely different, Mother. I have no desire to entertain circus people."

"But they're our guests. Won't you reconsider?" Mary cajoled.

"No Mother. I won't be there and that's the sum of it."

Elizabeth overheard this and wanted to walk over and slap the taste out of Robert's mouth. How could a son be so ungenerous to his mother? As Mary turned away from Robert, Elizabeth saw something more than mere disappointment in Mary's eyes; she also saw resignation. Sometimes the most momentous decisions are made on the thinnest data. Elizabeth recalled that she had decided to divorce James Keckley because of the way he had grabbed her hand to lead her across a busy street in Richmond. The grasp was not brutal or oppressive; it was just not 'loving'. It was the way one might grab a rein to walk a horse across a street. But at that instant Elizabeth knew that whatever she had felt for James Keckley was extinguished in that simple gesture, and it would never be rekindled. Elizabeth saw something similar happening now in Mary. Mary had simply exiled Robert to some distant part of her soul and although he would be allowed to visit as often as he wished, he would never be an invited guest again.

When Mary caught Elizabeth peeking into the window of her soul, she quickly pulled the curtains shut. "Elizabeth, could you help Tad with his tie? It's almost eight o'clock. The Strattons will be here any moment."

Soon Mary led her little contingent down the stairs and into the East Room, where they sat upon a sofa and awaited the announcement of the Strattons. The Army band struck up a patriotic ditty, and in walked what appeared to be two puppets, unassisted by wires or ropes or pulleys. The Lincolns were awed. Formal introductions were made and Mr. Lincoln folded his long body like a jack-knife and grasped Mr. Stratton's hands gently in his over-sized paw.

"Thank you for coming. It's certainly a pleasure. For the last two years every general that's been in the White House has been the bearer of bad news. I read about your recent victory in New York where you captured the hearts of all the citizens and Mrs. Lincoln and I are pleased and honored that you not only marched south to our little town, but that you also brought the captured treasure with you."

With that he warmly enfolded his hands around those of Mrs. Stratton. Lavina Warren Stratton stood 2-ft 8inches tall and weighed less than 30 pounds.

"Allow me," said Mr. Lincoln as he lifted Lavina and sat her on the sofa beside Mrs. Lincoln. He cast a glance at the assemblage and said, "God likes to do funny things, and here you have the long and the short of it."

As the crowd laughed politely, Mr. Lincoln hoisted the 54 pound Mr. Stratton and sat him on the sofa to his left. The wine stewards came in with flutes for everyone and bottles of champagne, the notable exceptions being Mr. Lincoln, a life-long teetotaler, and Tad, a life-long minor. The male Lincolns were given apple cider.

When all glasses were filled, Mr. Lincoln stood and toasted, "Here's to the Strattons! May their happiness endure all the days of their lives."

After everyone had toasted, Tad leaned in between his mother and Livina and said, "Mother, if you were a little woman like Mrs. Stratton, you would look just like her." Both ladies smiled. And it was true, Lavina looked like a copy of Mrs. Lincoln that had been left out in the rain and had shrunk to a smaller size.

General Tom Thumb turned his attention to Tad. "Why don't you come join Mr. Barnum's show with us. It would be quite educational." Tad's eyes lit up.

"Can I, Pa? Can I?"

"And what would your talent be, Tad?" asked Mr. Lincoln.

Tad looked pleadingly at General Tom Thumb.

"Perhaps we could bill you as the world's smallest giant? Or maybe we could call you the world's tallest midget?

Everyone except Tad laughed as he turned the options over in his mind.

"We're going back to England in the spring, Tad. You'd love it there."

Chapter XX

"Is this another command performance for the Queen?" Mary asked.

"No, we're going to visit a friend that I met on our last tour, the Earl of Portarlington. Interesting story, if I may be allowed." Mr. Stratton removed a large handkerchief from the inside pocket of his expensively tailored suit and spread it across the sofa. He then stood up atop the handkerchief so as to be better heard by those in attendance.

"Lord Portalington invited Mr. Barnum and me to visit his castle in Ireland, which he was presently renovating. As he was giving us the grand tour, I noticed a portrait of a stately looking woman accompanied by a 'little person,' such as myself, hanging above the mantle of the main fireplace. The Earl saw me studying the painting and said, 'Ah, that's Queen Henrietta Maria and Sir Jeffery Hudson, painted by Anthony van Dyke.

'Sir Jeffery?' I asked.

'Yes, his father was a bull baiter on the estate of the Duke of Buckingham. At the age of five, his father gave him to the Duke as a present. The King of England had just taken a young French princess as a bride, the aforesaid Henrietta Maria.'

Mary noted how craftily he had engaged the audience. Everyone was leaning in so as not to miss a word. He took a sip of Champagne.

"To ingratiate himself to the new young Queen, he invited her to a supper, at which time he cold-baked the 18-inch Jeffery inside a pie. When the pie was placed before the Queen, out bounced Jeffery. Maria was so taken with admiration for the little fellow, she persuaded the king to knight him." The crowd gave a round of warm applause at the amusing story.

"But there's more," said Mr. Stratton. "This King Charles granted a large part of the New World to a Lord Baltimore to settle for the Crown. When asked what the new settlement should be called, Jeffery said, 'Let it be named after your wife

– call it Terre Maria – or Mary land! So the very soil we are standing on today is due, in a circuitous fashion, to the artifice and stratagem of a dwarf."

The crowd was bewitched. *Small wonder that people would pay $75.00 to see him perform,* Mary thought.

"Would you allow us to give you a tour of the White House?" asked Mrs. Lincoln.

Mr. and Mrs., Stratton turned onto their stomach and slid feet first to the floor, having long before learned to adjust to an over-sized world. Once the tour of the first floor was complete, Mr. Lincoln lifted Mr. Stratton in his arms intending to ascend the stairs to the second floor.

Seeing this, an excited Tad sprang in front of his mother. He grabbed the diminutive Mrs. Stratton and lifted her perfectly, not counting the fact that he was standing on the hem of her gown. The rip was audible. Everyone gasped. Lavina just laughed.

"It's only the hem. It can be re-sewn easily enough."

"We're in luck," Mary said. "Elizabeth is still here and we can have her do it now." Mary led the way up the stairs and Tad carried his precious cargo up the stairs and into the sewing room.

"Shoo, Tad. Shoo. This is women's work. Go join the men."

Once the women were alone introductions were made and Elizabeth was apprised of the situation. Lavina slipped off her gown and handed it to Elizabeth. She studied the garment for the briefest moment, turning it in her hands and then reached for her sewing basket. "I don't know who your seamstress is, Mrs. Stratton, but I would keep her as close as possible. This is quality work."

"Would you like me to get you a chair, Mrs. Stratton?" Mary inquired.

"Mrs. Lincoln, I'm a three day bride. It's good to be on my feet. I felt at times as though I would never be vertical again."

Chapter XX

Mary and Elizabeth laughed. "It's good that Mr. Barnum gave Charles the name of 'General Tom Thumb' at the age of five. If he had waited he might have chosen another appendage." The hen party was in session.

"Men fizzle out pretty quickly," Mary offered. "Enjoy it while it lasts. They start out as intrepid explorers, but soon they're only railroad conductors, punching tickets with no enthusiasm and impatiently awaiting the final terminal where they can debark and get back to doing whatever it is they do all day long."

"And they make unscheduled stops," Elizabeth offered. "Sometimes they ask you off long before your station."

"And sometimes the train barely gets out of the station," chimed in Mary

"Oh yeah! Oh yeah!"

The unlikely trio rolled forward, down that rutted road that women had traversed since the beginning of time. Elizabeth noted to herself that they three could stand for women all across America: one is admired because she represented access to a powerful man; one is disdained because she falls short of men's expectations as to what a woman should be in terms of complexion and hue; and one is viewed simply as a doll because of nature's quirk of physical attributes.

"Perhaps we should invite Mrs. Stratton to one of our medicine parties. Wouldn't that be a rhubarb?" said Mrs. Lincoln.

Elizabeth was heartened to see Mary rising from the depths of her anguish.

"Elizabeth, you should steal a glance at Mr. Stratton's brother. He could rival that photographer for sheer good looks. Plus, he's in uniform." Elizabeth warmed remembering how Jack Radcliffe had flattered and charmed Mrs. Lincoln.

"And," Lavina narrowed in on Elizabeth, "at Sunday dinners he always reaches for the dark meat first." Mary laughed out loud for the first time since the death of Willie.

"I've been the guest at such a dinner and I stayed full for nine months," Elizabeth said.

"Speaking of childbirth and Mr. Stratton's brother, is that typical? One child being born large and one diminutive?" Mary asked.

"To be exact, they were both born normal. Charles weighed close to nine pounds at birth. He matured like all babies for six months and then he simply stopped growing. Most little people have growth spurts where they'll add an inch or two over several years. I've forbidden Charles to grow another inch lest he cease to be a curiosity and people no longer pay to see him perform. It's somewhat debasing to be exhibited, but it's also quite lucrative. Charles has become a wealthy man. If he does have any more growth spurts, I pray to God that it's upward."

"You are randy, Mrs. Stratton. You would fit in so nicely at one of our medicine parties. Please give us advance notice of your next visit to Washington."

Elizabeth completed the stitching and began helping Mrs. Stratton into her gown. They could hear the footsteps of the men coming down the hall.

"Well, it's been a pleasure meeting you both. Perhaps you could come over to the Willard Hotel tomorrow for tea. I'm sure I'll be able to give you a detailed lecture on the ceiling medallions of the rooms at Willard's," offered Lavina.

Mary and Elizabeth smiled. "Like I said, you would fit in so nicely."

Mary opened the door and gave her farewells to Mr. Stratton in the hallway. "Mr. Lincoln will escort you to the front door. I need to discuss a matter with Elizabeth. And let someone more sure-footed than Tad carry Mrs. Stratton down the stairs."

When the voices became faint echoes, Mary closed the door. She looked at Elizabeth with worried eyes. "Do you think Mr. Lincoln has any chance of re-election next year?"

Elizabeth was taken aback by the question. She couldn't conceive why this was suddenly such a matter of urgent concern.

"Yes, I think Mr. Lincoln will serve four more years. People trust Mr. Lincoln. They may not always agree with him, but they know that his motives are above reproach. The war isn't going well at the moment, but that will change. The North has too many resources and people for the war not to be a success. The South used his election as an excuse for rebellion. But if the North voted him out of office, it would look like a capitulation on our part. No, I feel strongly that he will be re-elected."

"I hope that your assessment is correct. I have grown to feel that he wouldn't be re-elected, but your argument has merit. God help us all if he's not given another four years. It would be my undoing."

"Whatever do you mean?"

"I am heavily in debt, Elizabeth. I have contracted large debts, mostly at clothing stores. Particularly at Stewarts in New York. Mr. Lincoln has no idea as to the magnitude of these debts and if he is defeated, they will all become due and he'll have no way of paying them. Mr. Lincoln has no guiles and is violently opposed to those who do. Once he finds out that I have deceived him, I shudder to think what the consequences will be. Mr. Lincoln is clueless in so many ways. He thinks that the few hundreds of dollars that he gives me occasionally are enough to keep me outfitted in clothes. You know how I'm constantly sniped and critiqued every time I appear in public. I'm only trying to dress in a manner that reflects credit and taste upon him and the White House. I must have money to stay in step with the fashions, and Mr. Lincoln has none to give. He's probably the only politician to ever enter this town and leave poorer than when he arrived. We are destined to die as poor as Job's turkey."

"How much is the debt?" Elizabeth asked, thinking that perhaps she and Artemas could lend her a few thousand dollars to clear the books.

"Something over forty thousand dollars."

Elizabeth collapsed in her chair.

"So you see, if Mr. Lincoln is not elected it will be the ruin of us all."

Elizabeth and Mary sat in silence. Finally Mary spoke, "Did you know that Mr. Barnum sold tickets to the Stratton's reception at $75.00 per person. And 5,000 people attended. What's that, Elizabeth? Almost $400,000.00. I guess Mrs. Stratton was accurate when she described her husband as being a wealthy man. Maybe I can go on tour as the disgraced wife of a President."

Again they sat without talking. Mary abruptly stood up, "I've detained you long enough. Thanks for listening. Like Mrs. Stratton, I'll probably be staring at the ceiling all night, but for a far, far different reason."

Chapter XXI

Charles J. Colchester was an exacting man. He didn't like to leave anything to chance. He realized that if he were to perform a useful service to his clients, then everything needed to be scripted beforehand and well-rehearsed. He looked upon his calling with great reverence. That's why he was reading the Bible so intently, searching through the Old Testament for the exact quote; that perfect nugget of wisdom that would set the tone for tonight's performance. And there it was in Daniel. It was a passage that Charles had never read before. He wasn't surprised since his reading of the Bible was cursory at best. Yet he was always amazed that no matter where he opened the Bible, he could usually find the near-perfect passage on that page. He began to memorize the verse as he loaded his basket with the musical instruments he used as props. He glanced out of the hotel window to reassure himself that it was still a moonless night. Darkness was very important to his calling.

He always arrived seventeen minutes late. Everyone expected you to be ten minutes late. But after fifteen minutes, a tension grows as to whether there was some misunderstanding or as to whether, God forbid, there was some accident. Charles could see the look of concern on their faces as he walked into the White House at exactly seventeen minutes past nine o'clock.

"You must forgive me. I was so deep in meditation that I lost all connection with this astral plane. On the positive side, in the past that has always presaged a rich and rewarding encounter with our brothers and sisters on the other side of the veil.

Allow me to introduce myself – to you I'm Brother Charles, seeker and searcher of the vast mysteries of the Universe. To the outside world I'm referred to as Lord Colchester – a dubious distinction at best, since I am the illegitimate son of Sir Henry Bartle Abbot, 1st Baron Colchester. But enough about me – allow me to recite a verse from the book of Daniel that my mother taught me as a young boy. *'Praise be to the name of God for ever and ever; wisdom and power are his. He changes times and seasons; he sets up Kings and deposes them. He gives wisdom to the wise and knowledge to the discerning. He reveals deep and hidden things; he knows what lies in darkness, and light dwells with him.'* Amen. So let's see what deep and hidden things we might have revealed tonight"

He extended his hand to Mary. "You must be Mrs. Lincoln. I had been foretold of your magnetic aura, but I must admit, it's stronger than I had been prepared for. You're a clairvoyant yourself – that I can plainly see. Have you developed your talents yet?"

Mary gushed. "I'm still a novice."

"*And about as psychic as your average chamber pot,*" he noted to himself.

"Allow me to introduce you to Mrs. Drake."

Mrs. Drake curtsied quickly. Charles summed her up to himself, "*Must be a war widow. Mid thirties. Husband probably killed early in the war. I don't blame him; I'd have gone out and got myself shot as well if my only prospect was another fifty years with this beast.*"

"And this is Mrs. Gillespie."

"Charmed," he said. He thought to himself, *"Not as bad as Mrs. Drake but still nothing to get excited about. I've never been fond of these pear shaped women. All that meat and no potatoes."*

"And this is Katie Fryer."

"Eureka!" Charles drooled to himself. Katie was exactly what he had been praying for. Young – gorgeous – and breasts that seemed to defy the laws of gravity.

"If I may ask, whom would you like to contact tonight if we can open the door to the other side?"

"My husband, who was killed at Manassas," Katie answered.

Charles nodded thoughtfully as his fantasies spiraled, *"Thank God for Rebel marksmanship."*

Mrs. Lincoln drifted back to the other guests, leaving Charles and Katie isolated in one corner of the room.

"Have you ever felt that your husband was trying to reach out from the great beyond and contact you?"

Katie blushed, as Charles hoped she would. This was a maneuver that Charles had used successfully many times in the past. He was getting so proficient at his little games of seduction that he was considering giving them names like the standard openings in a chess match. He could call this one 'The Lord's gambit accepted' or 'The widow's capitulation.'

"Yes, sometimes at night." Katie looked uncomfortable and turned crimson.

"Mrs. Fryer, I would like you to pay especial attention to what I am about to tell you. What you are experiencing is very common amongst women whose husbands are desperately trying to reach them from the veil. They generally have something of utmost importance to impart. Sometimes a warning of imminent danger – sometimes a solution to a problem – most always a reflection of love so deep that its bonds cannot be severed by death. Believe me, I can help you in this area. I know that it's very personal, but I urge you to look on me not as a man, but rather as a porous membrane that betimes provides access to the vast beyond, merely ferrying messages between people who have temporarily lost the ability to communicate."

Katie nodded agreeably. *"Your King is in jeopardy, Mrs. Fryer,"* he said to himself.

"These matters may be too delicate for a public reading as we are having tonight, but in special instances I give private sessions."

"Oh yes, if it wouldn't be too much of an inconvenience. I would like that very much."

"Check and Mate!" thought Charles. He had pulled this off numerous times. It wasn't too much of a leap to convince a lonely widow that the departed husband was not only speaking through him but also inhabiting his body and would finally be at peace if only he could once again hold her in his arms.

"Let's speak after tonight's session. We can make arrangements then."

Katie grabbed his hand in both of hers and squeezed affectionately.

"Anyone for Polo? You saddle the horse; I already have the mallet."

Charles turned and rejoined the group. Mrs. Lincoln extended her hand towards the only male in the assemblage. "You of course know Noah Brooks. He's been present at several of your readings, I believe."

"Of course. I'm well acquainted with Mr. Brooks."

"And these two ladies are responsible for arranging tonight's reading. You are familiar with Elizabeth Keckley and Eunice LaRon?"

"But, of course," Charles said. *"The dead son and the cow killer. They don't have much money but they are good bird-dogs. I'll work 'em in some how."*

Charles met Elizabeth and Eunice at a previous séance at Mrs. McClean's. At that evenings conclusion Charles found himself alone with the two women as Mrs. McClean went upstairs to search her purse for what turned out to be a sizable offering. Not entirely comfortable making small talk with Negro women, Charles asked Eunice how her husband had died. Charles regretted that question for weeks to come. Eunice relayed the events so eloquently and so graphically that Charles was troubled by a recurring dream in which the cows were replaced by people that he had fleeced at his séances. They would slide down the long chute and Charles would hit them between the eyes with a maul that had been crafted by tying a hard cover Bible to the end of a pool cue. Before he hoisted them up and over to the next worker, Charles would rifle through their pockets and purses for money. He would take their rings and watches and check their teeth for gold fillings. He would wake up and the sheets would be wet with his sweat.

"Let us begin," said Charles Colchester in his most clerical voice. He reached into his basket and removed a banjo, a drum and a cow bell and scattered them around the table. "There is gauze between the two worlds. Those on the other side have as much trouble penetrating that gauze as we do. They want desperately to assist us, but they can't make themselves heard. That's where I come in. For some reason that I don't fathom to understand, I have been selected as a guide, an interpreter, a medium as it were, to assist in this communication. Believe me when I tell you there is nothing special about me at all. Why I was chosen to lead these excursions, I have no idea. I'm just like anyone else in this room. Oh, I may pray more and I may meditate more on the mysteries of life, but that's simply owing to the fact that I perhaps have more free time, being unencumbered by wife or family."

Here he always paused to make sure that the hook was

in their mouths before he gave the line a quick jerk to set it firmly.

"I say I have no family, unless you count the forty-five children I support in the mountains of Chile. They are family enough for me. The tithings that are tendered me for these little readings are dispatched directly to Father Eugene Garcia in Santiago. Once every week or so he'll lead his burro down that mountain pass and convert your offerings into beans and corn and tortillas for those poor, wretched, starving children."

The vapid smiles on their collective faces let Charles know they were all on board. In fact, Charles had often dreamed of going to Chile after a sea-faring man told him of the numerous brothels in Santiago and the unending supply of nubile women who plied their trade there.

"A word of caution – those on the other side are not as bound by the details of our world as we are. They frequently misname things and confuse dates and sometimes even forget names of those they knew intimately on this side." Bitter experience taught Charles to add this caveat to his spiel. It made things go smoother. "My very own mother insisted on calling me 'Jeremy' throughout one session. Don't fixate on things like that; just remember that they are here because they have a profound interest in helping us." They nodded in unison. Charles thought to himself, "*Well, the hay's in the barn on this one. Let's get the money.*"

"Please take your seats and I'll draw the curtains." He was pleased to see Katie had chosen the chair immediately to his left.

"Spirits prefer total darkness. Please join hands and close your eyes and concentrate on the faces of your loved ones."

Before closing the door he glanced at his petitioners and noted they were following his instructions to the letter. "*Sheep to the slaughter,*" seemed entirely appropriate. Immediately before the door closed and encased the room in total darkness, he looked at

Mrs. Drake and thought *"I suppose it's customary to slaughter the fattest cow first."*

He had noted that the distance from the door to his chair was seven paces. As he walked across the floor in complete darkness, he reached inside his coat and procured two halves of a billiard cue, painted dark black, and began screwing them together.

"Mrs. Drake, I have a gentleman here who wishes to say 'hello'. He's a handsome chap attired in an officer's uniform of Union Blue."

"Franklin?" she almost squealed.

"He wants to know if his appearance here tonight will fulfill the promise he made to you to return safely from the war. And he wants me to assure you that he is safe, but in a way that you can't fully understand yet."

Mrs. Drake began to sob and Charles mentally marked her down for $50.00.

Charles continued to work the room. Occasionally he would reach out with his billiard cue and plunk the banjo or do a rat-a-tat on the drum. Mrs. Lincoln was particularly easy – everything about her was either covered in the newspapers, or bandied about by the gossip mongers in every tavern and salon in Washington. He began with the lowest hanging fruit first: her known distrust of Mr. Lincoln's cabinet members, her background in the South, her paralyzing grief over the death of Willie. Charles was chalking her off in his mind for at least $100.00 when he was suddenly washed over with the oddest sensation.

———•◆•———

Upstairs and down the hall, Tad lay on his bed staring at the ceiling and thinking of the day when he could finally join Mr. Barnum's Show. He still had not finalized his plan, but he was certain that General Tom Thumb would come up with something.

Tad felt an invisible hand prodding him to get up and look out of the window and down into the stables. He had already looked once, but without the aid of moon-light he could see nothing. Yet the urge was uncontrollable. He went to the window and peered down, and there, sitting on his pony and holding a lantern, was Willie. Willie was wearing the same soldier's uniform that he was wearing when he galloped away almost two years ago.

<hr />

Charles didn't like to improvise, but tonight had been so flawless he decided to drift with the tide and see where he landed. "Mrs. Lincoln, your husband is in danger. This hand of evil that I see does not belong to a political enemy. It's someone in a completely different arena. He seems to be on a stage, as though he's an actor in a play."

Charles was beginning to have fun with this line of thought. Perhaps with a little showmanship he could nudge Mrs. Lincoln to the $200.00 level. He extended the billiard cue into the hanger loop of the cow bell and eased it into the air.

"This actor has a derringer in one hand and is walking up behind Mr. Lincoln." He gave the bell a little jingle for emphasis.

Bam! A thunderclap echoed around the room as Tad burst in and pushed the door so violently that it slammed against the plaster wall. "Ma! I seen Willie! I seen Willie!"

Unfortunately the unfurled door had allowed the newly installed gasolier in the hallway to flood the room with light, showing Lord Colchester, illegitimate son of Sir Henry Bartle Abbot, 1st Baron, dangling a cow bell on the end of a pool cue.

Noah Brooks seized him forcibly by the wrists. "You, sir, are a fraud and a humbug. I'll have you thrown in jail."

Charles hastily gathered his props and mumbled, "Believe me; I'm as baffled as you. It must be a miracle that this stick materialized in my hand. I must hasten back to my room and pray on it." He hesitated at the door and said, "Remember the poor orphans in the Andes. If anyone would care to donate..."

Noah Brooks advanced menacingly.

"Well, probably not tonight. Another time then."

Elizabeth glanced at Mary, who seemed to be shrinking in her chair. She reminded Elizabeth of a puffball; that children's delight of a mushroom that when kicked would spray its brown spores into the air and deflate into a hollow carcass. Elizabeth wasn't certain of everything that Mary was leaking into the night air, but she was positive that it held the last vestiges of her hope and sanity.

Chapter XXII

Not only was Mr. Lincoln re-elected, but his war machine had turned into a juggernaut. The talk was no longer if the war would ever end; it turned to predicting the month in which the South would finally capitulate. General Sherman had severed the South, cutting a swath of destruction from Atlanta to Savannah, destroying the railroad arteries that carried the necessary nutrients to the heart of the Confederate resistance; General Robert E Lee. Lee and his Army of Northern Virginia were presently dug in and under siege at Richmond. General Sheridan's army had annihilated the Rebel forces of Jubal Early at Cedar Creek, Virginia and had turned east to assist General Grant in his relentless pressure on Lee. In reality, Lincoln and the other politicians had turned their thoughts on how to proceed with the South after their final surrender. The outcome was no longer in doubt. So certain was Grant of the pending capitulation of Lee's army, that on March 20th, 1865 he wired Lincoln and invited him down to Virginia to witness the death throes of the Confederacy.

Lincoln wired back and said he would arrive at City Point on March 23rd.

The retinue of the victorious and triumphant presidential party would include Mary and Tad and Elizabeth.

"Elizabeth, don't forget to pack some of Tad's warmer clothes. You know how changeable this weather can be in early spring."

William knocked on Mrs. Lincoln's door.

"Yes, William."

"There's a lady down stairs that barged her way in and demanded to see President Lincoln. We told her the President was in a cabinet meeting and not available, but she won't leave. And she has three little children with her."

"I'll come down."

When Mary entered the spacious East Room, a baby and two toddlers crawled around the floor. The woman had her back to the children and was staring at the wall. She turned as Mary entered and Mary could see the desperation in her eyes.

"My husband was killed in battle and I have no way to care for these children so I'm bringing them to the President and leaving them with him."

There was something more than desperation in the woman's face; there was also a touch of madness. Mary walked over and put her arm around the woman and gently told her which departments she needed to go to and whom to ask for.

"I'll be out of town for a week or so, but I will instruct Mr. Nicolay, upstairs, to assist you if you run into any bureaucratic delays. Have those children had their lunch yet? William, take them down to the kitchen and have the cooks whip up something tasty. Then come upstairs and I'll write down the names of the people she needs to see."

When she returned to the bedroom Mary said nothing but sat on the edge of the bed and stared out the window.

"I shudder to think of the number of widows we've made with this war, North and South. We'll have to pay, Lizzie – one way or another – in this life or the next. What will history say about us, Lizzie? Will they be kind to Mr. Lincoln and me?"

"History will be well disposed towards you and Mr. Lincoln. It's true – many have died, but many millions more have been freed."

"I imagine that St. Peter will have some sharp questions for us before he throws open those Pearly Gates."

"Can I ask you a personal question, Mrs. Lincoln?"

"You and I have no secrets, Lizzie. You know that."

"While I was packing your clothes for the trip, I noticed a new wardrobe of mourning clothes. There must be six dresses. Why are you buying mourning clothes?"

"I can't answer that, Elizabeth. I was shopping and I had this overwhelming compunction to buy mourning clothes. I can't explain it, but I had no choice. I had to do it."

Elizabeth had seen Mary in a buying frenzy before, so she was not surprised by the activity, only by the choice of clothing.

"Have you ever been on a boat for thirty hours before?" Mary asked Elizabeth.

"No, but Artemas says that after a certain amount of time at sea, different for each sailor, the salt water gets in your blood and changes you forever. After that there's always a lure and a pull to the sea. Do you think that after our little voyage we'll be petitioning Gideon Welles to muster us into the navy?"

"I just hope that I don't throw up before we clear the Potomac," said Mary.

———•◆•———

The *River Queen* docked at City Point, at the conflux of the James and Rappahannock Rivers, at 9:00 p.m. on March 24th. General Grant hastened down the hill from his headquarters and met with Mr. Lincoln for over an hour. The next morning the President trudged up the hill to join General Grant in a review of the battle positions. The Confederates had attacked

Fort Stedman early that morning and Grant advised against an outing that day due to the hostilities. Lincoln, ever callous to his physical safety, overrode the general and insisted that they proceed as planned. A train was stoked and proceeded to take them near the most recent battle site. At that point Mr. Lincoln mounted a horse and, accompanied by General Meade, rode through the most recent battle field. It was the first time that Lincoln had actually been on a battle field and the site sickened him. There were dead and dying littered over many acres. The ambulance corps, under the white flag of truce, was busy tending the injured and near dead.

Mary and Elizabeth had debarked the train with Mr. Lincoln, but their mode of conveyance was a two-seated hospital wagon. They sat together on one seat facing Julia Dent Grant and Colonel Badeau. The ride was horrendous. Every time a wheel found a hole in the road the occupants of the cart were bounced upwards. Mrs. Lincoln started to complain about being separated from her husband and the inconvenience of the hospital cart. Colonel Badeau off-handily mentioned that no ladies remained at the front, save General Griffen's wife, who had been issued a special pass from the president.

"What do you mean by that, sir? Do you mean to say that she saw the President alone? Do you know that I never allow the President to see any woman alone?"

Colonel Badeau was flustered. He didn't know how to respond. Fortunately at this time General Meade rode up next to the carriage. He escorted Mary off some distance from the carriage and spoke to her in soothing tones. When she returned she addressed Colonel Badeau directly, "General Meade is a gentleman, sir. He says it was not the president who gave Mrs. Griffen the pass, but the Secretary of War."

On March 26th, Lincoln once again ascended the hill to Grant's headquarters. In addition to Grant, General Sheridan, who had just arrived, was present, along with General O.C. Ord, Commander of the Army of the James. Today's plan was to load the horses and carriages onto the *River Queen* and navigate further up river to the USS Malvern. There the Lincoln party was to be the luncheon guests of the U.S. Navy. After lunch the party were to motor to Aitkin's Landing and off-load in the same manner as the previous day, men on horses and women in carriages. Mary was even more distraught today about being separated from her husband. Elizabeth could see the ox-eye rising in some distant part of the sky. Matters were not helped when a severe rut in the road propelled Mary skyward until the planks of the carriage arrested her ascent. Mary Ord was exempt from the order that restrained women to the rear, for her husband was the commander of the troops. She rode along with the men.

The recent rains retarded the progress of the wagon. The slogging was slow. When Lincoln reached the troops, it was well after 2:00 p.m. The men had missed lunch and were tired. Instead of waiting for the carriage, Lincoln decided to review the troops at once. Mrs. Ord, excellent horseman that she was, fell into position.

A young major, oblivious to the disturbed hornets nest, rode up to the carriage and said, "The president's horse is very gallant, Mrs. Lincoln. He insists on riding by the side of Mrs. Ord." The ox-eye was now a 12 on the Beaufort Scale and rising.

About half way down the reviewing line, the carriage came into view and Mrs. Ord trotted her horse over to join the women. She was hardly prepared for the barrage with which she was greeted. "How dare you take my place and ride along side my husband! No doubt you have desires of assuming my conjugal duties as well. You harlot! You Jezebel! You strumpet!"

This was past anything that Elizabeth had ever witnessed. Mary had lost all sense of reason. Her face was contorted into the snarl of a half starved coyote, circling its final chance for a meal. Spittle ran down from her parted lips and onto her plump jowls. Elizabeth was enthralled. *"Well, that's it,"* she said to herself. *"She'll never make it back to port in this storm. She's lost at sea forever."*

Mary had one parting volley for Mrs. Ord, "You are a whore and will forever be a whore until your dying day."

Mrs. Ord, blinded by tears, jerked her horse around and ran back towards the formation. Mary collapsed in tears, sobbing from the darkest and murkiest regions of her soul.

Mary sulked around her cabin aboard the *River Queen* for the next several days, mortified at her own behavior. She was finally able to secure passage back to Washington aboard a steamer with William Seward, Secretary of State, who had come bearing documents that needed the President's signature. The departure of that little steamer seemed to create a vacuum as it left and sucked the oppressiveness and gloom down the James River. No one would dare say that they were glad Mary was gone, but there was a palpable difference in the moods of everyone, including Mr. Lincoln.

After several lazy spring days spent leisurely on board, word came that Richmond had fallen and the government had fled. It was Tad's birthday and as a present, Mr. Lincoln decided to take him into Richmond on a tour. The small party, flanked by a handful of sailors as guards, strolled into the city. It didn't take the local citizenry long to spot the lanky Mr. Lincoln. Crowds of Negroes gathered around him, singing and shouting praises. As he entered the home of Jefferson and Varina Davis, Mr. Lincoln became solemn and melancholic. He walked into the study and seated himself at Davis's desk. "May I have a drink of water please?"

A black man in fine livery entered bearing a tray with water and a bottle of whiskey. "Mrs. Davis ordered me to have the house in good condition for the Yankees." He then looked at Elizabeth. "You must be Mrs. Keckley. Mrs. Davis heard that you were on the boat. She said to tell you to keep the books as a present. It doesn't look like she will be returning to Washington as planned."

"Isn't that just like Varina? Always the perfect hostess."

Chapter XXIII

"In like a lion, out like a lamb!" This old chestnut about March had certainly proven true for Washingtonians in the year of 1865. The lion that charged north in April from Richmond carried so much good news that the newspapers had to print extra editions to keep up. The young men apprenticed as printer's devils were forced to sleep at the offices rather than go home to their mothers at night.

In early April, General Grant smashed through the Confederate lines at Petersburg, scattering the Rebel army into disarray. The next day Richmond fell and Jefferson Davis and his cabinet scurried south. Six days later, on April 9th, General Robert E. Lee surrendered his Army of Northern Virginia at the Appomattox court house. The North was jubilant. Elizabeth, as she had promised, gave the girls the day off to join in the festivities.

About mid-morning Elizabeth decided to stroll downtown to watch the revelers. The warm rays of the sun had barely begun their magical massage on Elizabeth's face when she, not just literally, bumped into J.L. DeBonet at the intersection of E and 6th streets. J.L. was dressed to the nines. He looked like a plantation owner out for a casual stroll around his grounds.

He wore a planter's coat of worsted wool with matching vest and high-waisted pants, and the entire ensemble capped with a fashionable top hat.

"Why Mr. DeBonet, I don't think I've ever seen you so sartorially resplendent. Are you out to celebrate the cessation of hostilities?"

"Quite the contrary, Mrs. Keckley; I'm out to celebrate the death of a distant aunt. She was kind enough to remember me ever so slightly in her will. I received the funds yesterday and am off to spend them recklessly. As for the clothes, they are a memento of my brilliant performance as Largo Kincaid, dashing river boat gambler and hero to the downtrodden. I insist that you be my guest for lunch."

"Thank you for your generous offer, but may I remind you that these deafening cannon salutes from the 68 forts that surround Washington are heralding only the end of war; they are not ushering in a new era where a Negro can enter a restaurant and order a meal."

"You underestimate me, Mrs. Keckley. I know of just such an eating establishment." With that he offered Elizabeth his arm.

"I remember what you said years ago about physical altercations and how you dread them. You must promise me that if anyone objects to my presence in the least, that we'll up and vacate the premises immediately."

"Agreed! But have no fear, this is a place frequented only by actors and their guests. I'm their most loyal client."

"What's the name of the restaurant?"

"It's called 'Forres Heath.' That's the place where the three witches in Macbeth stir up their poisonous cauldron. The owner is a onetime actor named Dixon Powell whose career was cut short by a freakish accident at Grover's National Theater. Dixon was working one evening assisting the prop manager. He asked Dixon to ignite the limelights; something

Dixon had done dozens of times prior. Do you know how lime lights work?"

Elizabeth shook her head 'No.'

"Oxygen and hydrogen are created in two separate containers, or gas bags. Pressure is applied to the bags and the gases are forced together through a tube and lit. The flame is applied to a block of lime that creates a very intense white light. That's what makes the actors on stage so clearly visible in a dark theater. Anyway, something went wrong and the gases exploded, blinding Dixon in one eye and severely disfiguring his face. In acting it's probably an asset if you have a disfigured soul, but roles are quite limited for those with disfigured faces. So Dixon began preparing lunches for the actors from noon 'til 2:00 and suppers from 10:00 p.m. to 2:00 a.m. If you're not accompanied by an actor, you would be refused seating."

"All the same, I would feel better if you would ask if my seating would present a problem."

"As you wish."

The entrance was five steps down from street level. J.L. rapped on the door. A small metal peep-hole was opened and a man said, "Your business?"

"Let us go in together,
and still your fingers on your lips, I pray.
The time is out of joint—O cursèd spite,
That ever I was born to set it right!
Nay, come, let's go together." said J.L.

Elizabeth heard the lock tumble and the door opened. A six-foot man with an eye patch and dressed as a nun stood in vestibule, calmly smoking a cigar.

"You are welcome, masters; welcome, all. I am glad to see thee well. Welcome, good friends. O, my old friend!" said the nun as she gave an exaggerated theatrical bow.

"That would be Hamlet, Scene 2," said J.L. He paused for

a moment and said, *"Mislike me not for my complexion, the shadow'd livery of the burnish'd sun."*

The nun pondered these words briefly and responded, "Merchant of Venice, Act 2 – Scene 1."

J.L. next countered with, *"Why, therefore fire; for I have caught extreme cold. Where's the cook? Is supper ready?"*

This one seemed to stump the nun momentarily, but she finally said, "All's Well That Ends Well- Act 3 – Scene 7."

J.L. continued, *"The better part of valor is discretion, in the which better part I have sav'd my life."*

The nun looked pensive; *"O, it offends me to the soul to hear a robustious periwig-pated fellow tear a passion to tatters"*, and, *"Yond Cassius has a lean and hungry look, He thinks too much; such men are dangerous."*

"Well spoken," said J.L.

"The lady doth protest too much, methinks," said the nun as she walked away.

"Do you always speak so to each other?"

"It's a game that Dixon and I play. Every thought must be a quote from a play, in this case a quote from any of Shakespeare's plays. Just another way in which actors try to break up the tedium of life."

"And what did you say?"

"I merely relayed your concerns, as I promised. The sun baked complexion referred to you, of course. The reference to the cooking stated our desire to dine. The 'better part of valor is discretion' told him of our mutual desire not to be thrashed for breaking customs. The part about bad acting was a reference to John Wilkes Booth, a fellow actor who dines here often and is expected for lunch today. Obviously, the 'such men are dangerous' refers to Booth. He has strong Southern sympathies. But Dixon doesn't think there will be a problem, ergo 'the lady doth protest too much.' Perhaps I should have forewarned you that Dixon always dresses in costume. And lunch is always only one entrée. At suppertime, you have a choice of two entrees.

The nun returned with a tray that held two mugs of beer and two bowls of lamb stew. Setting them on the table the nun said, "Indulge me for a moment, sir. It's two weeks before I take my final vows and enter the nunnery. As a test to the sincerity of my calling, I thought I would have a last night of debauchery and lust. I was wondering, sir, if you would assist me in my undertaking?"

"I think it would be my undertaking, madam, for a night with a wench as homely as you would certainly kill me. Thy face looks as though it was beaten by the leg of lamb ere you turned it into this stew. I do, however, have a possible solution to your problem. We passed a blind man not three blocks from here. Perhaps he could be persuaded, being unable to gaze on that dart board that you call a face."

The nun looked hurt. "I believe that I have at least one advantage on you in life, sir. The sightless would not be aware of my affliction, whereas your affliction, that odious smell, that knee buckling aroma of chicken coop droppings, would precede you by two blocks. Even to the blind, you would be unacceptable." He turned to Elizabeth. "If you are unable to maintain an appetite sitting so close to a walking pig sty, I can happily accommodate you at the other end of the room. You might have to dine alone, but the conversation would not be so boring." He then adopted an accent that sounded exactly like J.L. "Enough talk about me. Let's talk about you for a while. What do you think about me?"

Elizabeth had never encountered such zany people. "Have you always possessed such an excellent memory?" she asked J.L. after the nun had moved on to another table.

"Practice assuredly helps. But even as a child, I had the ability to remember and repeat most everything I heard and read."

"Did that lead you into the theater?"

"My widowed mother enrolled me in a Catholic school at the age of five. Nuns of the Ursaline Order ran the school. Education of the mind was their second objective, their first being to mold us into obedient Catholics. Every day we had a one hour class on religion, mostly the New Testament, immediately prior to lunch. One of our first assignments was for everyone to memorize a verse from the Bible. I was younger than the other children and paralyzing shy. As Sister Marcellus Janine called us up alphabetically, I began to physically shake in my seat. Only Melvin Daniels stood between me and death by embarrassment. As he regurgitated his inspired rendition of Jesus turning water into wine, I tried to will myself into shrinking, hoping to escape detection. I sat there trying to get smaller and smaller.

"Finally Sister Marcellus Janine said in her booming voice, 'We're waiting, J.L.'

"I walked to the front of the class and without stopping said, 'Jesus wept. John 11:35.'

"'There's always someone who tries to slide by without any effort,' said the Sister. 'I trust that you can learn another verse by the time the other children are finished. If not, you can stay here while they go to lunch.'

"My mortification was complete. When Margaret Williams finished telling of Lazarus being raised from the dead, I was wishing I could crawl into his tomb, seeing that he had no further use for it. Again without stopping I passed the front of the room and said, 'Pray without ceasing. Thessalonians 5:17.'"

"Sister Marcellus Janine looked like a thermometer in a heat wave. You could see the crimson rising from her neck to the top of her scalp where it disappeared under her wimple. I didn't know what I had done that was so offensive. 'Since you care so little about your classmates and the effort that they put into learning their verses, then they can sit here with you during the lunch break until you learn a suitable verse.' They whined in unison."

"I didn't know what she wanted so I walked to the front of the class and began at John 1:1. I held my eyes shut and started, *'In the beginning was the Word, and the Word was with God, and the Word was God.'* I felt that if I didn't have to open my eyes, I wouldn't faint. I continued to recite."

"I must have been half way through John when she said in a calm voice, 'that's quite sufficient, J.L.' I opened my eyes and saw the entire class looking at me with wonder and amazement on their faces. I never forgot that look. I had no idea that the mere recitation of words could have such an electrifying effect on people. I didn't realize it at the time, but I had just chosen my life's work."

"Are you still a Catholic?"

"I was never a Catholic. My mother only enrolled me there because they would take me as a five year old. The entire business never made any sense to me, and my freakish memory kept me as a constant irritant to the nuns. 'How can Matthew say this when John says that?' or 'Why doesn't Mark mention that? Wasn't he there?' I wasn't trying to cause trouble; I just had an inquisitive mind. I've always liked things neat and tidy and consistent, be it Greek mythology or Biblical stories or Aesop's Fables. It didn't take the nuns long to figure out that they were plowing a barren field, so they suggested that my education could best be pursued at a secular institution."

Dixon returned with fresh mugs of beer. "Are you on tonight?"

"Mr. Ford is canceling tonight's performance. Everyone will be out watching the fireworks. No sense in paying us to play to an empty house."

Dixon returned to the bar.

"What are your feelings, Mrs. Keckley, now that this bloody business has ended? Was it worth it?"

"I don't know, Mr. DeBonet. I don't know. The part of me that's black says, 'Yes! Worth it at any price.' The part of me that's white questions the deaths of hundreds of thousands of men to uphold an unsettled principle. My son George died in this war and I would say let slavery die its natural death like it has in so many parts of the world if George could have been spared. Maybe the Quakers are correct; maybe the world needs to seek solutions to its problems in some way other than war. I honestly don't know."

They drank in silence for a long time.

Dixon responded to a knock on the door by allowing four men to enter and seated them at the other end of the room.

"That's John Wilkes Booth in the riding jacket. And that's our cue to exit stage right."

The giant nun said to J.L. as a parting volley, "If you would eat here every day you just might get into the habit."

"Our friend Shakespeare said, *'Costly thy habit as thy purse can buy'* and I don't believe my purse can bear such a huge price - the price being the loss of any sense of self esteem that I may have. But I would tender you one piece of the bard's advice, you gorgon from hell, *'get thee to a nunnery.'*"

"Thank you, Mr. DeBonet," Elizabeth said as they walked down the street. "I've been in an asylum before but I've never been allowed to dine with the inmates. It was an experience that I shan't forget."

Chapter XXIV

For the first time in over four years the mood in Washington was light and airy. Spring, that sly temptress, was strutting around town enticing people to believe that this was a good place to live. The trees had all budded and the migratory birds had been lured back. The sun was cocked at a pleasant angle during the day, promising that the temperature would never exceed 80 degrees. No wonder that people were seduced into actually moving here and building homes. People were friendly on the streets and greeted each other warmly. There was no longer the fear that when you asked someone how they were doing, that the answer would come back "We just got news that our other son was killed at...," or "my husband lost his leg at..." Now, for the first time in almost half a decade, people expected and received answers like, "I'm fine," or "We're having a tea for Aunt Jennie this Saturday. Won't you come?" It was too soon for people to assess the price paid for such an ethereal and abstract idea as the 'preservation of the Union.' Negroes were certain that the carnage had been well worth the price, having led them one step closer to freedom and emancipation. White people were glad the war was over; black people were ecstatic. This ecstasy was felt no where deeper than at the house/factory of Elizabeth Keckley.

The girls were singing a catchy tune, as they had been for two days following the surrender of Robert E. Lee at Appomattox. Elizabeth occasionally joined in although Portia was quick to remind her that she "couldn't carry a tune in a bucket."

It was amidst this festivity that Mary Lincoln had arrived this morning to drop off some of Tad's clothes in need of alteration. "He's growing like Topsy," Mary exclaimed. Elizabeth could recall no sudden burst of growth attributed to Topsy in Harriett Beecher Stowe's novel, but the phrase was certainly gaining traction. As she was leaving she said to Elizabeth, "Mr. Lincoln will be addressing a crowd from the White House tonight. You've frequently lamented that you have never heard him give a speech. Why don't you come about six and help me dress, and then be my guest for the oration?"

"Splendid! I'd love to."

Elizabeth was five minutes early to the White House.

"I think I would like to wear my lavender dress tonight. It's fitting for such a festive occasion, don't you think?"

"I think it would be perfect. Lavender does so much for your cheeks." Elizabeth noted.

Tad and Mr. Lincoln walked into the room accompanied by Noah Brooks, the newspaper man. Noah Brooks held a notable distinction in Elizabeth's eyes; he was the only man who was a close friend of both the President and Mrs. Lincoln.

"Madame Elizabeth, you're acquainted with Mr. Brooks, I believe?"

"Yes I am. I haven't seen you since our evening with that dreadful Lord Colchester." Embarrassment of some sort prevented either of them from pursuing that line of thought. "And may I say how anxious I am to hear you speak tonight, Mr. Lincoln. It's an honor I've never had before."

"You'd best reserve the accolades until after the speech. I'm afraid you might be disappointed. Tonight's speech is directed solely to Congress. It's about the re-admission of the Southern States into the Union. I'm afraid it's as dry as a popcorn fart."

"Father! Don't be coarse," Mary said in mock exasperation. Tad could not stop laughing. Noah Brooks looked amused, but uncomfortable.

"Then I'll make it interesting, Mr. Lincoln. I'll do a call and respond in the African tradition. I've seen it done so well by the black preachers that Lucifer himself came up to the altar to testify. We'll whip that crowd up to a frenzy. We'll beat 'em like egg whites."

Mr. Lincoln was amused. "Another time, perhaps. Tonight I want to engage their minds, not their hearts. I could have sorely used you at my debates with Senator Douglas however."

"Then I'll do it silently. You'll still feel the extra energy."

Mr. Lincoln, Tad, and Mr. Brooks walked toward the window over the main entrance to the White House, pausing to light a kerosene lantern.

"You certainly seem chipper tonight, Elizabeth," said Mary.

"I reached a big decision today, Mary. In the fall, I'm moving to the Eastern shore and marrying Artemas."

Mary reacted as though she had caught a 12 pound Dahlgren cannon ball directly in the stomach. She staggered over towards the divan in a near-by sitting room. Tears over flowed her eyes. "I'm all alone now, Lizzie. I'm all alone. You're my only true friend and now you're deserting me. What will become of me? What will I do?"

"You have Mr. Lincoln and Tad. Besides, I won't be that far away."

"Men! They're good for cold nights, but most of life is spent in the daytime and it's in the daytime that you need someone to talk to and tell how you really feel and what's bothering you. Men have no depth and no sense of subtlety," Mary sobbed. Finally she wiped her eyes and said, "And even on cold nights they're still susceptible to popcorn farts." With that Mary had changed as quickly as a quarter horse cutting a heifer out of a herd. Mary and Elizabeth laughed. She wiped her eyes and said, "Artemas is as rich as cream. How are you going to spend his money?"

"First I'm going to Vienna to see a zoo. Then I want to go to Italy to see some marble sculptures, and then I want to go to Spain to see a bull fight. Will you come with me?"

"Mr. Lincoln and I were talking of traveling to Europe and the Holy Land after we serve out the rest of our sentence here. I've always wanted to go to Scotland," said Mary.

"You know how I detest cold weather, but for you, Scotland it is. But can we do it in June or July?"

"What will you do with your business and the girls?"

"I'm selling it to Portia. She's been running it for over a year now, anyway. The girls will all be fine."

Mary embraced her in a warm hug. "Let's sit here in this room and listen to Mr. Lincoln." They sat and Mary rested her head on Elizabeth's broad chest. They could not see Mr. Lincoln from where they sat, but they could hear every word. Mary held Elizabeth tightly, as though Elizabeth might evaporate into the night air if she loosened her grip.

He began in that tinny voice that was so characteristic of him. "We meet this evening, not in sorrow, but in gladness of heart."

As Lincoln spoke, he dropped the completed pages at his feet. Tad scrambled to retrieve them and place them in order. When his speech was completed, he walked back into the White House and asked Elizabeth, "Well, were you disappointed?"

"Not in the least, Mr. President. Not in the least."

Not everyone was as warmed by the President's speech as Elizabeth. The crowd below applauded politely, but the President could have done no more to dampen the festivities had he thrown wet blankets from the balcony. They drifted away in twos and threes; seeking some way to rekindle their earlier euphoria. Ultimately there were only three of the audience that remained; John Wilkes Booth and two of his plotting cohorts.

"Did you hear what he said? Do you know what this means? This means nigger citizenship. That'll be the last speech that son-of-a-bitch ever makes."

Chapter XXV

In one way or another, all men are superstitious. The malady may be as mild as wearing a "lucky" hat or coat when meeting someone whom one wishes to impress, or it may be as severe as the rituals that bedeviled J.L. DeBonet. For instance, he was walking south on 10th Street approaching Ford's Theatre. He knew that he wouldn't enter through the front door, but continue walking around the block to E Street and down the alley and enter through the stage door. The door would be open, but he would still knock three times before he entered. This was one of his rituals, and he performed it as faithfully as a priest performing the Eucharist. He had executed this maneuver six days a week for two years without varying. He had secured steady work at Ford's Theatre since its re-opening in 1863. The former edifice was a dilapidated wooden building, totally consumed by fire.

The Phoenix that rose from the ashes was a magnificent Italianate structure that J.L. DeBonet was now entering. This building occupied more of his waking hours than the modest row house that he shared with fellow actor, George Spear. They likewise shared a dressing room at Ford's. They never walked to the theatre together as George always left first and usually stopped at Harvey's Oyster House for his daily intake of a half dozen oysters and two mugs of lager beer.

George was seated at his dressing table reading a copy of the Herald.

"Big night tonight! Paper says that Mr. and Mrs. Lincoln and General and Mrs. Grant will be in attendance this evening. Fitting way for Laura Keene to conclude her 1,000th performance, don't you think?"

George was well aware of the simmering animosity between J.L. and Laura, stemming from some unpaid wages that J.L. had earned working at Mrs. Keene's theatre in New York in the mid-50's. J.L. had subsisted for four months on little more than meal money before he was forced to return to Washington to avoid starvation. It was her reprisal of the play "Our American Cousin" that led to her reversal of fortune. She had produced and starred in it for over 2 years, a record for longevity in American theatres. Now that she was successful and relatively wealthy, she still refused to settle the account with J.L.

"I think it would be a fitting conclusion to her 1,000th performance if she fell off the stage and broke her goddamn back," J.L. said matter-of-factly.

"Isn't life strange?" George asked. "A woman endowed with, at best, a modicum of talent, picks an English play that ran with limited success in London, that no one wished to produce in America, and turns it into such a cash cow. God must have a perverse sense of humor."

"I wish I could believe in your God; so I could hate Him."

"That's a terrible thing to say."

"Oh, is it? Was it your loving God's perverse sense of humor that made us different from other men, and then decreed that if we were ever exposed to the light of day we should be stoned?"

George hated it when their conversations veered toward religion. He was thinking of how to nimbly change the topic, when he was saved by a knocking on the door.

"Come!"

In walked fellow actor J.W. Booth. "Mr. Ford said I had received a letter and that he left it in your safe-keep."

George opened his desk drawer and retrieved a fattish letter. Booth pulled a long hunting knife out of a leather sheath and used it as a letter opener.

"Are you coming to the production tonight to see history made?" George asked.

"History will certainly be made tonight," Booth said dryly.

J.L. didn't like Booth either, but the animus that he felt towards him sprang from a different well than that which he felt towards Laura Keene. At least Laura Keene had some talent: Booth had none. Aside from the fact that his father and brother were noted actors, and that he commanded a certain presence due to his handsome good looks, there was no valid reason for Booth to ever grace a stage. Except for the historical impossibility, J.L. often thought Shakespeare had Booth in mind when he penned his blistering attack on over-acting:

"O, it offends me to the soul to hear a robustious periwig-pated fellow tear a passion to tatters, to very rags, to split the ears of the groundlings, who for the most part are capable of nothing but inexplicable dumbshows and noise: I would have such a fellow whipped."

"No doubt that envelope carries a billet-doux from one of the ladies in your harem," teased George.

"Yes, it's from Lucy Hale."

"Which one is she?"

Booth rifled through his inside coat pocket and pulled out a stack of carte-de-visites. He thumbed through the lot and selected one. "This is Lucy," Booth said as he thrust the picture toward George. "I may have to dismantle the harem, as I have extended an offer of betrothal to Lucy." He returned the carte-de-visites to his inside pocket. "I'm good for a libation at Deery's Tavern, if you gentlemen would favor me with your presence."

"Thanks, but 'no,' said George. "I had my performance day quota at Harvey's."

"And I wouldn't drink with you if my intestines were on fire," J.L. thought to himself.

Booth gave an exaggerated theatrical bow and exited, securing the door as he left.

"There goes enough ham to ration the entire Union Army for a month," said J.L. bitterly. "That lack-of-talent bastard made over $20,000.00 last year, and I can't afford to buy a wrestling jacket for a piss-ant. Is this another example of your God's wry sense of humor?"

George was again saved by a rapping on the door. "Come!"

In walked James R. Ford, business manager of the theatre, and brother of John T. Ford - builder and proprietor. "Gentlemen, I have a crisis and beg your assistance. Laura Keene has taken ill and won't be able to perform tonight."

"Something terminal, I trust," said J.L.

Undeterred, James forged ahead. "J.L., I need you to play the part of Florence Trenchard tonight."

"Why not one of the women?" asked J.L.

"Those dunderheads would have to carry the script onstage. It's either you or I'll have to turn away a full house and refund the advance ticket money. And I'll have hell to pay when John returns from Richmond."

George sensed that J.L. had already accepted the challenge, as his body subtly began to molt into character. His face softened and his voice changed pitch, ever so slightly.

"I'll do it on two conditions: first, you send a carriage for Elizabeth Keckley to come and do some alterations on that frumpy dress that Laura so illy wears, and second, I want what you pay Laura.... Doubled!"

James stared blankly while his mind raced through his options. Finding none more palatable, he said "Agreed! But you should pay me for the chance to dress up like a woman in front of 1400 people and parade around on stage."

They all smiled. "In another situation, I probably would, but tonight I want to extract some of the money rightfully owed me by Mrs. Keene."

"How should I introduce you to the audience? I would prefer that they not know your true gender."

"Well, I've never known, so we might as well keep them in the dark as well."

"I think it would be a hoot to introduce him as Miss Nancy Buchanan," said George. "Remember how President Buchanan insisted that we call him 'Miss Nancy' at those parties?"

"Unnecessarily risky. How about Nancy Butler?" asked James.

"Call me what you wish, just don't forget to call me when the money's ready," said J.L. in an increasingly effeminate voice.

J.L. spent the next two hours preening and applying make-up and reading the script. At precisely 3 p.m. Elizabeth knocked on the door. J.L. welcomed her into the room. "Before we get started, I need your word that you're going to be as silent on this matter as a cloistered nun who's taken a vow of perpetual silence. Not a word of this to anyone, particularly the Lincolns." Elizabeth nodded assent.

With that he handed her the dress and said, "Now help me grow a bosom by 8 o'clock."

For two hours Elizabeth measured and tucked and pinned and sewed. Finally, she retreated several paces, eye-fondled him from neck line to hem line and said, "I wish I looked that good. Now, let's do your hair."

J.L. sat in his chair as Elizabeth fitted him with several wigs. "This one frames your face the best, but I need to trim the length."

As Elizabeth tweaked the hair piece, J.L. asked "How is Mrs. Lincoln doing?"

"Better. She's still off her feed over Willie's death; but better. That's one wound that I suspect will never completely heal. She still bursts into tears at any mention of his name or any reminder of him. I suspect that all of those tears may have rusted the hinges of her mind. I doubt if it will ever swing open and shut smoothly."

"Have the séances provided any comfort?"

"I think so," said Elizabeth.

"And what about you, Elizabeth? Have the séances deepened your belief in the here-after? Are you a kneeler and a groveler like my friend George?"

"I'm like Mr. Lincoln: I keep an open mind on the subject."

There came an anxious knock from the other side of the door.

"Come!" shouted George, thinking how fortuitous it was that for the third time today he was spared from a religious conversation by a visitor.

Booth strolled in and nodded to the women. "George, will you be so kind as to post this letter to the editor of 'National Intelligencer' tomorrow. I will be out of town."

"Certainly," said George as he slid open his desk drawer and deposited the letter.

Booth slowly surveyed the women and asked, "Where's J.L.?"

"He's off chasing a fantasy," George said.

"Ladies," Booth nodded to the women and made his exit.

"Obviously we're a success," said J.L. "If we can fool Booth within three feet, we can surely fool 1400 strangers in a dark theatre. I would feel so much more comfortable if you would stay for the play, Elizabeth. Just in case I need some adjustments."

"Gladly."

"I'll have Peanuts place a chair for you in the wings. Next to the Lincolns, you'll have the best seat in the house."

"Places everyone! Five minutes to curtain! Places everyone!" warned the prop manager.

———·•·———

Audible disappointment ran through the crowd when James Ford announced that Laura Keene would be replaced by Nancy Butler for the night's performance. But within two minutes of her entrance, her elegance and charm as Florence Trenchard had captivated the audience.

Acts 1 and 2 were flawless and seamless. At the intermission, Elizabeth walked around backstage to relieve the stiffness in her knees, while the stage hands shifted scenery. She noticed Mr. Booth pacing back and forth. He was dressed so oddly. He looked not like a theatre patron, but rather like someone going for a horse ride. He was even wearing spurs. The actors began returning to the stage and Elizabeth reclaimed her chair.

About fifteen minutes in, one of the actors was scolded for impertinence because he lacked 'the manners of good society.' The actor responded, "Well, I guess I know enough to turn you inside out, old gal – you sockdologizing old man-trap!" The audience erupted in the biggest laugh of the evening.

Through the laughter Elizabeth heard a muted pop. As the laughter petered out, she heard several screams. From out of nowhere, John Wilkes Booth jumped on the stage. He didn't land smoothly as his spurs were entangled with an American flag. He hit with a thud. In his right hand he clutched a hunting knife. He shouted something in what sounded to Elizabeth like a foreign language. He then raised the blood-soaked knife and shouted, 'The South is avenged." He bounded to the stage door exit, flung the door open and there stood Peanut, holding the reins to a horse.

The theatre was frantic with activity. People were running in all directions. Soldiers were pouring in, their weapons at the ready. J.L. grabbed Elizabeth's hand and led her to the changing room.

"What in God's name has happened?" asked Elizabeth.

"They say Booth has shot someone in the audience," said George.

"I had always assumed that someone in the audience would finally shoot Booth," said J.L.

James Ford ran into the room and said, "The President has been shot!"

"Oh, my God! I must find Mrs. Lincoln." Elizabeth ran down the steps and out the front door of the Theatre. An angry crowd was milling in the street across from Mr. Peterson's house. Soldiers were blocking the entrance. She approached the soldier in command and said, "I'm a friend of Mrs. Lincoln, and I think she would like for me to be with her."

The soldier seemed to be weighing whether a simple denial was best, or if a derisive comment was called for. He settled on the former. "Sorry, no one allowed."

"Let's burn the Theatre!" someone shouted. The soldier in command dispatched several of his minions across the street to stand guard in front of the Theatre.

George approached Elizabeth and said, "This could turn ugly. I've seen crowds turn into mobs before, and believe me, you don't want to be anywhere near. Let us walk you home."

Chapter XXVI

At eight o'clock the next morning, Elizabeth sat at her kitchen table sipping on her second cup of coffee when she heard a forceful rapping on her door. Upon opening the door she saw Captain David Derickson, the man who led the brigade that guarded Mr. Lincoln at those times when he resided at the Soldier's Home, and the man with whom Lincoln would sleep when Mary was out of town. The angle of his cap protected his eyes from the morning sun.

"What's the news on Mr. Lincoln?" Elizabeth felt compelled to ask, but feared the answer.

"Lincoln lives, but the doctors say he's in mortal danger. Mrs. Lincoln has requested that I escort you to the White House. She is in distress and much desires your company."

"Will you and your men come in for coffee while I dress?"

"Duty forbids, but thanks. We'll wait here."

As the carriage carrying Elizabeth neared the White House, the crowd that glumly stood vigil on Pennsylvania Avenue parted and allowed them to pass. Elizabeth noted that there were as many black faces in the crowd as there were white. The mood was unlike that of the crowd last night in front of Ford's Theater. The initial pall of anger had burned out and had resolved itself into a watchful vigil. A phalanx of soldiers girded the White House but they parted as the escorted carriage approached.

As Elizabeth ascended the stairs to the second floor, she noticed a somber cabal spilling into the hall outside of Mr. Lincoln's office. She saw Gideon Welles, Secretary of the Navy, talking in hushed tones to Stanton, Secretary of War. Another bakers dozen of politicians that Elizabeth had seen come and go in the White House stood awkwardly and looked rudderless. She followed the wails and sobs down the hall and into Mary's room.

Mary was splayed across the bed, a wet towel compressed and resting on her forehead. She still wore the dress, caked with dried blood, which she had on last night.

"Why didn't you come last night when I sent for you?"

"I tried, but the soldiers turned me away."

"Didn't I always say there was a curse on this house? First, poor Willie. And now, my husband." This was the first time in over two years that Mary had said the name of Willie aloud.

"Mr. Lincoln perseveres. Let's not count him out yet. He's the strongest and most resolute man I've ever met," Elizabeth offered optimistically.

"The army doctors aren't so hopeful. They say that wounds to the head this severe are always mortal. And well they should know. We certainly supplied them with ample cases to study with this infernal war." Mary began to sob again.

Elizabeth removed the towel from Mary's forehead, dipped it into the wash basin sitting on the night stand, squeezed out the excess water and returned it to Mary's head. "I'll tell William to fill the tub with hot water and I'll give you a bath."

As Elizabeth pivoted to turn, Mary caught her quickly by the wrist. "There's a Judas in this house. I've always felt it. And I'll wager that he's in that crowd down the hall right now." Her eyes darted swiftly from side to side like an injured animal beset by a pack of predators. "What would an actor have to gain by shooting the President? Nothing!" She answered her own question. "He's just a hired pawn. Shake the grates of this stove hard enough and sooner or later a politician will fall out. Be very cautious, Elizabeth. Sleep with one eye open and keep your ears pinned back. I doubt if our Brutus is done with the blood letting yet."

Elizabeth walked down the hall and neared a knot of men. They fell eerily silent as she approached. The only sound was the hushed swish-swish as her furbelow scraped the wooden floor. Finally, Robert stepped towards her. "How's mother? Is she resting?"

"She's been up all night. I'm going to have the servants prepare a hot bath and I'll get her out of those bloody clothes. Any improvement with Mr. Lincoln?"

"No better – no worse. The doctors have staunched the bleeding and are discussing whether to attempt to locate and remove the bullet."

Just once, I'd like to see Robert show some real human emotion Elizabeth thought. *I'd like to see him cry, or get angry, or kick something or act like it was his father lying in that room with a bullet in his brain and not some distant acquaintance.* Elizabeth never saw him show any emotion when Willie died and she guessed it would be the same now that his father... she let the thought drift off. *He's not necessarily going to die.*

Elizabeth descended the stairs. After making arrangements for the hot water and some tea, she returned to Mary's room. Mary was sitting up in bed with her feet pointing out behind her. *I could sit like that as a little girl*, Elizabeth thought.

"Do you not find it odd that General Grant would have cancelled going to the theater with us at the last moment? Or that John Parker, the President's body-guard, would have abandoned his post last night right before Mr. Booth entered our box? There's treachery afoot, Lizzie. I doubt if I'll see another sun rise."

Mary rolled over onto her stomach and buried her face in the pillow.

This muffled her sobs somewhat, but it also had the effect of making them deeper. Elizabeth recalled the time on Mr. Burwell's farm when she watched the slaves hold down the young calves and castrate them. One man would be on each leg and a fifth would wield the knife. The noise that the calves made was similar to the ones now escaping from Mary. However, when the procedure was over and the calf released, he would quickly jump to his feet and scamper off. Elizabeth didn't think that Mary would ever scamper again. She just lay there and lowed. Elizabeth sat on the bed and gently rubbed her shoulders.

Chapter XXVII

"No better – no worse!" Robert's words were proving prophetic as the days drifted into weeks. Mr. Lincoln was comatose. He breathed, he swallowed, and he peed. The only change in his condition was a slow growing edema above his right eye. The surgeons were in agreement that this steady growth was due to an accumulation of blood and fluids in the cranium. Their consensus on the cause did not lead to a consensus as to the treatment. One wanted to re-enter the bullet hole and trace down the lodged missile. One suggested entering the brain through the right eye socket, believing the bullet to be the cause and source of the edema. It was only a chance visit by Dr. Squier that precipitated decisive action. He was in Washington discharging his duties as the Ambassador to Peru. He called on the White House to offer his sympathies to Mrs. Lincoln and in the hope of seeing Elizabeth and especially Artemas. He masked his disappointment well when Elizabeth told him Artemas was on the Eastern Shore.

Elizabeth ushered him into the upstairs bedroom where Mr. Lincoln lay across his oversized bed, hesitating between life and death. There were two physicians present whom Dr. Squire recognized immediately. The eldest, Dr. Brown, the esteemed

Army surgeon, looked at Dr. Squire and said, "Have you ever seen anything like this in your practice?"

"Just once. And I'm happy to report the outcome was entirely beneficial. He needs to be trepanned and I know precisely the man for the job. My friend Artemas has built the necessary apparatus and has perfected its use." Dr. Squier neglected to mention that said perfection was carried out only once and that was on a Dorset sheep. "I'll wire him on the Eastern Shore and we'll have him here in a fortnight. No time to waste; every minute is vital." As usual in medical situations, the voice sounding the most absolute carried the day.

When the other doctors had left, he pulled Elizabeth aside and asked, "How quickly can we get Artemas over here?"

"I'll wire him today. Probably two days."

"Tell him to bring the apparatus for trepanning - and it wouldn't hurt my feelings if he brought it inside a tureen of terrapin gumbo."

———•••———

Mary had not fared much better than Mr. Lincoln since that dreaded evening at Ford's Theater. She had a few more bodily functions than Mr. Lincoln, but not many.

Spending her days and nights secluded in her room with the curtains drawn, she alternated between pacing the floor and rocking in her favorite chair. Elizabeth had not seen her with dry eyes even once.

Tad was not much better. Mr. Lincoln had doted on him ever since Willie died, and the two had become practically inseparable. Occasionally Tad would go outside and play with his animals, especially Nanko, the goat. Once when Elizabeth could not find him in his room, she looked out his window and saw him in the pen with Nanko. Tad had his arms around the goat's neck and he was crying heavily. Elizabeth started to cry, too. Then she felt a rage boiling in her stomach.

She wanted to run down the hall into Mr. Lincoln's room and slap him across the face. She hated this war and every thing about it, and it was his war. Everybody else would have quit years ago if it weren't for his unbendable will. This war had killed George and hundreds of thousands of other mothers' sons. He had held out the promise of freedom to the black race, but now they sat huddled in squalid slums cannibalizing each other because they had no means to adapt. He had torn the arms and legs off boys like the hapless Bobby, who were now ill-fitted to live in the world. He had stoked the hatred of men like Booth, who had widowed, sooner or later, her insane friend Mary. God, she wanted so much to slap him.

And then, like a blacksmith dousing a glowing poker into a bucket of water, it was gone. That white-hot anvil of hatred that burned so recently in her stomach was not only extinguished, it was cold to the touch. She no longer wished to strike out at Mr. Lincoln. Her quarrel was with Life itself, or with God. *Like all of us, he had no good choices. He did the best he could.*

Chapter XXVIII

As Elizabeth neared Mary's bedroom, she heard something floating down the hall she had not heard for over two years; Mary was singing. And it was neither a lilting lullaby nor a sweet hymn; Elizabeth was giving a rowdy rendition of "Dixie."

She stopped singing when she saw Elizabeth and smiled broadly. "And why shouldn't I sing? I'm moderately happy. Did you know that little ditty was one of Mr. Lincoln's favorites? Remember, he had the band strike it up when he received the news of the fall of Richmond? I noticed something today, and mark that I said I 'noticed,' not I 'decided,' I noticed I'm all out of grief. I've cried out every last drop of grief my body and soul contained. I think when we're born we're allotted so many heartbeats, so many laughs, so many breaths, and so many tears. And after Eddie and Willie and Mr. Lincoln, I've simply used up all of my grief. It's all been wrung out like a wet towel run through a wringer. There's simply no more. If someone walked through that door this very instant and told me, God forbid, that something mortal had befallen Robert or Tad, I would feel sad, but I couldn't grieve. There's no more left. It's all used up."

"Well, I came in to tell you we are going to start trepanning Mr. Lincoln soon," said Elizabeth.

"Elizabeth, Mr. Lincoln is dead. He died at Ford's Theatre on April 14th. He's never going to be any different than he is now. I know it, you know it, and the doctors know it. Once Robert told me how they give cadavers to the medical students at Harvard so they can dissect them and learn anatomy. That's how I think of Mr. Lincoln now – he's a cadaver who's retained the use of his lungs, but precious little else. If these experiments further medical science, then I say 'hallelujah!' But when one of the experiments fail and he loses the ability to breathe, I'm not going into mourning all over again, anymore than if we had donated his body to Harvard and someone told me that the dissection classes were over and they were done cutting on him and were burying the remains tomorrow. I know this may sound cold, but it's honestly how I feel. So let them trepan Mr. Lincoln, take out his tonsils, or cut his toe-nails. It's all the same. Mr. Lincoln died on April 14th and we're just going to have a delayed funeral, but I won't be having a delayed grieving. It's done."

Elizabeth didn't have an appropriate response.

"I'm not going to delude myself any longer," Mary continued. "My energies are all devoted to Tad and caring for his creature comforts. And to that end, if Mr. Lincoln could somehow detach himself from that suspended state and look at things with his cold, lawyerly mind, he wouldn't wish to persist in that comatose state for another day. Mr. Lincoln fought life with his mind, battling other lawyers in court, writing laws and directing legislation. If told that he could no longer do these things, but had to lie unknowingly while we ladled soup down this throat twice a day, while nightly changing a pigs bladder that we afastened to him to catch his run-off water, I bet he'd pay Booth to come back and shoot him in the other side of the head. Or, better yet, he would ask for the gun and do it himself." Mary hummed a few more bars of 'Dixie'.

"Do you know they're preparing to swear in Andrew Johnson

as President?" Mary asked. "Do you know what that means? Mr. Lincoln's salary will cease. Tad and I will be unceremoniously tossed overboard from the Ship-of-State. All of the creditors to which I owe money will start to move in like jackals to a wounded lamb. It's odd, but our only salvation will be Mr. Lincoln's official death, which will entitle us to a $200,000.00 death benefit." Mary not only started to hum again, but she lifted her skirt about eight inches from the floor and began to dance a little jig across the room. Elizabeth had to smile.

"I had a dream about Mr. Lincoln two nights ago. Are you familiar with the Greek myth of Charon? Or maybe it's Roman, I don't know. Anyway, when you die Charon ferries you across the River Styx in his boat, taking you from this world to the next. Well, there they sat in the ferry, Charon and Mr. Lincoln, not moving, but run aground. They were sitting there playing chess, waiting for God knows what. Mr. Lincoln looked at me and said, 'get 6469.' I didn't figure this out until this morning. 6469 is Mr. Lincoln's patent for freeing a river boat from a sand bar. He's asking me to free him. He wants to go. I only wish I knew how."

Elizabeth had once overheard Mr. Lincoln talking to Noah Brooks and he made a passing reference to Mrs. Lincoln's 'partial insanity.' That phrase had always seemed apt, but particularly so today. There was lucidity to her thoughts, but there was also a detachment that didn't seem altogether normal. It was easy to see when her behavior and actions veered from the norm, when she wildly and without cause would verbally lunge at someone over the slightest provocation. But this wasn't behavioral; it was all in the realm of her thought processes.

It was as though someone had thrown a switch on the train tracks of her mind and she was steaming off on an altered course. When train tracks are switched, it feels no different to the riders. They are going just as fast, only in a slightly different direction. It takes an outside observer to notice the alteration. So it was with Mary. Elizabeth sensed this new track may be headed directly toward an on-coming locomotive. Mary had not noticed the shift in direction, but continued speeding along towards some distant destination, having left important baggage on the depot platform.

As Elizabeth vacated Mary's room and began her return to the make-shift operating room at the end of the hall, Mary began to sing a popular Stephan Foster song called 'Willie, We Have Missed You.' Mary's voice was true and clear. Elizabeth paused to listen:

Oh! Willie, is it you, dear,
Safe, safe at home?
They did not tell me true, dear;
They said you would not come.
I heard you at the gate'
And it made my heart rejoice;
For I knew that welcome footstep
And that dear, familiar voice
Making music on my ear
In the lonely midnight gloom:
Oh! Willie, we have missed you;
Welcome, welcome home!

Perhaps she is better, Elizabeth thought. *Two months ago she couldn't suffer to hear Willie's name, let alone utter it herself – and here she is now singing a dirge to him.*

Chapter XXIX

Dr. Squier stood on the left side of the wooden table, built some seven feet in length to accommodate the long frame of Abraham Lincoln. He wore a seersucker suit that Elizabeth thought was perfect attire for the doctor. It gave Elizabeth some assurance that he did not expect the procedure to be too bloody. Katie Fryer was to assist as nurse, having been selected and recommended by Clara Barton herself. Miss Barton, head of the Army Nursing Corps, said Katie was the best surgical nurse in the country.

Artemas stood on the other side of the table holding the metal apparatus he had built following Dr. Squier's instructions. Elizabeth stood beside him with her bag of sewing tools resting on a small table.

Dr. Squier nodded at Elizabeth, signaling she should begin. She reached into her bag and grabbed a pair of scissors. She grabbed a shock of Mr. Lincoln's dark, oily hair in her left hand and started cutting. A small wicker basket sat on the table next to Elizabeth's bag. She deposited the severed hair into the basket. After she had removed about an eighth of his hair on the right side of his head, Katie began stirring a gelatinous cake of soap in Mr. Lincoln's shaving mug with a soft horse hair brush. When she had stirred up a generous amount of foam, she transferred it to the stubbled area Elizabeth had prepared. With long measured strokes, Katie Fryer scraped the foam and hair away from the head until it was completely smooth. She rinsed the area with water, careful to avoid the large, base-ball sized node protruding from Mr. Lincoln's right brow. She then dabbed the bald spot with a tincture of red oak bark and water to sterilize and deaden the area. She slipped her hands around Mr. Lincoln's throat and squeezed until the veins in his head became visible.

Dr. Squier leaned in to look. He covered parts of the bald patch with gauze and cheese cloth, leaving an opening about the size of a pocket watch, avoiding the largest surface veins. He was holding a small scalpel in his right hand and deftly cut an x into Mr. Lincoln's scalp. Nurse Katie grabbed one flap of the cut skin and exerted pressure to lift it up and away from the skull. Dr. Squier worked the tip of his scalpel between the skin flap and the skull until the flap was completely free. Katie laid it back across the gauze. They repeated this procedure with the other three sections of skin. There was some minor amount of blood, which Katie irrigated away with a solution of sodium chloride.

Artemas set his apparatus over Mr. Lincoln's head so that its base was resting on the wooden table. He adjusted it until the drilling bit was cleanly above the exposed skull. He lowered the bit until it touched the bone. The apparatus was akin to a bracing bit that carpenters use. There were two wooden handles. One of them, when turned, caused the rotation of the drilling bit; the other would lower and raise the bit. Artemas began to methodically turn the drill and it began to slowly grind away the bone. He would occasionally raise the bit out of the hole so Katie could irrigate, flushing away the bits and scraps of bone.

Elizabeth was surprised she could watch this procedure without feeling squeamish in the least. The area under siege being the only area visible offered a sense of detachment to the operation. It could have easily been a coconut that Artemas was boring into. The only moment of apprehension came after about thirty minutes of drilling where Artemas drilled through a vein running through the interior of the skull. Blood gushed immediately but quickly subsided.

Elizabeth was thinking she could possibly be a nurse when the final assault on the bone breached the cranial area. The foul and fetid material that was responsible for the large edema on Mr. Lincoln's forehead rushed out of the new hole under great pressure. Katie blunted its departure by holding a towel over the wound as best she could. Elizabeth lost all aspirations for a new career. She was amazed to see the edema visibly shrinking. After the pressure was released and the contents flushed away by the sodium chloride solution, Artemas switched bits and began to widen the hole.

When the hole was approximately 2 inches in diameter, Elizabeth fished the bung out of her pocket. It was the one Artemas had carved on the Eastern Shore to be used on the Dorset ram. She had kept it on her desk at home and enlisted it as a paper weight in her unending war against loose invoices. Artemas had to cut a groove into the skull to accept the bung. He was employing a set of ever widening carving needles that Uncle Salty had used to carve scrimshaw. Finally he screwed the bung into place. Katie folded the skin flaps back into their original position and Elizabeth sewed them back together.

The entire procedure had taken less than four hours and Mr. Lincoln looked much improved without the baseball size lump on his head. But Elizabeth had to admit that Mary was right: Mr. Lincoln, as the world had known him, was dead.

Chapter XXX

Lincoln hovered between life and death for well over a month. As Elizabeth closed the massive front door to the White House she saw William walking towards her. William shook his head from side to side.

"The wheels are falling off the hay wagon, Miss Elizabeth. They are sho 'nuff falling off." He glanced up the stairs to make certain no one was listening, and as a further precaution, held his fingers to his lips and guided her into the waiting room. "It's Mrs. Lincoln. She's past peculiar, Miss Elizabeth. She's well past peculiar."

"What on earth do you mean?" Elizabeth asked.

"I don't think she's slept in three days. I can hear her walkin' back and forth, back and forth, at all hours of the night. And when I bring her supper to her room, she makes me bring an extra fork and I have to taste every thing before she'll eat a bite. The wheels are falling off for sho."

Elizabeth chewed on this information.

"And she asked me to buy her a gun. I said 'Why you need a gun, Mrs. Lincoln?' and she said, 'I hear enemies trying to break into my room at night and I want to be ready.' 'What enemies?' I say. 'Why, the same ones who killed Mr. Lincoln,' she sez.

"She forced this money on me and sez, 'And buy plenty of bullets. I think there are a large number of them.' I sez, 'Why don't I give this money to Mr. Robert and let him buy the gun?' Well she got this wild look in her eyes, like a rabbit cornered by a cat in a barn, and she sez, 'Trust no one, William. Trust no one.' You could have pushed me over with a spoon. Not trusting her own son." William again shook his head. "The wheels are off the wagon."

"I'll talk to her," said Elizabeth.

"What should I do with this money, Miss Elizabeth? It's almost $200.00."

"Just keep it for now. I'll talk to her."

Elizabeth made her way to Mary's room, making as much noise as possible so as not to startle her. "Mrs. Lincoln, it's me, Elizabeth, "she called out as a precaution in case Mrs. Lincoln had procured firearms from another source.

"Come in."

Mary was sitting at her little Jacobean desk she had purchased on one of buying sprees in Philadelphia. She was reading a copy of the *Intelligencer*.

"I've almost got it deciphered, Elizabeth. It's complicated; but I've almost got it. Try to follow along. I had two dreams last night. Well, one dream about Mr. Lincoln and one of my nighttime visitations from Willie. The visitations aren't dreams. Willie stands at the foot of my bed, every much a person as you are now. Last night he brought along little Eddie. I asked how they were doing, and Willie said 'fine.' I asked how they spend their time and Willie said Eddie likes to play tag. 'Eddie runs away and I have to chase and chase and chase.' Now remember those exact words, Elizabeth. Then I fell asleep and had another dream about Mr. Lincoln and Charon. They were still stranded on that little spit of sand, but this time Mr. Lincoln was reading a book. I asked him what was he reading and he said poems by Alexander Pope. I asked him which one and he said *The Rape of the Lock*. It was always one of Mr. Lincoln's favorites. And then he quoted:

> But since, alas! frail beauty must decay,
> Curl'd or uncurl'd, since locks will turn to grey,
> Since painted, or not painted, all shall fade,
> And she who scorns a man, must die a maid,
> What then remains but well our pow'r to use,
> And keep good humour still whate'er we lose?

Now keep that thought suspended as well. I'm reading the *Intelligencer* this morning and there's an article about John Cardinal McClosky being inducted into the College of Cardinals by Pope Pius IX. Don't you remember, Lizzie, they're the ones that wanted Mr. Lincoln to allow a Vatican Embassy in the United States. Mr. Lincoln said 'No.'"

Elizabeth was truly puzzled.

"Don't you understand, Lizzie, it's the papacy that was behind Mr. Lincoln's death. They want to take over the country and turn it into a Theocracy. Don't you remember the first attempt on Mr. Lincoln's life was in Baltimore, the largest congregation of Catholics outside of Ireland? That's why Booth was killed. They were afraid he would reveal the plot during a trial. Why else would you need to shoot a man with a broken leg when you had him cornered in a barn and surrounded by fifty soldiers? And the man who shot Booth, that Sergeant Boston Corbett, was certainly a fanatic to the cause. Do you know he castrated himself with a pair of scissors because he was afraid of falling into the temptations of prostitutes? And do you know his real name wasn't 'Boston?' He adopted the name because that was the city in which he had his religious epiphany. And John Surratt, indicted in the plot but as yet uncaptured, is a strong Papist. But it's more than just the Catholics. Chase is part of it. I just know it. And he's Episcopalian. Remember what Willie said in the dream, 'chase and chase and chase.'"

Elizabeth felt dizzy. There were connections but did it constitute proof?

"I don't think it was coincidence that Mr. Lincoln was reading Pope last night. I've said before he's trying to lead me somewhere. I think the poem about the cutting of the locks of hair is also a clue, but I haven't figured it out yet. Did you perchance keep the locks you cut away for the trepanning? That must be what he's hinting at, but I don't understand. Not yet anyway, but I will. I assure you, I will."

Part of Elizabeth agreed with William; the wheels had not only fallen off the wagon, but the axle was broken as well. Another part of Elizabeth was intrigued. The facts did line up in an arresting way.

"You look as though you could use a nice bath. I'll tell William to heat some water and I'll do your hair."

"I'm afraid of the water. I think they're putting something in it that soaks into your body like a poison. Stand there and make sure nobody comes near the pots. Don't let them out of your sight for a moment. I still maintain it was the water that killed Willie."

After the water was poured and Mary was soaking, Elizabeth said, "How would you fancy a glass of port? You know how it relaxes you."

"Fine! But bring an unopened bottle. We can't be too careful."

Elizabeth was correct. The port leeched out most of the tension from Mary's face.

"I have a mission for you Lizzie. I need your help. Have you been following the assassination trials in the papers?"

Elizabeth nodded her head in assent.

"They'll never get to the bottom of the barrel because they only have the flunkies on trial. But I know one thing without a shadow of a doubt – Mrs. Surratt is completely innocent. She was used by her son and Booth and is guilty only by association. I can't go to her myself because the press would hound me every step of the way. There would be no end to it. I want you to go and see if we can do anything for her. She already has an attorney but perhaps she needs funds to assist in his payment. I believe she's being held at the Arsenal Prison. If she needs new clothes, just put them on my bill." Insane or not, Mary was at heart a caring person.

"Tell me again about this soap that Artemas has so kindly given us."

"It's a sailor's soap. It's made from coconut oil. It's the only soap that will foam in salt water. That's why there are so many bubbles."

"Good old Artemas. You're making the right choice, Lizzie. I envy you your happiness."

"The invitation is still there for you to come live with us on the Eastern Shore."

"Thank you, Lizzie, but I've decided to move to Chicago. However, if I don't find a way to parry my creditors, Tad and I may be living under the Long Bridge at the Potomac River. Even today, two of the vultures called on me. Needless to say, I didn't receive them, but they both left their cards."

Mary burst into tears again. Elizabeth reached for the pitcher with the fresh warm water in it and began pouring it over Mary's hair. When her hair was lather free, she said, "Stand up and let me dry you off." Looking at Mary standing there, tears still running down her sagging cheeks, Elizabeth thought, *I've said it before; white women just don't age well. Gravity gets 'em every time.*

As she dried Mary off, something prompted her to say, "Don't worry about a thing. I'll come up with a plan. Don't you worry a muscle? I'll handle it."

Chapter XXXI

Elizabeth was always loath to venture down to the waterfront. Status in Washington, along with other cities, was measured in how far from the shoreline one resided. The docks were infested with rats of both persuasions – two and four legged. At least Mary had offered to allow William to drive her down in the carriage. This was the strangest mission Mary had ever asked Elizabeth to undertake. "Go down and see if we can do anything to help the woman accused of being complicit in shooting my husband in the head." For years it was only Mary's emotions that whirled so wildly; lately it was her thought processes. Elizabeth didn't know how to help. She was beginning to think Mary had drifted too far from shore and that no one could help.

The Arsenal Prison was a non-descript red brick building used as an ammunition depot during the war. When the government got out of the business of wholesale slaughter, it reverted back to its peace time mission of incarceration. And · this was a building well-suited to that purpose. There was only one entrance and the only windows were on the second floor. It looked impenetrable.

Elizabeth walked to the front desk and addressed the soldier sitting there, "I would like to see Mrs. Surratt, please."

"What is the nature of your business?" the young captain asked coolly. Elizabeth reached into her bag and produced the letter Mrs. Lincoln had written. The captain snapped to attention as soon as he saw it was written on White House stationery.

"Mrs. Surratt is with a visitor now. If you would be so kind as to sit here, I'll tell her you're waiting." The captain disappeared; letter in hand.

"She's with her priest," offered the captain as he returned. "They said it wouldn't be long."

Priest? Elizabeth thought. *Could Mary in her madness be onto something?*

After an interval of about 15 minutes, a young man with a clerical collar rounded the corner. "I'm Father Jacob," he said as he extended his hand.

"I'm Elizabeth Keckley."

"Are you a parishioner? I don't recall seeing you at mass."

"No, I just came by to see if I could be of service to Mrs. Surratt." Elizabeth could see the tumblers of his mind rolling, but he couldn't latch onto the combination that would open the vault. She let him twist.

"Well, I must be off," he said. "Thank you for helping minister to Mrs. Surratt."

As he disappeared down the stairs leading to the door, the captain said, "This way, please."

He led her into a small room with bars on a small window and a table with two chairs. One chair was occupied by a lady with her hands shackled and resting in her lap. She made no effort to rise.

"You're Elizabeth Keckley, the seamstress, aren't you? You live north of my boarding house. I'm on H, near 6th Street. I've seen you walking by dozens of times."

Mary Surratt, surprisingly, was the most composed woman Elizabeth had ever encountered.

"Do you mind if we visit for a while?"

"Mrs. Keckley, when you leave, they'll take me back to a room about 1/4th this size with nothing but a straw mattress and a bucket, and put a leather hood over my head. Please, stay a week if you're so inclined."

"I work for Mrs. Lincoln."

"Yes, I've heard. I'm also given to believe by overhearing the guards that the bullet that Mr. Booth fired did as much damage to her brain as it did to Mr. Lincoln's. They say she's as mad as a hatter." Mrs. Surratt said this conversationally, not bitterly.

"She's under a bit of a strain, to say the least."

"Aren't we all? Aren't we all?" Mrs. Surratt measured her with a level gaze. "And exactly why did Mrs. Lincoln send you? Does she want some admission of guilt on my part? Some scrap of information that didn't come out at the trial? Well, I hate to disappoint, but it's all there in the court record. Everything is exactly as I said at the trial."

"No, Mrs. Lincoln thinks you're completely blameless. She wanted me to come to see if we could assist you in any way."

Mrs. Surratt turned thoughtful. "I'm innocent, but I'm not completely blameless. I suspected there was skullduggery afoot, but I didn't know exactly what kind. And precisely what kind of assistance is she proposing? Did you bring a hacksaw? Can she get me a civil trial instead of this military tribunal where the outcome was decided before it ever began? I don't understand."

"If it's apparent to Mrs. Lincoln that you're innocent, don't you think it'll be apparent to the court?"

"Do you know anything about mobs, Mrs. Keckley? Have you ever seen a mob in action? I saw a lynching of a young black man in St. Mary's County in southern Maryland about 10 years ago, and believe me, I know about mobs. There are two types of mobs, Mrs. Keckley. There's the hot mob, like the one that strung up that young man, and there are cold mobs. Cold mobs are just as deadly, but they act slower, more deliberate. The dynamics are the same, but the cold mob acts under the guise of reason and civility. But the end result is the same; someone ends up swinging from a rope. Political parties are an example of a cold mob. They make speeches appealing to patriotism and founding fathers and the Constitution, but their ultimate end is the same - whip the crowd into a frenzy until they have their opponent swinging by his neck. People are blood thirsty by nature. They like human sacrifices to appease their gods. They want to be atoned. This trial is only to satisfy the blood lust of a cold mob. But the finale is already written; someone must die. Sadly in this case that someone is me."

Elizabeth could think of nothing to say.

"You asked what Mrs. Lincoln could do for me? The answer is nothing. There are, however, four things that you can do for me."

"Just ask."

"Before I ask, I want us to be clear. My sympathies are now, and always have been, with the South. I wanted to see that way of life preserved. I think the southern states should have been allowed to go in peace. You and I both know that slavery is a dying institution, as well it should be. I just think it should have been allowed to die a natural death, not smothered in its dotage as it lay upon its death bed." Mrs. Surratt paused and studied Elizabeth's face. "Do you eat meat, Mrs. Keckley?"

"Of course."

"Have you heard of the *Vegetarian Society*? They were founded in England about twenty years ago. Their mission is to enlighten people about the barbarism of eating animals. I have no doubt that in a hundred years or so their views will hold sway with most people and they'll look back on us in the same way we look back on the Inquisition, or on cannibals, or the Roman circuses where thousands would go to spend a leisurely afternoon and watch lions devour the Christians." She paused. "I say this, Mrs. Keckley, because when people look back on our generation and our indulgence of the institution of slavery, they'll never understand how gentle, God-fearing people could ever have participated. They'll call us monsters – or worse. But I know, and I think you know, that the people of the South are for the most part good people – they're just prisoners of the times. You're in the fashion business, Mrs. Keckley; you know fads come and go. You, of all people, should have some appreciation for the fact that black was the color that was selling best."

Elizabeth didn't entirely agree, but she wasn't offended by the remark. She didn't come to get into a debate.

Finally Mrs. Surratt spoke, "These are the four things you can do for me. First, they are reading our verdicts on June 30th. Would you consent to cut my hair before hand so I look somewhat presentable?"

Elizabeth nodded assent.

"Second, Captain Christian Rath, the hang man, is mistakenly convinced they will not hang a woman. Bolstered by these false beliefs, he has told me everything there is to know about hangings. I know short drops don't break the neck immediately and you are left to dangle and suffocate. I know long drops can actually decapitate you. Captain Rath says he can gauge the proper drop based on a person's weight. I don't doubt he is an expert technician, but I remember at the hanging I witnessed, the young man struggled for long minutes and ultimately lost all control of his bowels. I know that can't be prevented, but can you make me something I can wear so it won't be apparent to the spectators. I don't know why, but I'm vain in this area."

Again Elizabeth nodded assent.

"Thirdly, I may look calm to you, but I'm not. I'm frightened to my soul. And I'm sure that as the day approaches, I'll be even more frightened. Can you procure some laudanum, or something equally as effective, that will help calm me on that dreadful day?"

"I agree with Captain Rath, I don't think that's a reasonable concern. But if it ever gets to that point, you can rely on me."

"Fourthly, as one woman to another, I have a rash and an infection that almost makes me yearn for the noose. Do you know of any potions or balms that could provide relief?"

"I'll be back within an hour."

As Elizabeth stood to go, Mrs. Surratt asked, "Are you familiar with the quote from Samuel Johnson that 'the prospect of hanging concentrates the mind wonderfully?' Well my mind is concentrated and I sense Mrs. Lincoln has another thought in her mind. Would you be willing to divulge that to me?"

Elizabeth took a deep breath. "She wonders if there was a plot on the President's life involving the Papacy?"

Mrs. Surratt shook her head slowly, "Mad as a hatter. Mad as a hatter."

When Elizabeth returned to the carriage, William was napping across the wooden seat. "Let's go to my house, William. I'll fix us lunch and then we need to come back here."

They were maybe eight blocks from the prison when Elizabeth spied a young man turning a corner not ten feet in front of them. Elizabeth would never forget that sycamore skin.

"Stop the carriage, William." Elizabeth reached into her purse and pulled out a twenty dollar bill. "Take this to that young man. He tried to assist me in carrying my bag one day, but I demurred. Give him this money for his efforts."

William overtook the man in half a block. He stared blankly towards the carriage as William relayed the message. He took the money and nodded blankly toward the carriage before he turned and ran away. William returned and they began the long, uphill slog to the top of Washington.

Chapter XXXII

It's strange how friendships develop, Elizabeth thought as she approached the Arsenal Prison. Who could have predicted that Elizabeth and Mary Surratt would have ever found enough common ground to grow a friendship? They shared no mutual acquaintances; their outlooks on life were worlds apart, if not diametrically opposed, and they seemed to have no interests in common. Mrs. Surratt's interest in fashion extended no further than opting for the black dress with the narrow collar or the black dress with the wide collar.

Yet, in what had become almost daily visits for the last month, the women had scarified that common ground and planted seeds of understanding and caring. Unfortunately those fast growing seedlings stood a good chance of being harvested today. To the surprise of most everyone in Washington, Mrs. Surratt had been found guilty, along with three men, and sentenced to hang at 1:00 p.m. today, July 7th, 1865. The prevailing sentiment was that Andrew Johnson, the newly sworn President, would surely issue a pardon. Even now, her lawyer and her daughter, Anna, were on their way to see the president. After all, the United States had never executed a woman before in its septuagenarian history.

As usual she played tag with Father Jacob; him leaving as soon as they announced Elizabeth's arrival. As they passed in the hallway this morning, Elizabeth noticed his overgrowth of stubble and concluded that he had been with Mrs. Surratt all night. He grabbed her hand as she walked past and gave it a caring squeeze.

Mary Surratt looked as distraught and troubled as anyone in such a situation with a grain of sense would look. Her eyes were beet red from crying. Elizabeth opened her bag and recovered a pint size mason jar. Unscrewing the top she extended it to Mary and said, "Drink this and you'll feel better." Mary complied. Elizabeth thought she would give the potion a couple of minutes to take effect before she launched into her hollow assurances and consolations. "Let me do something with that hair." Elizabeth gathered a fat handful and scooped it up to the top of Mary's head. "What do you feel like today?"

"Do you think you could do something that's noose proof?"

Nothing like a little gallows humor to break the ice, thought Elizabeth. "You do know that they're in the process of securing your pardon as we speak?" she offered optimistically.

"Yes, but I don't feel that they're going to be successful. We're also trying to produce Booth's diary. The government has it and it was suppressed at the trial. David Herold, who was with Booth in the barn in Virginia, stated that Booth had the diary on his person and had noted in it that the plan was changed from a kidnapping to murder only at the last moment. Stanton had the diary, but somehow now it's nowhere to be found. Like I said when we first met, Elizabeth, it's a mob and they'll only be satisfied by a letting of blood. As afraid as I am, Elizabeth, I'm also resigned. I will go down in history as a murderer, and Stanton will go down as a distinguished member of Lincoln's cabinet, fighting to preserve the Union and uphold the laws. I don't want to die, but it will be nice to be shed of all the hypocrisy that life offers." Mary managed a smile. "This is some good libation, Elizabeth; in less than two hours I'm to be hanged, and here I am offering a critique on politicians. What's in this stuff?"

"Some laudanum, as you requested; some Laughing Jim, a mushroom, and some other herbs that I'll only reveal to you when you come to a celebration party at my house after your release."

"I've really grown fond of you, Elizabeth. I don't think I'll be able to attend, but please have the party in my honor anyway. And ask my daughter Anna to attend. There are so many things about me that I think you can tell her better than I."

Mary drank more of the elixir from the Mason jar. "Let's pull my hair straight back and fasten it in a bun behind. That's what Captain Rath recommended. Long hair can interfere with the noose doing its job properly, he says."

"Your face is one of the few in Washington that is pretty enough to sustain such a severe style, but I think it's your best look."

Elizabeth parted her hair in the middle of her head and began to form a knot along the top of her nape. Mary took another sip from the jar. "Will you do me one last favor, Elizabeth? I have forbidden Anna from attending this afternoon's carnival. I don't want her last memory of me to be so grotesque and awful. But I would like to have someone in the crowd whom I care about. It would be a real comfort to me if I knew that you were there. Would you do that for me?"

Elizabeth's reply was in two parts. Audibly she said, "Yes," and silently she said, *I'll be there but I can't watch. I simply can't watch.* "In response to your earlier request, although I don't think it's necessary, I've brought you these leather britches. I had to guess at the correct size, but I'm pretty good at that."

As Mary wiggled into the britches, Elizabeth thought, *Why do they always wait to the last minute to deliver a pardon. Why can't they do it a day ahead of time? As J.L. DeBonet says, 'everybody loves a drama.'*

"Here comes Father Jacob to hear my last confession. I can't thank you enough Elizabeth. I wish we could have had more time together."

"I'll see you at my party."

"I'll see you in Heaven," said Mrs. Surratt through salty eyes.

Mary made her way down the stairs and out into the courtyard. There must have been a thousand people crowded there. Some of the families had brought their children. Exactly what lesson they hoped to impart to the young Elizabeth could not fathom. As she wormed her way to the back of the court yard she heard a voice from above, "You're Mrs. Keckley, aren't you? I'm Jack Radcliffe. We met at Brady's Studio one nightmarish morning in a futile attempt to photograph the Lincoln family. I heard that, regrettably, that was the beginning of the Lincoln boy's demise." Mr. Radcliffe was perched atop a make-shift structure about eight feet in the air. He was obviously setting up his equipment to capture the impending hanging.

"This is my last assignment for Mr. Brady. I'm moving to Baltimore and opening my own studio. You may recall that I mentioned on that day that I thought you had a wonderful face. I would still like to attempt to capture you in a photograph. Pardon me for saying this, but this doesn't seem like the type of event that you would attend."

"Thank you for saying that. No, this is something I would rather have no part in, but I recently befriended Mrs. Surratt and she asked if I would be here."

"I rather think that a rider with a pardon will appear at any moment," said Mr. Radcliffe. "Even the hangman thinks so. If you look carefully at the nooses, you will see that three of them have the traditional seven loops, but the one on the left has only five. It's probably all prearranged; the last minute pardon being part of the show."

Mr. Radcliffe continued with adjustments to his camera. "Here they come now."

Elizabeth turned for a final look at Mrs. Surratt. Her knees seemed to buckle as she walked down the platform. She was accompanied by Father Jacob. When in place, the executioner removed the veil from her face and covered her head with a thin white hood. That was all Elizabeth could bear to watch. She turned her body to face the brick wall of the prison yard. She stood with her back to the platform. She heard the clap of wood as the trap doors were sprung and she heard the collective groan of the crowd. It was neither ecstatic nor jubilant, but like the surprised expulsion of air that a boxer makes when he catches a sharp blow to the stomach. A boxer expects to be hit, but sometimes the delivery is so sudden and swift it catches him off balance. So it was with the crowd. They knew what to expect, but somehow the forcefulness of the act was so violent that the immediate reaction was involuntary.

The first individual sound that Elizabeth heard was the crying of a small boy. He was quickly drowned out by a collective murmur as everyone started to talk at the same time. They had not been disappointed. The morality play that they had come to watch had been performed to perfection. The leading actors were hanging around, figuratively, and taking their final curtain calls.

Elizabeth kept her eyes focused on Jack Radcliffe and his stand. He continued to take pictures, sliding the glass plates out and into the holding case and then inserting another plate. After several shots of what Elizabeth assumed were the twisting bodies, he adjusted the camera to record the crowd. After basking in the warm afterglow of fulfillment for five or so minutes, the crowd started to thin for the exits. Elizabeth was impelled to look to see if she could do anything for Mrs. Surratt, but she knew that thought to be an imposter and dismissed it immediately. She kept her eyes fixed on the dusty ground, and exited with the rabble.

Chapter XXXIII

As Elizabeth wended her way into Mr. Lincoln's darkened room, she saw Tad standing by his bedside. "You startled me, Tad. I was just coming to shave your father and trim his hair. You looked so grown-up standing there I barely recognized you."

She set her bag on the table and drew back the curtains to gain as much light as possible. As Elizabeth had suspected all along, Tad was evolving into a handsome young man. He had the tooth fairy working overtime as the majority of his extra teeth had decided to belatedly fall out. His speech was almost normal.

"I guess I need to grow up pretty fast. I'm no longer Tad, the President's son. I'm just another boy. I'm just like any other twelve year old boy."

Elizabeth smiled as she retrieved a shaving mug and a folding razor from the bag.

"Do you know that when Willie was 12, he was writing poetry? His poem about the death of Colonel Baker was published in the paper."

"Yes, I remember that. You're just as bright as Willie was, only in different ways," she fudged kindly.

"Do you know that I've always been good with numbers? Remember when Willie and I set up the table at the door of the White House and charged everybody a nickel to see Mr. Lincoln?"

Elizabeth paused from stirring up lather and laughed. "Yes, everybody except old pickle-puss Stanton paid. And he was the richest of all." Normally Elizabeth would not have said that, but she had not yet neutralized the bile that was churned up at the Arsenal.

"That was my idea to get enough money so we could go see a play at the National Theater. And I was the bookkeeper. I've just always understood about money."

Elizabeth brushed the lather onto Mr. Lincoln's face. "Do you have any idea why your father decided to shave off his whiskers before going to Ford's theatre that night? I've never heard anyone say."

"I don't think he said a word, not even to Ma."

Elizabeth flipped open the razor and began making short, smooth strokes down his face. "I think he's much more handsome without the whiskers. You can see the character in his face better."

Tad watched as Elizabeth scraped. When the razor was full of lather and hair, she would wipe it off on a towel that she had wedged under her belt.

"When we were in Springfield I liked to stand behind Pa as he shaved and listen to the sound that the razor made as it was pulled over his whiskers."

"I've always liked that sound myself."

"I know about the money problems that Ma is having now that Congress has sworn in Mr. Johnson. Pa's salary has stopped and they want us to move out of the White House. I don't think Ma can manage without you and the staff. Pa has a 'chalked hat' from all the work he did for the railroad when he was a lawyer, so I guess we could get him back to Springfield, but I don't think Ma could manage from there."

"You needn't worry yourself about matters like that. It'll work out."

"I don't know, Jib. Ma is no longer able to think for herself – and Robert doesn't seem to care."

Elizabeth was overcome with pride; Tad sounded so mature. It was a side of him that she had not seen blossoming before.

"Jib, did I ever tell you that our trip to the Eastern Shore was the best time of my life?"

"Why thank you, Tad. It's one of my fondest memories also. But you're young. Life is just beginning. You'll have many other wonderful times."

"I don't think so Jib. I think I'm getting ready to join Willie."

Elizabeth was glad she was wiping the razor onto a towel or she would have been in danger of cutting Mr. Lincoln. "What on earth do you mean?"

"I've got some kind of disease, Jib. It started about a month ago and it's getting worse."

Elizabeth thought she couldn't cram any more sorrow into the day, but this could not be ignored. "Have you talked to Dr. Stone? Does your mother know?"

"No, you're the first person I've told. That's why I was standing here today when you came in." Tad thrust his hand into his pocket and pulled out a half-pint jar with a screw top. "Remember this from our trip to the Eastern shore. This is the potion that Artemas mixed up for the rats and mice. Remember how sudden and how painless that ram died when this dripped into his head? I figure that since I'm about to die, I might as well do a good deed for Ma. Ma and Robert and the doctors all say that Pa is never going to recover, so if I do this, Ma can collect the benefit money from Congress. I think Pa would want me to."

"Tad, hand me that bottle and tell me why you think you're going to die."

Tad hesitated and lowered his gaze to the floor. "Every night or so I wake up and have a convulsion. And there's this strange discharge that comes out of my body."

Elizabeth had to support herself by grabbing the bed post to keep from falling to the floor she was laughing so hard. When she was finally able to control herself, she said, "Tad honey, you're not going to die – you're just starting to live. You're becoming a man. Those are the seeds of life and you're going to have more fun sowing them than just about anything you ever do." She proceeded to give Tad as much information as she could prudently impart, but he couldn't complete the picture. Finally, it became clear to Elizabeth that he had absolutely no conception of female anatomy.

"Tad, I need you to run an errand for me while I finish preening your father. Then after the errand come by my house. Portia and the girls have a watermelon floating in a tub of ice water and they're going to cut it this afternoon. This is the end of the season for watermelons, so you better take advantage. You can pick up your alterations at the same time. In my sewing room down the hall I have a bonnet that I just made. It's the one with the big blue ribbons. I need you to deliver it to Belle Boyd. You go fetch the bonnet and let me write a note to Belle."

Elizabeth pulled some stationery from her bag and wrote;

Belle,

I send to you the bonnet for Jane, being borne by a curious boy. Keep the bonnet and return the enlightened boy to me.

Elizabeth

"Now Tad, you take this note to Miss Belle and tell her what you and I were just talking about. She's an excellent teacher and I bet she just might be able to shed a little light on the matter. I'll see you at my house in an hour."

Elizabeth didn't think that Tad was ready for anything more than a lecture, but if a stereoscopic slide presentation went with it, so be it. Belle would not exceed boundaries.

Tad had certainly lifted the oppressive mood that had followed Elizabeth from the Arsenal. Every time she remembered the somber look on Tad's face and his dire prediction of doom, Elizabeth would laugh just as hard as she did the first time.

"I don't know if you heard that Mr. Lincoln, but if you did, I know you're smiling on the inside. Your Tad is becoming a man. I know there's a part of you that would like for him to stay a boy forever. I certainly felt that way about my boy, 'George,' but that's not the way of the world. I imagine you felt the same way about Robert as well."

Elizabeth began to trim his hair.

"I hope you don't object to me sending him to Belle Boyd. I've gotten to know Belle and I promise you, whatever she tells, or shows, or does to Tad, he will leave a better young man. Did you hear how mature and grown-up he sounded today? He is growing into the task of taking care of Mrs. Lincoln right nicely. He's got everything all figured out. And you know what? He's probably right."

Elizabeth carefully snipped the hair around the bald patch that had been shaved to allow for the trepanning.

"He'll do you and Mrs. Lincoln proud. He's growing into a fine boy. I'm sure you sense what a great act of love it would have been to carry out his little plan. But that would have been such a heavy burden for him to have to carry around for the rest of his life. But it was only an act of love."

Elizabeth cut the strings that held the four pieces of scalp together.

"I'm afraid Mrs. Lincoln is not faring as well as we had hoped. Even a strong person would have difficulty standing up under the heavy blows that life has dealt her over the past several years. First, Willie, and then you. I'm amazed that she's been able to stay as composed as she has."

Elizabeth unscrewed the bung.

"She's told me about you coming to her in your dreams and asking to be freed from the sand bar. She read me the verse about the 'locks.' I didn't know at first that you meant the locks that I cut off for the trepanning."

Elizabeth unscrewed the top from the Mason jar.

"I hope that I didn't cause you unnecessary suffering until I figured out what you meant. You know, of all the poetry and all the Shakespeare that you quoted and read to me, I think the most pure and heart-felt of all were the lines that the black barber from Springfield, William Florville, wrote to you upon Willie's death:

'I thought him a smart boy for his age, so considerate, so manly, his knowledge and good sense far exceeding most boys more advanced in years. Yet the time comes to all, all must die.'

You seemed to know that your time had come. Remember you predicted it down at City Point. By some misalignment in the universe you didn't die when you should have, but floated between life and death. I'm proud to have known you and proud to be allowed to right this wrong. Give my love to Willie and to George. Good night, Mr. President."

With that Elizabeth lovingly poured the contents of the Mason jar into the cranial cavity, re-screwed the bung, and basted the skin flaps. She returned all the items to her bag and walked down the stairs to the first floor.

William met her on the first floor near the door. "You want me to fetch the carriage, Miss Elizabeth?"

"No thank you, William. It's such a fine summer day; I think I'll walk home in the sun."

When Elizabeth reached the front door she heard music and laughter coming from the parlor. One of the girls was playing a fiddle and another was rubbing a stick over a home made percussion instrument. She had fashioned spools and bobbins together and was keeping time by running a wooden knitting needle along its length. *"So this is how they spend their time when I'm not around: they make musical instruments,"* Elizabeth joked to herself. Portia had Tad in the middle of the room and was trying to teach him to dance. It looked something like the Virginia reel, although there were only the two of them. He glanced at Elizabeth when she walked in with a self-assured look on his face. His lesson with Belle must have been productive as he looked fully five years older. The girls actually played quite well. Portia and Tad stepped and twirled, glided and bobbed, and the dance of life continued.

Acknowledgements

"No man but a blockhead ever wrote except for money."
—Samuel Johnson

Boy, he nailed me. I only started writing this as a lark for my friend Jack Radcliffe, renowned photographer. I read that Abraham Lincoln (a known camera Narcissus) had many dozens of photographs taken of himself and various family members, but none including the entire family. I thought that curious.

Jack showed me a Civil War era camera and explained how it worked. (Doesn't everyone have one of these in their basement?) So I wrote what ended up being Chapter 11. Jack was very supportive and urged (insisted) that I write more.

One might note Jack Radcliffe is cleverly disguised as Jack Radcliffe.

First to be impressed by this Flying Dutchman was my son, Duncan (a real writer). He stayed on for the entire voyage, and due to his patience and perseverance, a port is finally in sight.

Elizabeth Grady Carswell was one of my earliest readers. She understood the character of Elizabeth Keckley better than I, and guided me back towards refinement and gentility when I (frequently) strayed into crudity and crassness.

Anna Simons has a unique gift of rephrasing. Our literary flight was wonderful. We crash landed, but there were no fatalities.

Amy Thonnings' skills at editing are maximal, exceeded only by her skill in the art of friendship. I owe her big time.

Judith Campbell was a reader and insightful commentator.

Paige Espenshade was kind enough to guide a Luddite through the intricacies of these new-fangled machines.

Bonnie Ward (my daughter) surprised me by proving to be the equal of Sherlock Holmes in deduction and observation, and as dogged as a pit bull. She uprooted many inconsistencies and anachronisms. There was one ill she was unable to cure — my preference for dashes.

It took 4/5's of a century to get a gift that was gratefully received. For my 80th birthday my three children (Drew, Duncan & Bonnie) underwrote the publishing of my manuscript. It's a warm feeling to know they think it has enough merit to be readable. Thank you.

And thanks to Jessica Hill and her crew for herding this litter of stray cats to the finish line. If she ever takes up a strong drinking habit, she can probably trace it back to the month it began.

www.ingramcontent.com/pod-product-compliance
Lightning Source LLC
Chambersburg PA
CBHW031213260626
47169CB00007B/2037